Hunter waited until he [barcode: KU-530-671] **brass candlestick being set down upon the wooden surface of the desk behind him, then he cocked the pistol and swivelled his chair round to face the intruder.**

She was standing with her back to him, looking over his desk.

'Miss Allardyce.'

She started round to face him, gave a small shriek, and stumbled back against the desk. Her mouth worked but no words sounded.

He rose to his feet.

Her gaze dropped to the pistol.

He made it safe and lowered it.

'Mr Hunter,' she said, and he could hear the shock in her voice and see it in every nuance of her face, of her body, and in the way she was gripping at the desk behind her. 'I had no idea that you were in here.'

'Evidently not.' He let his gaze wander from the long thick auburn braid of hair that hung over her shoulder down across the bodice of the cotton nightdress which, though prim and plain and patched in places, did not quite hide the figure beneath. His gaze dropped lower to the little bare toes that peeped from beneath its hem, before lifting once more to those golden brown eyes. And something of the woman seemed to call to him, so that, just as when he had first looked at her upon the moor, an overwhelming desire surged through him.

AUTHOR NOTE

I love the rugged harsh beauty of the Scottish moorland, so much so that I've set A DARK AND BROODING GENTLEMAN on a moor in the West of Scotland, not so very far away from where I live. Blackloch, the fictional moor in the story, is based mainly on Eaglesham Moor (south of Glasgow), with a little touch of Rannoch Moor (near Glencoe) thrown in just for good measure. If you are interested, you can see pictures of the moors and read about the historical research behind the story on my website: www.margaretmcphee.co.uk

Blackloch is almost as dark and brooding as Sebastian Hunter. Readers who met him previously in UNMASKING THE DUKE'S MISTRESS might be surprised to find that he is a man much changed. Both Hunter and Phoebe have been in my mind for a long time, and I can only hope I've done them justice in the telling of their story. The story is one with many secrets, all of them to be discovered along the road to love, and I hope very much that you enjoy it.

A DARK AND BROODING GENTLEMAN

Margaret McPhee

Margaret McPhee loves to use her imagination—an essential requirement for a trained scientist. However, when she realised that her imagination was inspired more by the historical romances she loves to read rather than by her experiments, she decided to put the ideas down on paper. She has since left her scientific life behind, retaining only the romance—her husband, whom she met in a laboratory. In summer, Margaret enjoys cycling along the coastline overlooking the Firth of Clyde in Scotland, where she lives. In winter, tea, cakes and a good book suffice.

Previous novels by the same author:

THE CAPTAIN'S LADY
MISTAKEN MISTRESS
THE WICKED EARL
UNTOUCHED MISTRESS
A SMUGGLER'S TALE
  (part of *Regency Christmas Weddings*)
THE CAPTAIN'S FOBIDDEN MISS
UNLACING THE INNOCENT MISS
  (part of *Regency Silk & Scandal* mini-series)
UNMASKING THE DUKE'S MISTRESS*

Gentlemen of Disrepute

For Isobel, and her Glasgow.

Chapter One

The Tolbooth Gaol, Glasgow, Scotland—July 1810

'Blackloch Hall?' Sir Henry Allardyce shook his head and the fine white hair that clung around his veined, bald pate wafted with the movement. Upon his pallid face was such worry; it tugged at Phoebe's heart that her father, who had so much to endure in this dank miserable prison cell, was worrying not about himself, but about her. 'But I thought Mrs Hunter was estranged from her son.'

'She is, Papa. In all the months I have spent as the lady's companion I have never once heard her, or anyone else in the household, make mention of her son.'

'Then why has she expressed this sudden intent to travel to his home?'

'You know that Charlotte Street has been twice broken into in the past months, and the last time it was completely ransacked. Her most private things were raked through—her bedchamber, her dressing table, even her...' Phoebe paused and glanced away in embarrassment. 'Suffice to say nothing was left untouched.' Her brow furrowed at the memory. 'The damage was not so very great, but Mrs Hunter has arranged for the entire house to be redecorated.

As it is, every room seems only to remind her that her home has been violated. She is more shaken by the experience than she will admit and wishes some time away.'

'And they still have not caught the villains responsible for the deed?' Her father looked appalled.

'Nor does it look likely that they will do so.'

'What has the world come to when a widow alone cannot feel safe in her own home?' He shook his head. 'Such a proud but goodly woman. It was generous of her to allow you to come here today. Most employers would have insisted upon you accompanying her to Blackloch Hall immediately.'

'Mrs Hunter asked me to run some errands in town before my visit to you.' Phoebe smiled. 'And she has given me the fare to catch the mail to the coaching inn on Blackloch Moor, from where I am to be collected.'

'Good,' he said, but he gave a heavy sigh and shook his head again.

'You must not worry, Papa. According to Mrs Hunter, Blackloch is not so very far away from Glasgow, only some twenty or so miles. So, she has agreed that our weekly visits may continue. As you said, she really is a good and kind employer and I am fortunate, indeed.' She took his dear old hand in her own and, feeling the chill that seemed to emanate from his bones, chafed it gently to bring some warmth to the swollen and twisted fingers. 'And she enquires after your health often.'

'Oh, child,' he murmured, and his rheumy eyes were bright with tears, 'I wish it had not come to this. You left alone to fend for yourself and forced to lie to hide the scandal of a father imprisoned. She still believes that I am hospitalised?'

Phoebe nodded.

'And it must stay that way. For all of her kindness, she would turn you off in the blink of an eye if she knew the truth. Anything to avoid more scandal, poor woman. Heaven knows, there was enough over her son.'

'You know of Mrs Hunter's son? What manner of scandal?'

He took a moment, looking not at Phoebe but at the shadowed corner of the cell, his focus fixed as if on some point far in the distance and not on his ragged fellow inmate who was crouched there upon the uneven stone flags. The seconds passed, until at last he looked round at her once more, and it seemed that he had made up his mind.

'I am not a man for gossip. It is a sinful and malicious occupation, the work of the devil, but...' He paused and it seemed to Phoebe that he was picking his words very carefully. 'It would be remiss of me to allow you to go to Blackloch Hall ignorant of the manner of man you will find there.'

Phoebe felt the weight of foreboding heavy upon her. She waited for the words her father would speak.

'Phoebe,' he said and his voice was so unusually serious that she could not mistake the measure of his concern. 'Sebastian Hunter was a rake of the very worst degree. He spent all his time in London, living the high life, gambling away his father's money, womanising and drinking. Little wonder that old Hunter despaired of him. They say his father's death changed him. That the boy is much altered. But...' He glanced over his shoulder at the cellmate in the corner and then lowered his voice to a whisper. 'There are dark whisperings about him, evil rumours...'

'Of what?'

He shook his head again, as if he could not bring himself to convey them to her. But he looked at her intently. 'Promise me that you will do all you can to stay away from him at Blackloch.'

She looked at him, slightly puzzled by his insistence. 'My job is with Mrs Hunter. I doubt I will have much contact with her son.'

'Phoebe, you are too innocent to understand the wickedness of some young men.' Her papa sounded grim and his implication was clear. 'So do as I ask, child, and promise me that you will have a special care where he is concerned.'

'I will be careful. I give you my word, Papa.'

He gave a satisfied grunt and then eyed the bulging travelling bag that sat by her feet. 'You are well packed. Does Mrs Hunter not transport your portmanteau with the rest of the baggage?'

She followed his gaze to the worn leather bag that contained every last one of her worldly possessions. 'Of course, but it does not travel down until tomorrow and I thought it better to take my favourite dresses,' she said with a teasing smile.

'You girls and your fashions.' He shook his head in mock scolding.

Phoebe laughed but she did not tell him the truth, that there was no trunk of clothes, that all, save her best dress and the one she was now wearing, had been pawned over the months for the coins to pay her father's fees within the gaol so that he would not be put to work.

'I have paid the turnkey the garnish money and more, so you should have candles and blankets, and ale and good food for the next week. Be sure that he gives them to you.'

'You have kept enough money back for yourself?' He was looking worried again.

'Of course.' She smiled to cover the lie. 'I have little requirement for money. Mrs Hunter provides all I need.'

'Bless you, child. What would I do without you?'

The turnkey had reappeared outside the door, rattling his keys so Phoebe knew visiting time was at an end.

'Come, Phoebe, give your old papa a kiss.'

She brushed his cheek with her lips and felt the chill of his mottled skin beneath.

'I will see you next week, Papa.'

The turnkey opened the door.

It was always the hardest moment, this walking away and leaving

him in the prison cell with its stone slab floors and its damp walls
and its one tiny barred window.

'I look forward to it, Phoebe. Pray remember what I have said
regarding…'

The man's name went unspoken, but Phoebe knew to whom her
papa was referring—*Hunter.*

She nodded. 'I will, Papa.' And then she turned and walked away,
along the narrow dim passageways, out of the darkness of the gaol
and into the bright light of Glasgow's busy Trongate.

On the right hand side was the Tontine Hotel and its mail coaches,
but Phoebe walked straight past, making her way through the crowds
along Argyle Street, before heading down Jamaica Street. She kept
on walking until she crossed the New Bridge that spanned the River
Clyde. Half of Mrs Hunter's coins for the coach fare were squir-
reled away inside her purse for next week's visit to her father. The
rest lay snug in the pocket of one of the Tolbooth's turnkeys.

The road that led south out of the city towards the moor lay ahead.
She changed the bag into her other hand and, bracing her shoulders
for the walk, Phoebe began her journey to Blackloch Hall.

'Hunter, is that you, old man? Ain't seen you in an age. You ain't
been down in London since—' Lord Bullford stopped himself, an
awkward expression suddenly upon his face. He gruffly clapped a
supportive hand to Hunter's shoulder. 'So sorry to hear about your
father.'

Hunter said not one word. His expression was cold as he glanced
first at Viscount Linwood standing in the background behind
Bullford, and then at where Bullford's hand rested against the black
superfine of his coat. He shifted his gaze to Bullford's face and
looked at him with such deadly promise that the man withdrew his
hand as if he had been burnt.

Bullford cleared his throat awkwardly. 'Up visiting Kelvin
and bumped into Linwood. Thought we might drop in on you at

Blackloch while we were here. The boys have been worried about you, Hunter. What with—'

'They need not have been.' Hunter glanced with obvious dislike at Linwood as he cut off the rest of Bullford's words and made to step aside. 'And visitors are not welcome at Blackloch.'

He saw Bullford's eyes widen slightly, but the man was not thwarted.

'Kelvin knows an excellent little place. We could—'

'No.' Hunter started to walk away.

'Stakes are high but the tables are the best, and the lightskirts that run the place...' Bullford skimmed his hands through the air to sketch the outline of a woman's curves '...just your type.'

Hunter turned, grabbed Bullford by the lapels of his coat, thrust him hard against the wall of the building they were standing beside and held him there. 'I said no.' He felt rather than saw Linwood tense and move behind him.

'Easy, old man.' The sweat was glimmering on Bullford's upper lip and trickling down his chin. 'Understand perfectly.'

A voice interrupted—Linwood's. 'You go too far, Hunter.'

Hunter released Bullford, and turned to face the Viscount. 'Indeed?'

Linwood took one look at Hunter's face and retreated a step or two. But Hunter had already left Bullford and was covering the short distance to where his horse was tethered. The big black stallion bared his teeth and snorted a warning upon hearing his approach but, on seeing it was Hunter, let him untie his reins and swing himself up into the saddle. And as he turned the horse to ride away he heard Bullford saying softly to Linwood, 'Deuce, if he ain't worse than all the stories told.'

The July day was fine and dry; and Phoebe smiled to herself as, bit by bit, mile by mile, she left Glasgow behind her and passed through the outlying villages. The bustle and crowds of the city gave way gradually to quiet hamlets with cottages and fields and cows. The air grew cleaner and fresher, the fields more abundant. She could smell the sweetness of grass and heather and earth, and feel the sun warm upon her back, the breeze gentle upon her face.

Step by step she followed the road heading ever closer to Blackloch and its moor. Rolling hills and vast stretches of scrubby fields surrounded her, all green and yawning and peaceful. Sheep with their woolly coats sheared short wandered by the side of the road, bleating and gambling furiously ahead with their little tails bobbing as she approached. Overhead the sky was blue and cloudless, the light golden and bright with the summer sun. Bees droned, their pollen sacks heavy from the sweet heather flowers; birds chirped and sang and swooped between the hawthorn and gorse bushes. Two coaches passed, and a farmer with his cart, and then no more, so that as she neared the moorland she might have believed herself the only person in this place were it not for the two faint figures of horsemen in the distance behind her.

She walked on and her thoughts turned to Mrs Hunter's son and her papa's warning. *Dark whisperings and evil rumours,* she mused as she transferred the travelling bag from one hand to the other again, in an effort to ease the way its handles cut into her fingers. *You have no idea of the wickedness of some men...* Her feet were hot and her boots chafed against her toes as she conjured up an image of the wicked Mr Hunter—a squat heavy-set villain to be sure, run to fat with drink and dissipation, with eyes as black as thunder and a countenance to match. Living all alone on a moor miles away from anywhere. Little wonder his mother had disowned him. A man with a soul as black as the devil's. Phoebe shivered at the thought, then scolded herself for such foolishness.

Another mile farther and she stopped by a stile to rest, dumping the bag down upon the grass with relief and perching herself on the wooden step. She eased her stiffened fingers and rubbed at the welts the bag's straps had pressed through her gloves. Then she loosened the ribbons of her bonnet and slipped it from her head, to let the breeze ripple through her hair and cool her scalp, before leaning against the fence of the stile. She was quite alone in the peacefulness of the surrounding countryside, so she relaxed and let herself rest for a few minutes.

The clatter of the horses' hooves was muffled by the grass verge so that Phoebe did not hear the pair's approach. It was the jingle of a harness and a whinny that alerted her that she was no longer alone.

Not twenty yards away sat two men on horseback. Even had they not kerchiefs tied across their mouths and noses, and their battered leather hats pulled down low over their eyes, Phoebe would have known them for what they were. Everything of their manner, everything of the way they were looking at her, proclaimed their profession. Highwaymen. She knew it even before the men slid down from their saddles and began walking towards her.

She rose swiftly to her feet. There was no point in trying to escape. They were too close and she knew she could not outrun them, not with her heavy travelling bag. So she lifted her bag from where it lay on the grass and stood facing them defiantly.

'Well, well, what have we here?' said the taller of the two, whose kerchief obscuring his face was black. His accent was broad Glaswegian and he was without the slightest pretence of education or money.

Although she could not see their faces she had the impression that the men were both young. Maybe it was in the timbre of their voices, or maybe in something of their stance or build. Both were dressed in worn leather breeches, and jackets, with shirts and neck-cloths that were old and shabby and high scuffed brown leather boots.

'A lassie in need of our assistance, I'd say,' came the reply from his shorter, slimmer accomplice wearing a red kerchief across his face.

'I have no need of assistance, thank you, gentlemen,' said Phoebe firmly. 'I was but taking a small rest before resuming my journey.'

'Is that right?' the black-kerchiefed man said. 'That's a mighty heavy-looking bag you have there. Allow us to ease your burden, miss.'

'Really, there is no need. The bag is not heavy,' said Phoebe grimly and, eyeing them warily, she shifted the bag behind her and gripped it all the tighter.

'But I insist. Me and my friend, we dinnae like to see a lassie struggle under such a weight. Right gentlemanly we are.'

Gentlemen of the road, for they were certainly not gentlemen of any other description.

He walked slowly towards her.

Phoebe stepped back once, and then again, her heart hammering, not sure of what to do.

'The bag, if you please, miss.'

Phoebe's hands gripped even tighter to the handle, feeling enraged that these men could just rob her like this. She raised her chin and looked directly into the man's eyes. They were black and villainous, and she could tell he was amused by her. That fueled her fury more than anything.

Her own eyes narrowed. 'I do not think so, sir. I assure you there is nothing in my bag worth stealing unless you have an interest in ladies' dresses.'

He gave a small hard laugh and behind him the other highwayman appeared with a pistol in his hand that was aimed straight at her.

'Do as he says, miss, or you'll be sorry.'

'Jim, Jim,' said Black Kerchief, who was clearly the leader of the two, as if chiding the man. 'Such impatience. There are better ways to persuade a lady.' And then to Phoebe, 'Forgive my friend.' His gaze meandered over her face, pausing to linger upon her lips.

A *frisson* of fear rippled down Phoebe's spine. She knew then that she would have to give them the bag, to yield her possessions. Better that than the alternative.

She threw the bag to land at their feet.

Black Kerchief swung the bag between his fingers as he gauged its weight. 'Far too heavy for a wee slip o' a lassie like you.' She could tell he was smiling again beneath his mask, but in a way that stoked her fear higher. 'Search it,' he instructed his accomplice and did not move, just kept his eyes on Phoebe. 'Best relieve the lassie of any unnecessary weighty items.'

Red Kerchief, or Jim as he had been called, lifted the bag and, making short work of its buckle fastenings, began to rake within. He would find nothing save her clothing, a pair of slippers, a comb and some toiletries. Thankfully her purse, and the few coins that it contained, was hidden inside the pocket of her dress.

Phoebe eyed the man with disdain. 'I have no money or jewels, if that is what you are after.'

'She's right; there's nothin' here,' Jim said and spat his disgust at the side of the road.

'Look again,' instructed Black Kerchief. 'What we've got here is a bona fide lady, if her accent and airs and graces are anythin' to go by. She must hae somethin' o' value.'

His accomplice emptied the contents of her bag out onto the verge and slit open the lining of her bag. Further rummaging revealed nothing. He dropped the bag with its ripped lining on top of the pile of her clothes and spat again.

'Nothin'.'

Phoebe prayed a coach would pass, but the road ahead remained resolutely empty and there was silence all around. 'I did tell you,' she said. 'Now if you would be so kind as to let me pass on my way.' She held her head up and spoke with a calm confidence she did not feel. Inside her heart was hammering nineteen to the dozen and her stomach was a small tight knot of fear. She made to step towards the bag.

'Tut, tut, darlin', no' so fast.' The black-masked highwayman caught her back with an arm around her waist. 'There's a price to pay to travel this road, and if you've nae money and nae jewels...' His gaze dropped lower to the bodice of her dress and lower still to its dusty skirt before rising again to her face.

Phoebe felt her blood run cold. 'I have nothing to give you, sir, and I will be on my way.'

He laughed at that. 'I think I'll be the judge of that, hen.' He looked at Phoebe again. 'I'll hae a kiss. That's the price to continue on your way.'

She heard the other man snigger.

The villain curled his arm tighter and pulled her closer. The stench of ale and stale sweat was strong around him. 'Dinnae be shy, miss, there's no one here to see.'

'How dare you, sir? Release me at once. I insist upon it.'

'Insist, do you?' The highwayman pulled his mask down and leered at her to reveal his discoloured teeth. It was all Phoebe could do not to panic. Vying with the fear was a raging well of fury and indignation. But she stayed calm and delivered him a look that spoke the depth of her disgust.

He laughed.

And as he did she kicked back as hard as she could with her stout walking boots against his shins.

He was not laughing then.

A curse rent the air and she felt the loosening of his hands. Phoebe needed no further opportunity. She tore herself from his grip, hoisted up her skirts and, abandoning her bag, began to run.

The man recovered too quickly and she heard his booted foot-steps chasing after her. Phoebe ran for all she was worth, her heart thudding fast and furious, her lungs panting fit to burst. She kept on running, but the highwayman was too fast. She barely made it a hundred yards before he caught her.

'Whoa, lassie. No' so fast. You and I havenae yet finished our business.'

'Unhand me, you villain!'

'Villain, am I?' With rough hands he pulled her into his arms and lowered the stench of his mouth towards hers.

Phoebe hit out and screamed.

A horse's hooves sounded then. Galloping fast, coming closer.

Her gaze shot round towards the noise, as did the highwayman's.

There, galloping down the same hill she had not long walked, was a huge black horse and its dark-clad rider—rather incongruous with the rest of the sunlit surroundings. He was moving so fast that the tails of his coat flew out behind him and he looked, for all the world, like some devil rider.

Black Kerchief's hand was firm around her wrist as he towed her quickly back to where his accomplice still stood waiting. And she saw that he, too, had pulled down his mask so that it now looked like a loose ill-fitting neckerchief. Jim grabbed her and used one hand to hold her wrists in a vice-like grip behind her back. She felt the jab of something sharp press against her side.

'One sound from you, lady, and the knife goes in. Got it?'

She gave a nod and watched as Black Kerchief stood between her and the road, so that she would be obscured from the rider's view as he sped past.

Please! Phoebe prayed. *Please*, she hoped with every last ounce of her will.

And it seemed that someone was listening for the horseman slowed as he approached and drew the huge stallion to a halt by their small group. Not the devil after all, but a rich gentleman clad all in black.

* * *

'Step away from the woman and be on your way.' Hunter spoke quietly enough, but in a tone that the men would not ignore if they had any kind of sense about them.

'She's my wife. Been givin' me some trouble, she has,' the taller of the men said.

Hunter's gaze moved from the woman's bonnet crushed on the grass by the men's feet, to the neckerchiefs around the men's collars, and finally to the woman herself. Her hair glowed a deep tawny red in the sunshine and was escaping its pins to spill over her shoulders. She was young and pretty enough with an air about her that proclaimed her gentle breeding, a class apart from the men who were holding her, and she was staring at him, those fine golden-brown eyes frantically trying to convey her need for help. He slipped down from the saddle.

'She is no more your wife than mine. So, as I said, step away from her and be on your way…gentlemen.' He saw the men glance at each other, communicating what they thought was a silent message.

'If you insist, sir,' the taller villain said and dragged the girl from behind him and flung her towards Hunter at the same time as reaching for his pistol.

Hunter thrust the girl behind him and knocked the weapon from the highwayman's hand. He landed one hard punch to the man's face, and then another, the force of it sending the man staggering back before the villain slumped to his knees. Hunter saw the glint of the knife as it flew through the air. With the back of his hand he deflected its flight, as if he were swatting a fly, and heard the clatter of the blade on the empty road.

The accomplice drove at him, fists flying. Hunter stepped forwards to meet the man and barely felt the fist that landed against his cheekbone. The ineffective punch did nothing to interrupt Hunter's own, which was delivered with such force that, despite the villain's momentum, the man was lifted clear off his feet and driven backwards to land flat on his back. The shock of the impact was felt not only by the accomplice, who was out cold upon the ground, but seemed to reverberate around them. The taller highwayman, who had been trying to pick himself up following Hunter's first blow, stopped still and, as Hunter turned to him, all aggression evaporated from the scoundrel.

'Please, sir, we were only having a laugh.' It was almost a whimper. 'We wouldnae have hurt the lassie; look, here's her purse.' The highwayman fished the woman's purse from his pocket and offered it as if in supplication.

'Throw it,' Hunter instructed.

The man did as he was told and Hunter caught it easily in one hand before turning to the woman.

She was white-faced and wary, but calm enough for all her fear. In her hand she gripped the highwayman's knife as if she trusted him as little as the villains rolling and disabled on the ground before him.

Hunter's expression was still hard, but he let the promise of lethality fade from his eyes as he looked at her.

He held the purse aloft. 'Yours, I take it?'

She seemed to relax a little and gave an answering nod of her head. The man must have taken it from her pocket while they were struggling.

He threw the purse to her and watched her catch it, then barked an order for the highwayman, who was leaning dazed upon the stile, to pack the jumble of women's clothing lying in a heap at the side of the road into the discarded travelling bag. Only when the filled and fastened bag was placed carefully at his feet did Hunter move.

'To where are you walking?' His voice was curt and he could feel the woman's stare on him as he swung himself up into the saddle.

She glanced over at the highwaymen and then back at Hunter.

'Kingswell Inn.' A gentlewoman's voice sure enough. The pure clarity of it stirred sensations in Hunter that he thought he had forgotten.

He urged Ajax forwards a few steps and reached his hand down for her.

She hesitated and bit at her lower lip as if she were uncertain.

'Make up your mind, miss. Do I deliver you to Kingswell, or leave you here?' Hunter knew his tone was cold, but he did not care.

She took his hand.

'Place your foot on the stirrup to gain purchase,' he directed and pulled her up. As he settled her to sit sideways on the saddle before him the woman glanced up directly into his eyes. The attraction that arced between them was instant, its force enough to make him catch his breath. The shock of it hit him hard. For one second and then another they stared at each other, and then he deliberately turned his face away, crushing the sensation in its inception. Such feelings belonged to a life that was no longer his. He did not look at her again, just pressed the travelling bag into her hands and nudged Ajax to a trot.

'Did they hurt you?' The chill had thawed only a little from his voice.

Phoebe stared and her heart was beating too fast. 'I am quite unhurt, thank you, sir. Although it seems you are not.' She smiled to hide her nervousness. Clutching her bag all the tighter with one hand, she found her handkerchief with the other and offered it to him.

His frown did little to detract from the cold handsomeness of his face, but it did make it easier for Phoebe to ignore the butterflies' frantic fluttering in her stomach and the rush of blood pounding through her veins. The bright morning sunlight cast a blue hue in the ebony of his hair and illuminated the porcelain of his skin. Dark brows slashed bold over eyes of clear pale emerald. Such stark beautiful colouring upon a face as cleanly sculpted as that of the statues of Greek gods in her papa's books. A square chiselled jaw line and cleft chin led up to well-defined purposeful lips. His nose was strong and masculine, his cheekbones high, the left one of which was sporting a small cut that was bleeding. Phoebe could feel the very air of darkness and danger emanating from him and yet still she felt she wanted to stare at him and never look away. She ignored the urge.

'You have a little blood upon your cheek.'

He took the handkerchief without a word, wiped the trickle of blood and stuffed the handkerchief into his own pocket.

She could feel the gentleman's arm around her waist anchoring her onto the saddle, and was too conscious of how close his body was to hers even though he had taken care to slide back in the saddle to leave some room between them. He might not care for manners, but Phoebe's papa had raised her well.

'Thank you for your intervention, sir.' She was pleased to hear that her voice was a deal calmer than she felt.

The pale eyes slid momentarily to hers and she saw that they were serious and appraising. He gave a small inclination of his head as acknowledgement of her gratitude, but he did not smile.

'They meant to rob me and steal a kiss.'

'That is not all they would have stolen.' She could almost feel the resonance of his voice within his chest so close was she to it, deep and rich and yet with that same coolness in it that had been there from the very start.

She looked up into those piercing eyes, not quite certain if his meaning was as she thought. She was so close she could see the iris, as pale and clear a green as that of glass, edged with solid black. She could see every individual dark lash and the dark wings of his brows. The breath seemed to lodge in her throat.

'If you have no mind to lose it, then you will not travel this road alone again.' He looked at her meaningfully and then he gee'd the horse to a canter, and there was no more talk.

As the horse gathered speed she gripped the pommel with her left hand, and held her bag in place with her right. The man's arm tightened around her and their bodies slid together so that Phoebe's right breast was hard against his chest, her right hip tight against his thigh, his hand holding firm upon her waist. Her heart was thudding too hard, her blood surging all the more and not because of the speed at which the great black horse was thundering along the road. It seemed that the man engulfed her senses, completely, utterly, so that she could not think straight. The time seemed to stretch for ever in a torture of wanton sensations.

He did not stop until they reached the coaching inn.

The high moorland surrounded them now, bleak and barren and vast, stretching into the distance as far as the eye could see. The breeze was stronger here, the birds quieter, the air that bit cooler.

And when he lowered her gently to the ground and she looked up at him to thank him again, the words died on her lips, for he was staring down at her with such intensity she could not look away. All time seemed to stop in that moment and it was as if something passed between them, something Phoebe did not understand that shimmered through the whole of her body. Finally he broke his gaze and turned, urging the great horse out of the inn's yard, out onto the road and, without a backward glance, galloped away across the moor.

Phoebe stood there with the dust caked thick upon her boots and the hem of her faded blue dress, the travelling bag in her hand, and she watched him until the dark figure upon his dark horse, so stark against the muted greens and purples and browns that surrounded him, faded against the horizon. And only then did she realise he had not asked her name nor told her his. She turned away and walked over to the small stone wall by the side of the inn and sat down in the shade to wait. The clock on the outside of the inn showed half past six.

Chapter Two

Out on the moor the land was washed with a warm orange hue from the setting sun. At Blackloch Hall Sebastian Hunter stood, sombre and unmoving, by the arched-latticework window of his study and stared out across the stretch of rugged moor. A cool breeze stirred the heavy dark-red curtains that framed the window and ruffled through his hair. The clock on the mantel chimed nine and then resumed its slow steady tick. He swirled the brandy in the crystal-cut glass and took a sip, revelling in the rich sweet taste and the heat it left as it washed over his tongue and down his throat. He was only half-listening as Jed McEwan, his friend and steward, sitting in the chair on the opposite side of the desk, covered each point on his agenda. Rather, Hunter was thinking over the day, of Bullford and Linwood's appearance in Glasgow, and more so over the happenings upon the road—of the highwaymen and the woman. Inside his pocket his fingers touched the small white-lace handkerchief.

'And finally, in less than a fortnight, it is the annual staff trip to the seaside. Do you plan to attend, Hunter?' The inflection at the end of McEwan's voice alerted him to the question.

'I do.' It was a tradition passed down through generations of the Hunter family, and Hunter would keep to it regardless of how little he wanted to go.

'We have covered every item on the list.'

Hunter moved to top up McEwan's brandy glass, but McEwan put a hand over it and declined with thanks.

'Mairi been giving you a hard time?' Hunter asked as he filled his own glass.

'No, but I should be getting back to her.' McEwan smiled at the thought and Hunter felt a small stab of jealousy at his friend's happiness. The darkness that sat upon his soul had long since smothered any such tender feelings in Hunter. 'My father is arriving tonight.'

Hunter felt the muscle flicker in his jaw. He turned away so that McEwan would not see it.

But McEwan knew. And Hunter knew that he knew.

Through the open window, over the whisper of the wind and the rustle of the heather from the moor, came the faint rumble of distant carriage wheels.

Hunter raised an eyebrow and moved to stand at the window once more. He stared out over the moor, eyes scanning the narrow winding moor road that led only to one place—all the way up to Blackloch. 'Who the hell…?' And he thought of Bullford and Linwood again.

'Sorry, Hunter. I meant to tell you earlier, but I got waylaid with other things and then it slipped my mind.' McEwan picked up his pile of papers and came to stand by Hunter's side. 'That will be your mother's companion, a Miss Phoebe Allardyce. Mrs Hunter sent Jamie with the gig to Kingswell to meet the woman from the last coach.'

Hunter frowned. He did not know that his mother had a companion. He did not know anything of his mother's life in Glasgow, nor why she had suddenly arrived back at Blackloch yesterday, especially not after the way they had parted.

Hunter watched the small dark speck of the gig grow gradually larger and he wondered fleetingly what the woman would be like—young or old, plain or pretty? To the old Sebastian Hunter it would have mattered. But to the man that stood there now, so still and sullen, it did not. What did he care who she was, what she did? Hunter glanced at McEwan.

'My mother's companion is of no interest to me.' He felt only relief that it was not Bullford or any other of his old crowd. And gladder still it was not Linwood.

McEwan made no comment. He turned away from the window and its view. 'I will see you in the morning, Hunter.'

'That is Blackloch Hall, over there, ma'am,' said the young footman driving the gig and pointed ahead. 'And to the left hand side, down from the house, is the Black Loch itself, Mr Hunter's private loch, for which the house and the moor are named.'

Phoebe peered in the direction the boy was pointing. Across the barren moorland a solitary building stood proud and lonely, sinister in its bearing, a black silhouette against the red fire of the setting sun. And beyond it, the dark waters of the loch. The gig rounded the bend and the narrow track that had been winding up to this point straightened to become an avenue of approach to the house. At the front there was nothing to differentiate where the moor stopped and the house's boundary began. No wall, no hedging, no garden. The avenue led directly up to the house. With every turn of the gig's wheels Phoebe could see Blackloch Hall loom closer.

It was a large foreboding manor house made to look like a castle by virtue of its turrets and spires. As they drew nearer Phoebe saw the rugged black stonework transform to a bleak grey. All the windows were in darkness; not the flicker of a single candle showed. All was dark and still. All was quiet. It looked as if the house had been deserted. The great iron-studded mahogany front door, beneath its pointed stone arch of strange carved symbols, remained firmly closed. As the gig passed, she saw the door's cast-iron knocker shaped like a great, snarling wolf's head and she felt the trip of her heart. The gig drove on, round the side of the house and through a tall arched gateway, taking her round into a stable yard at the back of the house.

The young footman jumped down from the gig's seat and came round to assist her before fetching her bag from the gig's shelf.

'Thank you.' Phoebe's eyes flicked over the dismal dark walls of Blackloch Hall and shivered. It was like something out of one of Mrs Hunter's romance novels, all gothic and dark and menacing. Little wonder the lady had chosen to make her home in Glasgow.

The boy shot a glance at her as if he was expecting her to say something.

'What a very striking building,' she managed.

The boy, Jamie he said his name was, gave a nod and then, carrying her bag, led on.

Taking a deep breath, Phoebe followed Jamie towards the back door of the house. He no longer spoke and all around was silence, broken only by the crunch of their shoes against the gravel.

From high on the roof the caw of a solitary crow sounded, and from the corner of her eye she saw the flutter of dark wings…and she thought of the man against whom her father had warned her— Sebastian Hunter. A shiver rippled down her spine as she stepped across the threshold into Blackloch Hall.

Phoebe did not see Mrs Hunter until late the next morning in the drawing room, which to Phoebe's eye looked less like a drawing room and more like the medieval hall of an ancient castle.

Suspended from the centre of the ceiling was a huge circular black-iron chandelier. She could smell the sweetness of the honey-coloured beeswax candles that studded its circumference. The rough-hewn walls were covered with faded dull tapestries depicting hunting scenes and the floor of grey stone flags was devoid of a single carpet rug. A massive medieval-style fireplace was positioned in the centre of the wall to her left, complete with worn embroidered lum seats. A fire had been laid upon the hearth, but had not been lit so that, even though it was the height of summer, the room had a distinct chill to it. The three large lead-latticed windows that spanned the wall opposite the fireplace showed a fine view over the moor outside.

The furniture seemed a hodgepodge of styles: a pair of Italian-styled giltwood stools, a plainly fashioned but practical rotating square bookcase, a huge gilded eagle perched upon the floor beside the door, its great wings supporting a table top of grey-and-white marble, a small card table with the austere neoclassical lines of Sheraton, and on its surface a chessboard with its intricately carved pieces of ebony and ivory. Farther along the room was a long dark-green sofa and on either side of the sofa was a matching armchair and, behind them, in the corner, a suit of armour.

Mrs Hunter was ensconced on the sofa, supervising the making of the pot of tea. She watched while Phoebe added milk and a lump of sugar to the two fine bone-china cups and poured.

'How was your father, Phoebe? Does he fare any better?'

'A little,' said Phoebe, feeling the hand of guilt heavy upon her shoulder.

'That at least is something.' The lady smiled and took the cup and saucer that Phoebe offered. 'And you attended to all of my matters before your visit to the hospital?'

'Yes, ma'am. Everything is in order. Mrs Montgomery will send your invitation to Blackloch Hall rather than Charlotte Street. I delivered the sample books back to Messrs Hudson and Collier and to Mrs Murtrie. As you suspected Mr Lyle did not have your shoes ready, but he says they will be done by the end of the week.'

'Very well.'

Phoebe continued. 'I collected your powders from Dr Watt and have informed all of the names on your list that you will be visiting Blackloch Hall for the next month and may be contacted here. And the letters and parcel I left with the receiving office.'

'Good.' Mrs Hunter gave a nod. 'And how was the journey down?'

'Fine, thank you,' she lied and focused her attention to stirring the sugar into her tea most vigorously so that she would not have to look at her employer.

'The coach was not too crowded?'

'Not at all. I was most fortunate.' A vision of the highwaymen and of a dark and handsome man with eyes the colour of emerald ice chips swam into her head. The teaspoon overbalanced from her saucer and dropped to the flagstones below where it bounced and disappeared out of sight beneath her chair. Phoebe set her cup and saucer down on the table and knelt to retrieve the spoon.

'I would have sent John with the coach, but I do not wish to be at Blackloch without my own carriage at my dispos—' Mrs Hunter broke off as the drawing-room door opened and the movement of footsteps sounded. 'Sebastian, my, but you honour me.' To Phoebe's surprise the lady's tone was acidic.

Phoebe felt a ripple of foreboding down her spine. She reached quickly for the teaspoon.

'Mother, forgive my absence yesterday. I was delayed by matters in Glasgow.' The man's voice was deep and cool as spring water... and disturbingly familiar.

Phoebe stilled, her fingers gripping the spoon's handle for dear life. Her heart was thudding too fast.

It could not be.

It was not possible.

Slowly she got to her feet and turned to face the wicked Mr Hunter. And there, standing only a few feet away across the room, was her dark handsome rescuer from the moor road.

Hunter stared at the young auburn-haired woman he had left standing alone at the Kingswell Inn. Her cheeks had paled. Her lips had parted. Her warm tawny eyes stared wide. She looked every inch as shocked as he felt.

He moved to his mother and touched his lips to her cool cheek. She suffered it as if he were a leper, shuddering slightly with distaste. So, nothing had changed after all. He wondered why the hell she was here at Blackloch.

'Sebastian.' His mother's voice was cold, if polite for the sake of the woman's presence. 'This is my companion, Miss Allardyce. She came down on the late coach last night.' Then to the woman, 'Miss Allardyce, my *son*, Mr Hunter.' He could hear the effort it took her to force the admission of their kinship.

'Mr Hunter,' the woman said in that same clear calm voice he would have recognised anywhere, and made her curtsy, yet he saw the small flare of concern in her eyes before she hid it.

'Miss Allardyce.' He inclined his head ever so slightly in the woman's direction, and understood her worry given that it was now obvious she had palmed the money his mother had given her for her coach fare.

She was wearing the same blue dress, although every speck of dust looked to have been brushed from it. The colour highlighted the red burnish to her hair, now scraped and tightly pinned in a neat coil at the nape of her neck. His gaze lingered briefly on her face, on the small straight nose and those dewy dusky pink lips that made him want to wet his own. And he remembered the soft feel of her pressed against him on the saddle, and the clean rose-touched scent of her, and the shock of a desire he had thought quelled for good. She was temptation personified. And she was everything proper and correct that a lady's companion should be as she resumed her seat and calmly waited for Hunter to spill her secret.

Not that Hunter had any intention of doing so. After her experience with the highwaymen he doubted she would make the same mistake again. He watched as she set the teaspoon she was holding down upon the tray and lifted her cup and saucer.

His mother's tone was cool as she turned to her companion. 'My son has not seen his mother in nine months, Miss Allardyce, and yet he cannot bring himself into my company. This is his first appearance since my arrival at Blackloch.'

Miss Allardyce looked uneasy and took a sip of tea.

His mother turned her attention back to Hunter. 'Your concern is overwhelming. I think I can see the precise nature of the matters so important to keep you from me.' Her eyes were cold and appraising as they took in the small cut on his cheek and the bruising that surrounded it. She raised an eyebrow and gave a small snort.

'You have been brawling.'

He made no denial.

Miss Allardyce's eyes opened marginally wider.

'What were you fighting over this time? Let me guess, some new gaming debt?'

He stiffened, but kept his expression impassive and cool.

'No? If not that, then over a woman, I will warrant.'

A pause, during which he saw the slight colour that had washed the soft cream of Miss Allardyce's cheeks heighten.

'You know me too well, madam.'

'Indeed, I do. You are not changed in the slightest, not for all your promises—'

There was the rattle of china as Miss Allardyce set her cup and saucer down. 'Mrs Hunter...' The woman got to her feet. 'I fear you are mistaken, ma'am. Mr Hu—'

His mother turned her frown on her companion.

'Miss Allardyce,' Hunter interrupted smoothly, 'this is none of your affair and I would that it stay that way.' His tone was frosty with warning. If his mother wanted to believe the worst of him, let her. He would not have some girl defend him. He still had some measure of pride.

Miss Allardyce stared at him for a moment, with such depths in those golden-brown eyes of hers that he wondered what she was thinking. And then she calmly sat back down in her chair.

'Ever the gentleman, Sebastian,' said his mother. 'You see, Miss

Allardyce, do not waste your concern on him. He is quite beyond the niceties of society. Now you know why I do not come to Blackloch. Such unpleasant company.'

He leaned back in his chair. 'If we are speaking bluntly, what then has prompted your visit, madam?'

'I am having the town house redecorated and am in need of somewhere to stay for a few weeks, Sebastian. What other reason could possibly bring me here?' his mother sneered.

He gave a bow and left, vowing to avoid both his mother and the woman who made him remember too well the dissolute he had been.

After the awfulness of that first day Hunter did not seek his mother out again. And Phoebe could not blame him. She wondered why he had not told Mrs Hunter the truth of the cut upon his face or revealed that his mother's companion had not spent her money upon a coach fare after all. She wondered, too, as to why there was such hostility between mother and son. But Mrs Hunter made not a single mention of her son, and it was easy to keep her promise to her father as Phoebe saw little of the man in the days that followed. Once she saw him entering his study. Another time she caught a glimpse of him riding out on the moor. But nothing more. Not that Phoebe had time to notice, for Mrs Hunter was out of sorts, her mood as bleak as the moor that surrounded them.

Tuesday came around quickly and Phoebe could only be glad both of her chance to escape the oppressive atmosphere of Blackloch and to see her father.

The Glasgow Tolbooth was an impressive five-storey sandstone building situated at the Cross where the Trongate met High Street. It housed not only the gaol, but also the Justiciary Court and the Town Hall, behind which had been built the Tontine Hotel. There was a small square turret at each corner and a fine square spire on the east side, in which was fitted a large clock. And the top of the spire arched in the form of an imperial crown. The prison windows were small and clad with iron bars, and over the main door, on the south side, was built a small rectangular portico on a level with the first floor of the prison, the stairs from which led directly down onto the street.

Phoebe arrived at the Tolbooth, glad of heart both to be back in the familiar cheery bustle of Glasgow and at the prospect of seeing her father. She hurried along the street and was just about to climb the stone steps to the portico and the main door when a man appeared by her side.

'Miss Allardyce?'

She stopped and glanced round at him.

He pulled the cloth cap from his head, revealing thick fair hair beneath. He was of medium height with nothing to mark him as noticeable. His clothes were neither shabby nor well-tailored, grey trousers and matching jacket, smart enough, but not those of a gentleman. Something of his manner made her think that he was in service. He blended well with the background in all features except his voice.

'Miss Phoebe Allardyce?' he said again and she heard the cockney twang to his accent, so different to the lilt of the Scottish voices all around.

'Who are you, sir?' She looked at him with suspicion. He was certainly no one that she knew.

'I'm the Messenger.'

His eyes were a washed-out grey and so narrow that they lent him a shifty air. She made to walk on, but his next words stopped her.

'If you've a care for your father, you'll listen.'

She narrowed her own eyes slightly, feeling an instant dislike for the man. 'What do you want?'

'To deliver a message to you.' He was slim but there was a wiry strength to his frame.

'I am listening,' she said.

'Your father's locked up in there for the rest of his days. Old man like him, his health not too good. And the conditions being what they are in the Tolbooth. Must worry you that.'

'My father's welfare and my feelings on the matter are none of your concern, sir.' She made to walk on.

'They are if I can spring him, Miss Allardyce, or, should I say, give you the means to do so. Fifteen hundred pounds to pay his debt, plus another five hundred to set the pair of you up in a decent enough lifestyle.'

A cold feeling spread over her. She stared at him in shock. 'How do you know the details of my father's debt?'

The man gave a leering smile and she noticed that his teeth were straight and white. 'Oh, we know all about you and your pa. Don't you worry your pretty little head about that. Just think on the money. Two grand in the hand, Miss Allardyce, and old pop is out of the Tolbooth.'

'You are offering me two thousand pounds?' She stared at him in disbelief.

He threw her a purse. 'A hundred up front.' She peeped inside and felt her heart turn over as she saw the roll of white notes. 'The rest when you deliver your end of the bargain.'

'Which is?'

'The smallest of favours.'

She waited.

'As Mrs Hunter's companion you have access to the whole of Blackloch Hall.'

Her scalp prickled with the extent of his knowledge.

'There is a certain object currently within the possession of the lady's son, a trifling little thing that he wouldn't even miss.'

'You are asking me to steal from Mr Hunter?'

'We're asking you to retrieve an item for its rightful owner.'

The man was trouble, as was all that he asked. She shook her head and gave a cynical smile as she thrust the purse back into his hands. 'Good day to you, sir.' And she started to climb the steps. She climbed all of four steps before his voice sounded again. He had not moved, but still stood where he was in the street.

'If you won't do it for the money, Miss Allardyce, you best have a thought for your pa locked up in there. Dangerous place is the Tolbooth. All sorts of unsavoury characters, the sort your pa ain't got a chance against. Who knows who he'll be sharing a cell with next? You have a think about that, Miss Allardyce.'

The man's words made her blood run cold, but she did not look back, just ran up the remaining steps and through the porch to the front door of the gaol.

'Everything all right, miss?' the door guard enquired.

'Yes, thank you,' she said as she slipped inside to the large square hallway. 'If I could just have a moment to gather myself?'

The guard nodded.

Her hands were trembling as she stood aside a little to let the other visitors pass. She took several deep breaths, leaned her back against one of the great stone columns and calmed her thoughts. It was an idle threat, that was all. The villain could not truly hurt her father within the security of a prison as tough and rigorous as the Tolbooth. The man was a villain, a thief, trying to frighten her into stealing for him. And Phoebe had no intention of being blackmailed. She tucked some stray strands of hair beneath her bonnet, and smoothed a hand over the top of her skirts. And only when she was sure that her papa would not notice anything amiss did she make her way through the doorway that led to the prison cells. Once through that door she passed the guard her basket for checking.

He removed the cover and gave the contents a quick glance. 'Raspberries this week, is it?' With her weekly visits over the last six months Phoebe was on friendly terms with most of the guards and turnkeys.

'They are my papa's favourite.'

'Sir Henry'll fair enjoy them.'

'I hope so.' She smiled and followed him up the narrow staircase all the way up to the debtors' cells on the third floor in which her father was held.

But the smile fled her face and the raspberries were forgotten the moment she entered the cell.

'Papa!' She placed the basket down on the small wooden table and ran to him. 'Oh, my word! What ever has happened to you?' She guided him to stand in the narrow shaft of sunlight that shone down into the cell through the bars of the small high window. And there in the light she could see that the skin around Sir Henry's left eye was dark with bruising and so swollen as to partially conceal the bloodshot eye beneath. The bruising extended over the whole left side of his face, from his temple to his chin, and even on that side of his mouth his lower lip was swollen and cut.

'Now, child, do not fuss so. It is nothing but the result of my own foolish clumsiness.'

But the man's words were ringing in her head again. *Dangerous place is the Tolbooth. All sorts of unsavoury characters, the sort your pa ain't got a chance against.*

'Who did this to you?' she demanded; she did not realise her grip had tightened and her knuckles shone white with the strain of it. 'Who?' Her eyes roved over his poor battered face.

'I tripped and fell, Phoebe. Nothing more. Calm yourself.'

'Papa—'

'Phoebe,' her father said, and she recognised that tone in his voice. He would tell her nothing. He did not want to worry her, not when he thought there was nothing she could do.

Her gaze scanned the cell. 'Where is the other man, your cell-mate?'

'Released,' pronounced her father. 'His debt was paid off.' Sir Henry nodded philosophically. 'He was interesting company.'

Who knows who he'll be sharing a cell with next?

Phoebe felt her stomach clench and a wave of nausea rise up.

'You are white as a sheet, child. Perhaps this travelling up from Blackloch Hall is too much for you.'

'No. Really.' She forced herself to smile at him brightly, so that he would not be concerned. 'I have been taking very great care to keep my complexion fair. A difficult proposition with red hair and the summer sun. I do not wish to end up with freckles!' She pretended to tease and managed an accompanying grin.

He chuckled. 'You have your mother's colouring, and she never had a freckle in her life, God rest her soul.'

Her eyes lingered momentarily on his bruising and she thought for one dreadful minute she might weep. It was such a struggle to maintain the façade, but she knew she had to for his sake. The smile was still stretched across her mouth as she took his arm in her own and led him back to the little table they had managed to save from the bailiffs. Her blood was cold and thick and slow as she pulled off the basket's cover to reveal the punnet of raspberries within.

'Oh, Phoebe, well done,' he said and picked out the largest and juiciest berry and slipped it into his mouth. 'So, tell me all about Blackloch Hall and the moor…and Hunter.'

'Oh, I have rarely seen Mr Hunter.' It was not a lie. 'But he seems to be a gentleman of honour, if a little cold in manner perhaps.' She thought of how Hunter had rescued her from the highwaymen and his discretion over the same matter.

'Do not be fooled, Phoebe. From all accounts the words honour and Sebastian Hunter do not go together in the same sentence. Why do you think his mother has disowned him?'

'I did not realise there was such…' she hesitated '…bad feeling between them,' she finished as she thought of the one interaction she had witnessed between Hunter and his mother. 'What is the cause of it, I wonder?'

'Who can know for sure?' Her father gave a shrug, but there was something in his manner that suggested that he knew more of the matter.

'But you must have heard something?'

'Nothing to be repeated to such innocent ears, child.' She saw the slight wince before he could disguise it. He eased himself to a more comfortable position upon the wooden stool and she saw the strain and pain that he was trying to hide.

She pressed him no further on the matter, but tried to distract him with descriptions of the Gothic style of the house and the expansive ruggedness of the moor. And all the while she was conscious of the raw soreness of her father's injuries. By the time she kissed her father's undamaged cheek and made her way down the narrow staircase, her heart was thudding hard with the coldness of her purpose and there was a fury in her eyes.

The man was leaning against the outside of the gaol, waiting for her.

He pulled off his hat again as he came towards her. 'Miss Allar—' he started to say, but she cut him off, her voice hard as she hid the emotion beneath it. She looked at him and would have run the villain through with a sword had she one to hand.

'I will do it, on the proviso that no further harm comes to my father.'

There was a fleeting surprise in those narrow shifty eyes as if he had not thought her to agree so quickly.

'What is it that you want me to steal?'

And he leaned his face closer and whispered the words softly into her ear.

She nodded.

'We have been told Hunter keeps it in his study—in his desk.

Bring it here with you when you visit next Tuesday. And keep your lips sealed over this, Miss Allardyce. One word to Mrs Hunter or her son and your old pa gets it…' He drew his finger across his throat like a knife blade to emphasise his point. 'Do you understand?'

'I understand perfectly,' she said and as the crowd hurried past, someone jostled her and when she looked round at the man again he was gone.

Her heart was aching for the hurts her father had suffered and her blood was surging with fury at the men who had hurt him. She knew she must not weaken, must not weep, not here, not now. She straightened her shoulders, held her head up and walked with purpose the small distance to the Tontine Hotel to wait for the mail coach that would deliver her to the moor.

Chapter Three

The moor was bathed golden and hazy in the late evening light. Behind the house, out over the Firth of Clyde, the sun would soon sink down behind the islands, a red ball of fire in a pink streaked sky. There was no sound, nothing save the steady slow tick of the clock and the whisper of the breeze through the grass and the heather.

Hunter remembered the last day of his father's life. When he closed his eyes he could see his father's face ruddy with choler, etched with disgust, and hear their final shouted exchange echoing in his head, each and every angry word of it…and what had followed. Thereafter, there had been such remorse, such anger, such guilt. He ached with it. And all the brandy in Britain and France did not change a damned thing.

The glass lay limp and empty within his hand. Hunter thought no more, just refilled it and settled back to numb the pain.

Phoebe struck that night, before her courage or her anger could desert her. Mrs Hunter was in bed when she arrived back in Blackloch, having retired early as was her normal habit.

Within the green guest bedchamber Phoebe went through the mechanics of preparing for bed. She changed into her nightdress, washed, brushed her teeth, combed and plaited her hair, brushed the dust from her dress and wiped her boots. And then she sat down in the little green armchair and she waited…and waited; waiting as the hours crawled by until, at last, Phoebe heard no more footsteps, no more voices, no more noise.

Daylight had long since faded and darkness shrouded the house. From downstairs in the hallway by the front door she heard the striking of the grandfather clock, two deep sonorous chimes. Only now did Phoebe trust that all of Blackloch was asleep. She stole from her room, treading as quietly and as quickly as she could along the corridor and down the main staircase.

The house was in total darkness and she was thankful she had decided to bring the single candle to light her way. Its small flame flickered as she walked, casting ghostly shadows all around. There was silence, the thump of her heart and whisper of her breath the only sounds. Her feet trod softly, carefully, down each step until she reached the main hallway. She could hear the slow heavy ticking of the clock.

The hallway was expansive, floored in the same greystone flags that ran throughout the whole of the lower house and roofed with dark disappearing arches reminiscent of some ancient medieval cathedral. She held up her candle to confirm she was alone and saw a small snarling face staring down at her from the arches. She jumped, almost dropping her candle in the process, and gave a gasp. Her heart was racing. She stared back at the face and saw this time that it was only the gargoyle of a wolf carved into the stone. Indeed, there was a whole series of them hidden within the ribs of the ceiling: a pack of wolves, all watching her. She froze, holding her breath, her heart thumping hard and fast, waiting to see if anyone had heard her, waiting to see if anyone would come. The grandfather clock marked the passing of the minutes, five in all, and nobody arrived. She breathed a sigh of relief and looked across at the study.

Not the slightest glimmer of light showed beneath the doorway.

No sound came from within. Phoebe crept quietly towards the dark mahogany door, placed her hand upon the wrought-iron handle and slowly turned. The door opened without a creak. She held up her candle to light the darkness and stepped into Sebastian Hunter's study.

Hunter was sitting silently in his chair by the window, his eyes staring blindly out at the dark-enveloped moor when he heard the noise from the hallway outside his study. The waning half moon was hidden under a small streak of cloud and the black-velvet sky was lit only by a sprinkling of stars, bright and twinkly as diamonds. His head turned, listening, but otherwise he did not move. His senses sharpened. And even though he had been drinking he was instantly alert.

Someone was out there, he could feel their presence. A maidservant on her way down to the kitchens? A footman returning to bed following a tryst? Or another intruder, like the ones who had tried before? He set the brandy glass down and quietly withdrew the pistol from the bottom right-hand drawer of his desk, then turned the chair back to face the moor so that he would not be seen from the doorway; he waited, and he listened.

He listened to the light pad of footsteps across the stone flags towards his door. He listened as the handle slowly turned and the door quietly opened, then closed again. Within the small diamond-shaped lead-lined panes he saw the reflection of a bright flicker of candlelight. The soft even tread of small feet moved towards the desk behind him. He waited until he heard the clunk of the brass candlestick being set down upon the wooden surface of the desk behind him, then he cocked the pistol and swivelled his chair round to face the intruder.

She was standing with her back to him, looking over his desk.

'Miss Allardyce.'

She started round to face him, gave a small shriek and stumbled back against the desk. Her mouth worked, but no words sounded.

He rose to his feet.

Her gaze dropped to the pistol.

He made it safe and lowered it.

'Mr Hunter,' she said and he could hear the shock in her voice and see it in every nuance of her face, of her body and the way she was gripping at the desk behind her. 'I had no idea that you were in here.'

'Evidently not.' He let his gaze wander from the long thick auburn braid of her hair that hung over her shoulder, down across the bodice of the cotton nightdress which, though prim and plain and patched in places, did not quite hide the figure beneath. His gaze dropped lower to the little bare toes that peeped from beneath its hem, before lifting once more to those golden brown eyes. And something of the woman seemed to call to him so that, just as when he had first looked at her upon the moor, an overwhelming desire surged through him. Had this been a year ago... Had this been before all that had changed him...

He saw her glance flicker away before coming back to meet his own and, when she did, he could see she had recovered herself and where the shock and panic had been there was now calm determination.

'Mrs Hunter is having trouble sleeping. She sent me to find a book for her, in the hope that it would help.' She made to move away and he should have let her go, but Hunter stepped closer, effectively blocking her exit.

'Any book in particular?'

Miss Allardyce gave a little shrug. 'She did not say.' The backs of her thighs were still tight against the desk, her hands behind her still gripping to its wooden edge.

He leaned across her to lay the pistol down upon the smooth

polished surface of the desk and the brush of his arm against the softness of her breast sent his blood rushing all the faster.

Miss Allardyce sucked in her breath and jumped at the contact between their bodies. He saw the shock in her eyes…and the passion, and knew she was not indifferent to him, that something of the madness of this sensation was racing through her, too.

He was standing so close that the toe of his left boot was beneath the hem of her nightdress. So close that the scent of roses and sunlight and sweet woman filled his nose. His gaze traced the outline of her features, of her cheekbones and her nose, down to the fullness of her lips. And the urge to take her into his arms and kiss her was overwhelming. A vision of them making love upon the surface of the desk swam in his mind, of him moving between the pale soft thighs beneath the thick cotton of her nightdress, of his mouth upon her breasts…

Desire hummed loud. He had never experienced such an immediacy of feeling like that which was coursing between him and Miss Allardyce. Hunter slid a hand behind that slender creamy neck and her lips seemed to call to his. All of his promises were forgotten. He lowered his face towards hers…

And felt the firm thrust of Miss Allardyce's hands against his chest.

'What on earth do you think you are doing, Mr Hunter?' Her chest was rising and falling in a rapid rhythm, her breath as ragged as if they had indeed just made love.

It was enough to shatter the madness of the moment. He realised what he was doing.

She was staring at him, her eyes suddenly dark in the candle-light, her cheeks stained with colour.

'Forgive me.' He stepped swiftly back to place a distance between them. He was not a rake. He damn well was not. Not any more. He did not gamble. And he did not womanise. 'A book, you say?'

'If you please.' A no-nonsense tone, unaffected, except that when she picked up the candlestick he could see the slight tremor of it in her hand.

'Be my guest.' He gestured to the books that lined the walls and moved away even further to the safety of the shelves closest to the window. '*Evelina* used to be a favourite of my mother's,' he said and drew the volume from its shelf. He offered it to her, holding it by the farthest edge so that their fingers would not touch.

She accepted the book from him, said 'Thank you', and made her way to the door where she paused, hand resting on the handle, and glanced round at him.

'And thank you for both your assistance upon the moor and your discretion over the matter.' She spoke with hesitation and he could feel her awkwardness at both the situation and the words, but there was a strength in her eyes that he had not seen in any other woman before. 'I will catch the coach in the future.' And before he could utter a word she was gone, leaving Hunter staring at the softly closed door of his study with a firm resolve to keep a distance between Miss Allardyce and himself for the weeks that remained of his mother's visit.

Inside the green bedchamber Phoebe leaned heavily against the door. Her legs felt like jelly and she was shaking so badly that the candlelight flickered and jumped wildly around the room. She set the candlestick down upon her little table and tried to calm the frenzied beat of her heart, to no avail.

Her heart was hammering as hard as it had been when she had faced Hunter in his study. Standing there in just his shirt and breeches. No coat, no waistcoat, no neckcloth. The neck of his fine white shirt open and loose, revealing the bare skin beneath, a chest that she knew was hard with muscle from the hand she had placed upon it. Memories of his very proximity that made it difficult for her to catch a breath. She closed her eyes and in her mind saw again that piercing gaze holding hers, driving every sensible thought from her head, making her stomach turn a cartwheel and her legs melt to jelly. Images and sensations vivid enough to take her breath away, all of which should have shocked and appalled her. She *was* shocked. Shocked at the spark the mere brush of his arm had ignited throughout her body. Shocked that for the tiniest of moments she had almost let him kiss her. Phoebe had never experienced anything like it. She clutched a hand to her mouth and tried to stop the stampede of emotion.

What on earth was he doing sitting in there in the dark in the middle of the night anyway? And she remembered the rich sweet smell of brandy that had clung to his breath and the way his chair had been positioned to face out onto the moor. A man who did not sleep. A man who had much to brood upon.

She walked to the window and pulled the curtains apart. Unfastening the catch, she slid the window up and stared out at the night beyond. The bitten wafer of the moon shone silver and all around, scattered across the deep black velvet of the sky, were tiny stars like diamonds. Cool fresh air wafted in and she inhaled its sweet dampness, breathing slowly and deeply in an attempt to calm herself. Not so far away she could hear the quiet ripple of the Black Loch, its water merging with the darkness of the night. She thought of her father's warning about Hunter and his wickedness. And no matter how much she willed it, her heart would not slow or her mind dismiss the image of a raven-haired man whose eyes were so strangely and dangerously alluring.

In the cool light of the next morning after a restless night Phoebe could see things more clearly. Hunter had discovered her about to search his desk in the middle of the night. No doubt any woman's thoughts would be in such disarray and her sensibilities so thoroughly disturbed were a gun levelled at her heart by a gentleman with Hunter's reputation. The important thing was that he had appeared to believe her excuse and for that she could only be thankful.

Phoebe had bigger matters to worry about. She could not let the incident in the night deter her from securing her father's safety.

Phoebe tried again the next night and the night after that, but each time she stole down the stairs it was to see the faint flicker of light beneath the door to Hunter's study and she knew he was alone within, drinking through the night, as if he could not bear to sleep. As if he were haunted. As if he carried a sin so dark upon his soul that it chained him in perpetual torment. She shivered and forced the thoughts away, knowing that the days before Tuesday and her visit to the Tolbooth were too few. There had to be a way to search the study. Phoebe was in an agony of worry.

It was Mrs Hunter who solved the problem…when she told Phoebe of the Blackloch outing to the seaside planned for Saturday.

The morning of the trip was glorious. The sun shone down on a sea that stretched out in a broad glistening vastness before him. To the right was the edge of the island of Arran, and to the left, in the distance, the characteristic conical lump on the horizon that was the rock of Ailsa Craig. A bank of grass led down to the large curved bay of golden sand. It was beautiful, but nothing of the scene touched Hunter.

He and McEwan dismounted, tying their horses to a nearby tethering pole. The maids and footmen were milling around the carriages, chatting and laughing with excitement. McEwan looked to Hunter for his nod, then went to organise the party, to see that the blankets were spread upon the sands before collecting the picnic hampers and baskets containing the bottles of lemonade and elderflower cordial. Hunter stood there for a moment alone, detached, remote from the good spirits, and watched as the men peeled off their jackets and the women abandoned their shawls and pushed up their sleeves. There was such joviality, such happiness and anticipation amongst the entirety of his household that Hunter felt his very presence might spoil it. He moved away towards his mother's coach where her footman was already assisting her down the steps.

She threw him a grudging nod. 'I am glad that at least you have not let the old customs slip.'

He gave a nod of acknowledgement, his face cold and expressionless to hide the memories her words evoked.

His mother took her parasol from the maid who appeared from the carriage behind her. There was a silence as she surveyed the scene before her, a small half-smile upon her mouth there not for Hunter, but for the sake of the staff.

Hunter glanced round, expecting Miss Allardyce, but his mother's companion did not appear.

'The book was to your satisfaction?' he enquired.

'The book?' His mother peered at him as if he were talking double Dutch.

'*Evelina,*' he prompted.

'I have not seen that book in years,' she said and turned her attention away from him.

Hunter turned the implication of her answer over in his mind and let the minutes pass before he spoke again.

'Your companion does not accompany you,' he said, as if merely making an observation. His face remained forward, watching the staff as they carried the hampers down onto the sand.

'Miss Allardyce is feeling unwell. I told her to spend the day in bed, resting.' His mother equally kept her focus on the maids and the footmen.

'The timing of her illness is unfortunate.' *Or fortunate, depending on whose point of view one was considering,* he thought grimly.

His mother nodded. 'Indeed it is—poor girl.'

Once everyone was settled upon the blankets, his mother in pride of place upon a chair and rug, he and McEwan removed their coats, rolled up their sleeves and served plates of cold sliced cooked chicken, ham and beef to the waiting servants. There were bread rolls and cheese and hard-boiled eggs. There were strawber-ries and raspberries, fresh cooled cream and the finest jams, sponge cakes, peppermint creams and hard-boiled sweets. And chunks of ice all wrapped up and placed amongst the food and drink to keep it cool. Expense had not been skimped upon. Hunter wanted his staff to have a good time, just as his father had done before him and his father before him.

This was duty. He knew that and so he endured it, even though the laughter and light that surrounded him made him feel all the darker and all the more alone. Hunter stood aside from the rest and watched the little party, his mother in the centre of it, good hu-moured, partaking in the jokes and the chatter; the few staff that remained at Blackloch were as warm with her as if she had never left.

He slid a glance at his pocket watch before making his way over to his mother. The laughter on her face died away as soon as she saw him. And he thought he saw something of the light in her expire.

'There are matters at Blackloch to which I must attend. I will leave McEwan at your disposal.'

She smiled, if it could be called that, but her eyes were filled with disdain and condemnation. She made no attempt to dissuade him. Indeed, she looked positively relieved that he was leaving.

McEwan appeared by his side as Hunter pulled on his coat.

'Attend to my mother's wishes if you will, McEwan. I will see you back at Blackloch later.' Hunter brushed his heels against Ajax's flank and was gone, heading back along the road to Blackloch Hall.

Phoebe did not know where else to look in the sunlit study. All six desk drawers lay open. She had searched through each one twice and found nothing of what she sought. There were bottles of ink, pens and pen sharpeners. There was also a packet of crest-embossed writing paper, books of estate accounts, newspapers and letters, a brace of pistols and even a roll of crisp white banknotes, but not the object she must steal. She had searched all of the library shelves, even sliding each deep red leather-bound book out just in case, but behind them was only dark old mahogany and a fine layer of dust.

The faint aroma of brandy still hung in the air, rich and sweet and ripe, mixed with the underlying scent of a man's cologne—the smell of Hunter. She thought of him sitting in this room through the long dark hours of the night, alone and filling himself with brandy. And despite her father's words, and whatever it was that Hunter had done, she could not help but feel a twinge of compassion for him.

She slumped down into Hunter's chair, not knowing what to do. The man had said it would be in Hunter's study. But Phoebe had been looking for over an hour without a sight of it. She leaned her elbows on the dark ebony surface of Hunter's desk and rested her head in her hands. *Where else to look? Where?* But there were no other hiding places to search.

The sun was beating through the arched lattice windows directly upon her and she felt flustered and hot and worried. A bead of sweat trickled between her breasts as she got to her feet, her shoulders tense and tight with disappointment and worry. There was nothing more to be gained by searching yet again. The Messenger, as he called himself, had been wrong; she could do nothing other than tell him so.

She thought of Mrs Hunter, and the man who was her son, and of all the staff down at the seaside, with the cooling sea breeze and the wash of the waves rolling in over the sand, and up to the ankles of those who dared to paddle. Her fingers wiped the sweat from her brow and she felt a pang of jealousy. And then she remembered the loch with its still cool water and its smooth dark surface. She rubbed at the ache of tension that throbbed in her shoulders as she thought of its soothing peacefulness and tranquillity.

She knew she should not, but Mrs Hunter had said they would

not be back until late afternoon, and there was no one here to see. Phoebe felt very daring as she closed the door of Hunter's study behind her.

The glare of the mid-day sun was relentless as Hunter cantered along the Kilmarnock road. He would not gallop Ajax until he reached the softer ground of the moor. Sweat glistened on the horse's neck, but the heat of the day did not touch Hunter, for he was chilled inside, chilled as the dead. In the sky above it was as if a great dark cloud covered the sun, the same dark shadow that dogged him always.

He thought of Miss Allardyce and he spurred Ajax on until he reached Blackloch.

Hunter stabled his horse and then slipped into the house through the back door. All was quiet, and still; the only things moving were the tiny particles of dust dancing in the sunlight bathing the hall-way. He made his way into his study, his refuge. And, dispensing with his hat and gloves, scanned the room with a new eye.

Nothing looked out of place. Everything was just as he had left it. The piles of paperwork and books perched at the far edge of his desk, the roll of banknotes in the top drawer, the set of pistols in the bottom. He pulled out the money, counted the notes—not one was missing. Upon the shelves that lined the room the books, bound in their dark red leather with gold-lettered spines, sat uniform and tidy. No gaps caught the eye. His gaze moved to the fourth shelf by the window, to the one gap that should have been there. *Evelina* sat in its rightful place.

Hunter poured himself a brandy and sat down at the desk. She had been in here. He mused over the knowledge while he sipped at the brandy. Returning a book that she had lied about needing to borrow. His gaze moved over the polished ebony surface of his desk, and he saw it—a single hair, long and stark against the darkness of the wood. A hair that had not been there this morning, on a desk that she had no need to be near in order to return the book to its shelf. He lifted it carefully, held it between his fingers and, in the light from the window, the hair glowed a deep burnished red. Hunter felt a spurt of anger that he had allowed his physical reaction to the woman cloud his judgement. He abandoned his brandy and made his way to find Miss Allardyce.

It was no surprise to find the bedchamber empty and the bed neatly made. He undertook a cursory search of her belongings, of which it seemed that Miss Allardyce possessed scant few. A green silk evening dress, the bonnet she had been wearing upon the moor road the day he had encountered her with the highwaymen. A pair of well-worn brown leather boots, one pair of green silk slippers to match the dress. A shawl of pale grey wool, a dark cloak, some gloves, underwear. All of it outmoded and worn, but well cared for. A hairbrush, ribbons, a toothbrush and powder, soap. No jewellery. Nothing that he would not expect to find. And yet a feeling nagged in his gut that something with Miss Allardyce was not quite right. And where the hell was she?

He stood where he was, his gaze ranging the room that held her scent—sweet and clean, roses and soap. And then something caught his eye in the scene through the window. A pale movement in the dark water of the loch. Hunter moved closer and stared out, his eye following the moorland running down to the loch. And the breath caught in his throat, for there in the waters of the Black Loch was a woman—a young, naked woman. Her long hair, dark reddish brown, wet and swirling around her, her skin ivory where she lay beneath the surface of the water, so still that he wondered if she were drowned. But then those slim pale arms moved up and over her head, skimming the water behind her as she swam, and he could see the slight churn where she kicked her feet.

He stood there and watched, unable to help himself. Watched the small mounds of her breasts break the surface and fall beneath again. He watched her rise up, emerging from the loch's dark depths like a red-haired Aphrodite, naked and beautiful. Even across the distance he could see her wet creamy skin, the curve of her small breasts with their rosy tips, the narrowness of her waist and the gentle swell of her hips. She stood on the bank and wrung out her hair, sending more rivulets of water cascading down her body before reaching down to pull on her shift. Hunter felt his mouth go dry and his body harden. He knew now the whereabouts of Miss Allardyce—she was swimming in his loch.

Chapter Four

Phoebe hummed as she hurried up the main staircase, carrying her petticoats and dress draped over her arm. She resolved that once she was dressed she would retrace her route and wipe the trail of wet footprints she was leaving in her wake. The tension had eased from her shoulders; she was feeling clear-headed and much more positive about tackling the Messenger on Tuesday. She was padding down the corridor towards her bedchamber when one of the doors on the left opened and out stepped Sebastian Hunter.

Phoebe gave a shriek and almost dropped her bundle of clothes. 'What on earth…? Good heavens!' He seemed to take up the whole of the passageway ahead. She saw his gaze sweep down over her body where the thin worn cotton of her shift was moulded to the dampness of her skin; she clutched her dress and undergarments tight to cover her indecency.

'Mr Hunter, you startled me. I thought you were gone to the seaside with the rest of the house.' She could feel the scald of embarrassment in her cheeks and hear the slight breathlessness of shock in her voice.

'I returned early.' His expression was closed and unsmiling as ever.

'If you will excuse me, sir,' she said and made to walk past him, but to Phoebe's horror Hunter moved to block her way.

'My mother said you were ill abed.' His tone was cold and she thought she could see a hint of accusation in his eyes.

'This is not the time for discussion, sir. At least have the decency to let me clothe myself first.' She looked at him with indignation and prayed that he would not see the truth beneath it.

Hunter showed no sign of moving.

'I would hear your explanation now, Miss Allardyce.' His gaze was piercing.

'This is ridiculous! You have no right to accost me so!'

'And you have no right to lie to my mother,' he countered in a voice so cool and silky that it sent shivers rippling the length of her spine.

'I did not lie.' Another lie upon all the others. She could not meet his gaze as she said it.

'You do not look ill and abed to me, Miss Allardyce. Indeed, you look very much as if you have been swimming in the loch.'

She could not very well deny it. She stared at her the bareness of her feet and the droplets of water surrounding them, then, taking a deep breath, raised her eyes to his. And in their meeting that same feeling passed between them as had done on the moor and that night in his study. Hunter felt it, too, she could see it in his eyes. And standing there, barely clothed before him, at this most inopportune of moments she understood exactly what it was. An overwhelming, irrational attraction. Her mind went blank; she could think of not a single thing to say.

'I…'

Hunter waited.

With a will of iron she managed to drag her gaze away and close her mind to the realisation.

'I felt somewhat feverish and took a dip in the loch to cool the heat.' The excuse slipped from her tongue and, feeble though it was, she was thankful for it. 'As a result I am feeling much recovered.'

He gave no sign that he did not believe her, but neither did he look convinced. The tension hummed between them. The seconds seemed to stretch for ever.

'Sir, I am barely clothed! Your behaviour is reprehensible!' She forced her chin up and eyed him with disdain.

Hunter did not move. 'You were in my study today, Miss Allardyce.' That pale intense gaze bored into hers as if he could see every last thought in her head.

Phoebe's heart gave a little stutter. The tension ratcheted tighter between them. She swallowed hard and kept her eyes on his, as if to look away would be some kind of admission of guilt. She thought of her father and his poor battered face and the memory was enough to steel every trembling nerve in her body. She knew what was at stake here.

'I returned your book.' She could feel the water dripping from her hair over her shoulders, rolling down over her arms, which were bare to Hunter's perusal if he should choose to look, but his gaze did not stray once from her own.

'How did my mother enjoy *Evelina*?'

'Well enough, I believe.' Phoebe spoke calmly, and stayed focused.

He said nothing, but there was a tiny flicker of a muscle in his jaw.

She shivered, but whether it was from the cooling of her skin or the burning intensity of Hunter's eyes she did not know. 'And now, if you will excuse me, sir.'

His gaze shifted then, swept over her bare shoulders, over the dress she clutched to her breast, down to her bare feet and the puddle of loch water that was forming around them. And she blushed with embarrassment and anger, and most of all with the knowledge that she could be attracted to such a man.

'Really, Mr Hunter! How dare you?'

Hunter's eyes met hers once more. He did not look away, but he did step aside to let her reach the door.

She edged past him, keeping her back to the door so that he would not see the full extent of her undress. Her hand fumbled behind at the door knob.

The door did not open.

Phoebe twisted it to the left.

The door did not yield.

Then to the right.

Still nothing happened.

She rattled at the blasted knob, panicking at the thought she would have to turn round and in the process present Hunter with a view that did not bear thinking about.

Hunter moved, closing the distance between them.

Phoebe gave a gasp as his hand reached round behind her. He was so close she could smell his soap, his cologne, the very scent that was the man himself. Her heart was thudding so hard she felt dizzy. And as Hunter stared down at her she could see the sudden darkening blaze in his eyes, could sense the still tension that gripped his large powerful male body, could feel the very air vibrate between them. The edge of his sleeve brushed against her arm. And part of her dreaded it and, heaven help her, part of her wanted to feel the touch of those strong firm lips. To be kissed, to be held by such a strong dangerous man. She squeezed her eyes closed and clutched the dress all the tighter.

Cool air hit against her skin and she heard the sound of booted steps receding along the passageway. She opened her eyes to find Hunter gone and the door to her chamber wide open behind her.

Hunter paused as the clock upon his study mantel chimed eight and then looked across his desk at McEwan, who was sitting in the chair opposite and waiting with the air of a man much contented. Hunter swallowed back the bitterness.

'You are up and about early this morning, Hunter.' Hunter saw McEwan eye the still half-full brandy decanter, but his steward was wise enough to make no comment upon it.

'I have things on my mind,' said Hunter and frowned again as he thought of Miss Allardyce.

'What do you make of my mother's companion?'

'I cannot say I have noticed her,' McEwan confessed.

'Hell's teeth, man, how could—?' Hunter stopped, suddenly aware of revealing just how much he had noticed Miss Allardyce himself. In his time he had known diamonds of the *ton*, actresses whose looks commanded thousands and opera singers with the faces of angels, all of whose beauty far exceeded that of his mother's companion. And yet there was something about Phoebe Allardyce, something when she looked at him with those golden-brown eyes of hers that affected Hunter in a way no woman ever had. He took a breath, leaned back in the chair and looked at McEwan.

'She seems much as any other lady's companion I have met,' McEwan offered. 'Why are you asking?'

Hunter hesitated.

The clock ticked loud and slow.

'I do not trust her,' he said at last.

McEwan's brows shot up. 'What has she done?'

'Nothing…at least nothing solid I can confront her with.' He thought of her visits to his study, and the telltale hair upon his desk so vibrant against the polished ebony of the wood. He glanced up at McEwan. 'Let us just call it a gut feeling.'

'Is it a question of her honesty?'

'Possibly.' Hunter thought of her lies about the coach fare, *Evelina*, her absence at the seaside trip, all of which were trivial and might be explained away by a myriad of reasons. But his instincts were telling him otherwise. And that was not all his damnable instincts were telling him of Miss Allardyce. A vision appeared in his mind of her standing in the upstairs passageway, her shift clinging damp and transparent, and the pile of clothing that hid little, and he almost groaned at the pulse of desire that throbbed through him. He closed his eyes, clenched his teeth to martial some control and felt anger and determination overcome the lust. When he opened his eyes again McEwan was staring at him.

'Everything all right?'

Hunter schooled himself to dispassion. 'Why would it be otherwise?' He saw the compassion that came into McEwan's eyes and hated it. 'We are talking of Miss Allardyce,' he said and knew he should curb the cold tone from his voice. Jed McEwan was his friend and the one who had helped him through those darkest days. The man did not deserve such treatment. 'Forgive me,' he muttered.

McEwan gave a single nod and the expression on his face told Hunter that he understood. 'What do you want to do about Miss Allardyce?'

Hunter narrowed his eyes slightly. 'Find out a little more about her. There is a man I know in Glasgow who should be able to help.' A man he had used before for less honourable pursuits. 'Would you be able to act on my behalf?'

'Of course.'

Hunter scribbled the man's details on a sheet of paper; while he waited for the ink to dry, he opened the drawer and extracted one of the rolls of banknotes. 'The sooner, the better.' He pushed the money and the paper across the desk's surface to McEwan, who folded the paper before slipping both into his pocket.

'And while you are gone I will see what I can discover from my mother.'

Hunter waited until his mother and her companion had finished their breakfast and were playing cards within the drawing room before he approached.

His mother was dressed as smartly as ever, not a hair out of place in her chignon, her dress of deep purple silk proclaiming her still to be in mourning for his father, although it had been nine months since his death. Miss Allardyce sat opposite her, wearing the same faded blue dress he had last seen clutched raggedly against her breast, on the face of it looking calm and unruffled, but he saw the flicker of wariness in those tawny eyes before she masked it.

'If you would excuse me for a few minutes, ma'am.' Miss Allardyce set her cards face down upon the green baize surface of the card table and got to her feet. She smiled at his mother. 'I have left my handkerchiefs in my bedchamber and find I have need of them.'

His mother gave a sullen nod, but did not look pleased.

'Well?' she asked as the door closed behind her companion. 'What is it that you have to say to me?'

Hunter walked over to Miss Allardyce's chair and sat down upon it. 'How are you finding it being back at Blackloch?'

'Well enough,' she said in a tone that would have soured the freshest of milk. She eyed him with cold dislike. 'There are no amends that you can make for what you did, Sebastian. You cannot expect that I will forgive you.'

'I do not,' he said easily and lifted Miss Allardyce's cards from the table. He fanned them out, looking at them. 'Is Miss Allardyce to play?'

His mother gave a grudging nod.

Hunter gestured for another card from the banker's pile. And his mother slid one face down across the baize towards him. He noticed the arthritic knuckles above the large cluster of diamonds that glittered upon her fingers, and the slight tremor that held them.

'I did not know you had taken on a companion.'

'There is much you do not know about me, Sebastian.'

'You did not advertise the position in the *Glasgow Herald*; I would have seen it.' He narrowed his eyes and stared at the cards as if musing what move to make. His attention was seemingly focused entirely upon the fan of cards within his hand.

'Miss Allardyce came to me recommended by a friend. She is from a good family, the daughter of a knight, no less, albeit in unfortunate circumstances.'

'Indeed,' murmured Hunter and played his card.

His mother nodded appreciatively at his choice. She sniffed and regarded her own cards more closely, then filled the silence as he had hoped. 'She is left alone while her father, a Sir Henry Allardyce, is hospitalised. I offered my assistance when I heard of her situation.'

'You are too good, Mother, taking in waifs and strays.'

'Do not be sharp, Sebastian. It does not suit you.'

He gave a small smile of amusement.

She played a card.

Hunter eyed it. 'Your card skills have improved.'

His mother tried not to show it, but he could tell she was pleased with the compliment.

'Did she offer a letter of recommendation, a character?'

'Of course not. I told you, she is a gentleman's daughter with no previous experience of such a position.' His mother's eyes narrowed. 'You are very interested in Miss Allardyce all of a sudden. Do not think to start with any of your rakish nonsense. I will not stand for it. She is my companion.'

'Miss Allardyce is not my type,' he said coolly. 'As well you know.'

Her cheeks coloured faintly at his reference to the light-skirts in whom he had previously taken such interest. 'There is no need for vulgarity.'

'I apologise if I have offended you.' He inclined his head. 'My concern is with you, Mother, and if that warrants an interest in those you take into your employ, particularly in positions of such confidence, then I make no apology for that. What do you really know of the girl? Of her trustworthiness and her background?'

'Oh, do not speak of concern for me, for I know full well that you have none,' she snapped. The disdain was back in her eyes, their momentary truce broken. 'And as for Miss Allardyce, or any of my staff, I will not be dictated to, nor will I have my choice vetted by you. To put it bluntly, Sebastian, it is none of your business.'

'On the contrary, I owe it to my father—'

'Do not dare speak his name! You have no right, no damned right at all!' And she threw the cards down on the table and swept from the room.

Phoebe spent the next hour trying to pacify her employer in the lady's rooms.

'Come, cease your pacing, Mrs Hunter. You will make yourself ill.' Already the older woman's face was pale and pinched. She ignored Phoebe and continued her movement about the room.

'How dare he?' she mumbled to herself.

'Mr Hunter has upset you,' Phoebe said with concern.

'My son's very existence upsets me,' muttered Mrs Hunter in a harsh voice. 'I rue the day he was born.'

Phoebe masked her shock before it showed. 'I am sure you do not mean that, ma'am. Let me ring for some tea. It will make you feel better.'

'I do not want yet another cup of tea, Phoebe,' she snapped. 'And, yes, when it comes to Sebastian, I mean every word that I say.' She stopped by the window, leaning her hands upon the sill to stare out of the front of the house across the moor. 'I hate my son,' she said more quietly in a tone like ice. 'It is an admission that no mother should make, but it is the truth.' She glanced round at Phoebe. 'I have shocked you, have I not?'

'A little,' admitted Phoebe.

She turned to face her fully. 'If you knew what he has done, you would understand.'

Phoebe felt her blood run cold at the words. *Tell me,* she wanted to say.

Mrs Hunter looked at Phoebe for a moment as if she had heard the silent plea, then the anger drained away. In its place was exhaustion and a fragility that Phoebe had never before seen there.

Her face was pale and peaked and as Phoebe looked she realised Mrs Hunter looked old and ill.

'Do you wish to speak of it?'

There was silence and for a moment, a very small moment, Phoebe thought she would. And then Mrs Hunter shook her head and closed her eyes. 'I cannot.' And then she pressed a hand to her forehead, half-shielding one eye as if she might weep.

Phoebe moved to take Mrs Hunter's arm and guided her to sit in an armchair. She knelt by her side and took one of the lady's hands within her own. 'Is there anything that I might do to help?'

Mrs Hunter gave a little shake of the head and a weak smile. 'You are a good and honest girl, Phoebe.'

Phoebe felt the guilt stain her cheeks. She glanced down uneasily, knowing that she had been less than honest and that thieving made her very bad.

Mrs Hunter sighed as her hand moved to her breastbone and she rubbed her fingers against the silk of her dress, feeling the golden locket that Phoebe knew lay hidden beneath. 'My head aches almost as much as my heart.' Her voice was unsteady and there was such an underlying pain there that Phoebe felt the ache of it in her own chest.

'I could make you a feverfew tisane. It should relieve the pain a little.'

'Yes. I would like that.' Mrs Hunter patted Phoebe's hand, then she rose and walked from the little sitting room towards her bedchamber. 'And send Polly up. I wish to lie down for a while.'

Phoebe nodded and quietly left. Yet she could not stop wondering at the terrible deed in Hunter's past that had made his mother hate him so.

McEwan came to him that evening with the information he had discovered.

'Are you certain?' Hunter demanded.

McEwan glanced up at him. 'Absolutely. Sir Henry Allardyce was sent to gaol for an unpaid debt of fifteen hundred pounds some six months ago. He has been imprisoned in the Tolbooth ever since.' McEwan tasted the brandy. 'It seems that your instincts concerning Miss Allardyce were right, Hunter.'

Hunter said nothing, just toyed with the glass of brandy in his hand.

McEwan lounged back in the wing chair by the unlit fire. 'I suppose it is understandable that she would lie over the matter. She is unlikely to have found a decent position otherwise.'

'Indeed.' Hunter took a small sip of brandy.

'Will you tell Mrs Hunter?'

'My mother will not thank me for the knowledge.'

'Then we will leave Miss Allardyce to her secret.'

'Not quite,' said Hunter and set his glass down on the drum table between him and McEwan. He thought of Miss Allardyce in his study and of the lies she had spun, and he could not rid himself of the notion that there was more to the mystery surrounding the girl than simply hiding her father's fate.

McEwan listened while Hunter told him his plan and then left to rush back to his Mairi. Hunter lifted his glass and stood by the window, looking out over the moor. In all these months not once had he even looked at a woman. He was the man his father had wanted him to be. And yet it was all too little, too late. The past could not be undone. Some sins could never be washed clean. And Hunter would have to live with that knowledge for the rest of his life. All he had were the vows he had sworn and his determination to honour them. And now it seemed even they were to be tried.

Fate was taunting him, testing him. Throwing temptation in his path, and such a temptation that Hunter could never have imagined, wrapped in the guise of a plain and ordinary girl, except there was nothing plain or ordinary about Phoebe Allardyce. For the sake of his mother there could be no more thought of avoiding

Miss Allardyce. He sipped at the brandy and knew he would have to take an interest in the girl, whether he liked it or not. And in him burned a cold steady anger and a determination to honour the promises he had sworn.

Mrs Hunter was still in bed as Phoebe hurried down the main staircase two mornings later, reticule in hand, shawl around her shoulders. Through the window she could see the sky was an expanse of dull grey filled with the promise of rain, and all around her the air held a nip that boded of the end of summer. Phoebe's normally bright spirits on a Tuesday morning were clouded by the prospect of meeting the Messenger empty-handed. Ahead of her the front door of Blackloch lay open, rendering the house all the more chilled for the cold seeping breeze. But Phoebe barely noticed; her mind was filled with thoughts of her father as she crossed the smooth grey flags of the hallway.

She was through the doorway, down the stone steps and out onto the driveway before she realised that Jamie was not wearing his normal clothes, but a smart black-and-silver livery. Where the gig should have stood was a sleek and glossy black coach complete with coachman in a uniform to match Jamie's.

'Miss Allardyce.' The voice sounded behind her; his booted footsteps came down the steps, then crunched upon the gravel. And she did not need to turn to know who it was that had spoken for the whole of her body seemed to tingle and her heart gave a flutter.

She turned, showing not one hint of her reaction to him. 'Mr Hunter.'

'Forgive me for borrowing Jamie when you had asked him to drive you to Kingswell, but I have a meeting in Glasgow and as we are both travelling the same way I thought we might travel together.'

For just one awful moment Phoebe felt the mask slip and something of her horror show. They could not possibly travel together, not when she was going to the Tolbooth gaol. But she could think of not a single excuse to extricate herself from the situation. She forced the smile to her face and looked at him perhaps a little too brightly so that he would not fathom anything of her real thoughts on the matter.

'I thank you for your offer, sir, but I could not possibly put you to such inconvenience.'

'It is no inconvenience, Miss Allardyce.' He was standing close to her, looking down into her face with the same brooding intensity he always wore. Those stark ice-green eyes, the gaze that seemed to see too much. She glanced away, feeling uncommonly hot and flustered, and pretended to fix the handle on her reticule.

'Indeed, I insist upon it, the roads being as unsafe as they are these days.'

'I...'

But he was already walking the few steps to the coach.

Jamie had already opened the door and pulled down the step.

Hunter reached the door and turned to her. 'After you, Miss Allardyce.'

She stared at the coach, consternation filling her every pore, for she knew there was no means to escape this. Phoebe took a deep breath, thought of her father and climbed into the coach.

The interior was as dark as the outside. Black-velvet squabs upon black-leather upholstery. And at each window matching thick black-velvet curtains tied back to let in the daylight.

The ride was comfortable and smooth, but Phoebe could not relax, not with Hunter sitting opposite, his long black pantalooned legs stretched out by her side, so that his booted feet were close to the hem of her skirt; too close, she thought and she remembered the feel of him standing so near when she was half-naked, clutching the pile of clothes to her breast. She blushed and pushed the memory away.

His boots looked as if they were new, as black and gleaming as the horses that pulled the coach. Her eyes travelled up to his thighs, noting that the pantaloons did little to disguise the muscles beneath. Phoebe realised what she was doing, blushed again and averted her eyes to look out of the window at the passing moorland. But even then she was too conscious of him, of the sheer size of him, of his strength and his very presence. The coach seemed too small a space and the atmosphere held a strain. Her hands clasped tighter together.

'To which hospital do I deliver you?'

She ignored his question. 'Mrs Hunter has then told you something of my situation?' she said carefully.

'She has. If it is not too delicate a matter, may I enquire as to your father's ailment?'

'The doctors are not sure yet. Until they are, he must be confined.' She stuck to the story her father had devised.

'Confined, you say?'

She glanced up to find Hunter's gaze upon her. And it did not matter how many times she had told the story previously without the slightest betrayal, sitting there in the coach before him, Phoebe felt guilt scald her cheeks. 'Indeed. It is a most worrying situation.' At least that was truthful. 'I fear for him.' She glanced away out of the window, thinking of her father's poor swollen face the last time she had seen him and the threats so vilely uttered against him. 'More than you can imagine. Without these visits I do not know how either of us would survive the time.' Her words halted as she realised just how much of the truth she had revealed and when she looked back she found Hunter was watching her with a strange expression upon his face.

'What of your mother?'

'She died when I was a child.'

'And you have no other family?'

'My sister died almost two years past.' Phoebe could almost speak of Elspeth now, but it had taken such a long time.

'I am sorry for your loss,' he said and something of the chill had thawed from his voice.

She glanced round at the change in his voice, met his eyes once more. And something unspoken seemed to pass between them, some kind of shared experience that bound them together.

'And you, sir?' she asked. 'Do you have any other family?'

'None.'

'Your father, he—?'

'I do not speak of my father, Miss Allardyce.' And the coldness was back again just as if it had never gone.

'Please forgive me. I did not intend to stir painful memories.' Phoebe understood what grief felt like, how, just when you were not even thinking upon it, the smallest, most unexpected thing could trigger a rush of emotion so intense you were plunged into the depths all over again and the ache in your heart caught the breath from your lungs and made you weep. And she did not imagine a man like Hunter would wish to reveal such emotion. It was only nine months since his father had died.

She watched the blur of earthy colours through the carriage window, content to let the silence grow between them. And even though her focus was on the passing moorland she could feel the weight of Hunter's gaze heavy upon her. She did not look round. She wanted no more questions about her father.

The minutes passed.

'You do not know, do you?' he said at last, his voice softer than normal. And when she looked round at him there was almost disbelief on his face. And then as if to himself, 'She has not told you. I did not think—' He stopped himself.

Phoebe shook her head. 'I do not know of what you are talking, sir.'

He smiled; it was a cold smile, a mirthless smile and in his eyes there was an anguish he could not quite hide. 'I suppose that at least is something.' Their gazes held and for that brief moment there was such pain in his eyes that Phoebe could not help herself from reaching her hand towards him.

Hunter's gaze dropped to her hand and then slid back up to meet her eyes and the same stony control had slotted into place.

She froze, suddenly conscious of what she was doing, and pulled her hand back as if it had been bitten.

'You did not answer my question, Miss Allardyce—in which hospital is your father being treated?'

Only then did she realise that he was the only person since she had started as Mrs Hunter's companion to ask her that question.

'The Royal Infirmary.' It was the closest hospital to the Tolbooth. She dreaded what more he would ask and where his questions would lead. Her nervousness around him made it hard to think straight and she feared what she might be tricked into revealing. But to her relief Hunter made no further comment and the journey continued in silence. Part of her was willing the journey to be over, longing only for safety and to see her papa. And another part, a small perverse part that Phoebe did not understand, did not want it to end. Paradoxically, the minutes were both too long and too short until they reached Glasgow's Royal Infirmary.

She thanked Hunter and bade him good day as if she felt nothing of the roaring attraction to a man against whom she had been warned, a man she knew to be thoroughly wicked.

Phoebe stood and waited until the black luxurious carriage disappeared out of sight and only then did she release the breath she had been holding. Hunter was gone. Her secret was safe. *She* was safe.

She watched for a moment longer, thinking of the dark man in that dark carriage, then she turned and hurried off down Castle Street towards the gaol.

Chapter Five

The Messenger arrived at the Tolbooth's steps five minutes after Phoebe. He glanced around nervously before placing his hand on her arm and pulling her into the shadowed arches of the adjoining coffee rooms.

'You have it?' She could see the eagerness in his narrow grey eyes and felt a wave of revulsion and anger for him and the threat he posed to her father.

She had not time for preamble, and this man, whoever he was, deserved nothing of politeness. 'It was not where you said it would be.'

'You are lying.' His face hardened.

'It is the truth.' She stepped closer to him, the fury blazing in her eyes. 'Do you honestly think I would jeopardise my father's safety any more than it is already?' she demanded. 'I searched the whole of the study—every place I could find. Your information is wrong, sir. The item is not there.'

'You'd better be telling the truth, lady.' His voice was ugly.

'I assure you I am.'

They faced each other, Phoebe defiant and glaring, the Messenger suspicious and thinking. The drone of voices and traffic went on around them as if nothing was wrong.

'Everything all right, Miss Allardyce?' It was the one of the turnkeys who looked after her papa's cell, on his way home having finished his shift. His eyes flitted to the Messenger.

The Messenger's gaze met Phoebe's and it was filled with unspoken warning; not that she needed any reminders of what was at stake.

'Everything is fine, thank you, Mr Murray. I will be in to see my papa shortly.'

The turnkey gave a nod and was on his way, leaving them alone again.

'Good girl,' said the Messenger and smiled.

Phoebe narrowed her eyes and made no effort to hide her contempt. 'I have done as you asked and I trust that my father will be safe.'

'Old pop's safety can't be guaranteed till you deliver the goods, Miss Allardyce.'

'But—'

'Where else would a man keep such a thing?' When Phoebe did not respond the man answered his own question. 'In his bedchamber, perhaps?' The Messenger raised his eyebrows and looked at her expectantly.

'No,' she said firmly. 'You cannot expect me to—'

'If you care about your *dear papa*,' he emphasised the words horribly, 'then you will be as thorough with Hunter's bedchamber as you were with the study. The item is somewhere in that house, Miss Allardyce. And until you have found it and it is safely in my pocket then who knows when it comes to Sir Henry…?'

'You are a villain, sir!' she said quietly through gritted teeth. 'A rogue of the worst degree!'

He smiled. 'I've been called worse.'

'I cannot search the entirety of the house unseen in a week. I will have to wait until no one will catch me and that will take time.'

He looked at her, weighing up her words. 'At the start of September

Mrs Hunter'll be travelling down to London to visit a friend, no doubt taking her trusty companion with her.'

'She has no such plans. I would know—'

But he cut her off. 'Bring the item with you to London. I will contact you there. And remember, Miss Allardyce, I'll hear if you've talked. One word to Hunter or his mother and you know what'll happen…' His eyes narrowed in threat and glanced meaningfully at the prison building behind her. 'Best go and see how your pa is farin'.' He smiled and then turned and walked away, leaving Phoebe standing there looking after him. The Tolbooth clock struck eleven.

'I thought you were planning to confront her at the prison?' McEwan lounged back in his chair across the desk from Hunter.

'There was a change of plan.'

McEwan arched an eyebrow and transferred the calendar of appointments and notebook from his knee to the desk's surface so that he might concentrate on what Hunter was saying all the better.

'Miss Allardyce met with a man outside the gaol. It was a planned meeting. She waited for him before he showed.'

'An accomplice?' asked McEwan.

'Possibly.' Hunter's jaw tightened as he remembered the man's proprietorial grip on Miss Allardyce's arm. 'Miss Allardyce went with him readily enough to hide beneath the arches and sent the turnkey away when he ventured near them.' He wished he had been able to see her face or hear something of their words. 'Accomplice or not, I suspect there may be more to Miss Allardyce's deception than meets the eye.'

'You mean more than her guise to hide the truth of her father?'

'I believe so.'

'You do not think she means to harm Mrs Hunter, do you?' McEwan's eyes were serious with concern, his voice quiet.

'I hope for Miss Allardyce's sake that she does not,' said Hunter in such a steely voice that McEwan actually flinched. He softened his tone. 'But I doubt that is her intent.' He thought of her visits to his study and the insistent notion that she was looking for something. 'I think Miss Allardyce may have another purpose altogether.'

'Such as?'

'Theft, perhaps.' He looked at McEwan. 'I believe she has searched this study.' He made no mention of when he had found her here, or of what had so nearly passed between them.

McEwan gave a small shake of the head and a low whistle. 'Who would have thought it of Miss Allardyce? She seems so...'

Hunter raised a brow. 'So...?'

'So upstanding, so innocent, so honest,' finished McEwan.

'I think we have already established that whatever Miss Allardyce is, it is not honest. And as for the rest...'

'We should warn Mrs Hunter about the girl.'

Hunter thought of his mother's reaction to his enquiries over Miss Allardyce. 'Such an action would only make my mother all the more determined to keep Miss Allardyce.'

'What, then, can we do?'

'We must find another way to discover the nature of Miss Allardyce's game.' Hunter's face was grim. 'And in the meantime when she next visits the Tolbooth we will follow the man she meets with. Find out where he goes, who he is.'

McEwan gave a nod. Then the two men moved to discuss matters relating to the estate.

The door had not even closed behind McEwan when Hunter turned his chair round to face the moor once more. He left his brandy untouched, and as he looked over the windswept heather he brooded not upon his father, but upon Miss Phoebe Allardyce.

The window of the green guest bedchamber overlooked a garden that had been walled to gentle the harshness of the moor's wind and allow Blackloch to grow some of its own fruit and vegetables. To the right-hand side stood the stables and to the left, the still water of the loch where Phoebe had swum in the heat of the summer's day. She knew all that was there even though the darkness rendered it invisible. Dark shadows in a dark landscape beneath a sky of charcoal cloud. There was no moon to light the night, no stars to pretty the sky. Phoebe wrapped the shawl more tightly over her nightdress and stared out at the darkness, worrying about her father. Her eyes squeezed closed at the memory of what the Messenger had done to him and in her stomach was the familiar twist of horror.

Poor Papa who was gentle and kind and had never hurt so much as a fly, who was so lost in his science he barely knew the day of the week, and who could not even look after himself let alone offer a defence against such a savage assault. And she felt angry and frustrated and helpless, knowing there was nothing she could do to protect him from the Messenger's men if they chose to make good on their threats. Nothing save steal from Hunter just as the Messenger wanted. Steal from a man whose reputation was dark and dangerous as the devil's, and who, with one glance from those cool green eyes, could unnerve Phoebe completely.

It was that simple…and that difficult.

By midnight Blackloch was all silence. There was only the hush of the wind whispering against the glass of her window and the soft ripple of water. Everyone would be in bed, all save one. She shrugged off her shawl and, taking up her candle, Phoebe crept halfway down the staircase and peered over the banister at the darkened hallway below. A faint glow of light showed beneath the door to Hunter's study. She sighed with relief and made her way back up the stairs.

Hunter's bedchamber was opposite Phoebe's, but twice the size and with the door positioned as if it were one room up. She crept quietly past Mrs Hunter's room and stopped outside the bedchamber of the master of Blackloch.

McCabe would not be there. She had been careful to make her enquiries as to Hunter's valet. She supposed the man was too used to a master who, it seemed, did not sleep. Taking a deep breath, Phoebe opened the door and slipped into Hunter's bedchamber.

The room was lit only by the glow of coals upon the hearth. She closed the door softly behind her; even though she knew Hunter was downstairs in his study drinking alone through the night, her heart was racing as she held the candle aloft and scanned her surroundings.

It was undoubtedly a masculine room, as dark and sombre as Hunter himself. Dark curtains, dark covers, dark pillows. Every piece of furniture had been carved in ebony or deep mahogany or blackened oak. A huge four-poster bed, both wide and high, too luxuriant for a man who barely slept, sat between the two arched windows, facing into the room. The curtains framing the windows were thick and long, their hems just brushing against the polished floorboards. There was a large rectangular rug on the near side of the bed, the pattern a jumble of dark colours beneath the light of her candle. Her gaze swept around the bed, taking in the unlit wall sconces nearby, the matching chests of drawers on either flank and the large heavy studded chest at the foot. She moved her attention back to the room, her gaze moving over the large solid dark furniture and the internal doors on opposing walls. One she knew led to the bedchamber of the lady of the house, in which Mrs Hunter was currently sleeping. The other she guessed would be a bathroom.

Behind her was a heavy mahogany fireplace, above which hung a large painting of a dark-cowled man with a pet dog guarding its master. A monk and his dog. Such a peculiar choice of painting for a bedchamber that Phoebe peered closer, and gave a small breathy gasp when she realised that the dog was not a dog at all, but a wolf watching her with warning in its eyes. There were so many wolves at Blackloch that they must hold some significance to the Hunter family. She shivered, the sensation rippling right through her as if someone had walked over her grave, and such was her sudden overwhelming fear that it was all she could do not to turn and flee. But Phoebe could not run away from this, no matter how much she wanted to. She knew what she had to steal. And she knew, too, that, for the sake of her papa, there could be no room for failure. She turned away from the painting and forced herself to begin a calm, methodical search.

The bathroom contained a large oval bath with a shower device fixed above it, a screened water closet, a looking glass and a shaving accoutrements, and a comfortable armchair. Nothing in which the object was likely to be hidden.

She carefully searched each piece of furniture, one by one, every shelf, every drawer, every cupboard. By half past midnight she had reached the second set of drawers closest to the main door. As she set her candle down upon the surface she looked up and the curtains swaying in the draught caught her attention; she saw the looking glass and her own pale reflection staring back at her. And in that moment it seemed she felt the cold breath of foreboding whisper against her cheek. Phoebe ignored it, telling herself it was just her imagination at work, and pulled open the top drawer. And there, at last, was Hunter's jewellery casket.

He did not seem to be a man who favoured jewellery for there were few enough pieces. A diamond cravat pin, a gold-and-onyx signet ring engraved with the same crest that adorned the cushions of the dining-room chairs and the seats in the hall, a gold pocket watch and two silver snuff boxes, enamelled with such scandalous paintings of women upon their lids as to bring a blush to Phoebe's cheeks. She ran her fingers against the velvet lining of the casket's interior, searching insistently for something that was not there.

A sound whispered from the passageway, the soft tread of footsteps. Phoebe started and quickly piled all of the jewellery back into the casket, thrust the lid on and shoved the drawer shut. Last of all she grabbed her candle and turned to leave, just as the door to the bedchamber opened and in walked Sebastian Hunter.

He stilled, the intense gaze trained on her, the dark impassivity of his expression gone, replaced with surprise.

Phoebe could not move, could not speak, could not breathe. Everything in the world stopped.

She stared at Hunter.

'Miss Allardyce,' he said quietly and his voice was smooth and cool as silk.

She dropped her gaze to take in the tall black riding boots, the tight buckskin breeches and the coat slung haphazardly over his shoulder. His waistcoat and cravat were unfastened and his shirt gaped open at the neck, revealing something of the pale muscled skin beneath. The door closed behind him without a sound. As Hunter walked slowly towards her, relieving himself of the coat and cravat upon the armchair on the way, Phoebe's stomach dipped.

'I was about to ask what you are doing here.' He kept on walking until he was standing directly before her. 'But I suppose that would be a foolish question, when the answer is so obvious.'

She knew she had failed and she knew, too, the cost of that failure for her papa; the thought of it made her want to weep. There was nothing she could say, nothing she could do. She pressed her lips firm and waited for her dismissal.

'For why else does a woman come to a man's bedchamber in the night?'

Such was her anguish that it took a moment for his words to register. Phoebe blinked up at him in confusion. And as she looked up into his eyes she understood what it was he thought. Her heart skipped a beat and she felt the kindling of hope.

'Unless I am mistaken and there is some other reason that you are here...?' He waited, and everything about him seemed to still in that waiting.

She glanced down. Such a tiny second to make such a momentous decision, and yet, there was no decision to be made, not when her father's life was at stake. Time slowed. All that had happened with her papa and the Messenger ran through her head as she stood there.

'Miss Allardyce…?' Hunter pressed.

Phoebe knew what Hunter was offering her—the chance to save her papa. She raised her gaze to look through the soft flickering candlelight at the stark handsome man who so fascinated her. 'You are not mistaken,' she said and she heard the words as if they had been spoken by someone other than herself.

She saw something flicker in Hunter's eyes, and she could not tell whether it was surprise or anger or something else altogether. He made not one move and his expression was hard and thoughtful. 'But that night in my study…'

'I have changed my mind.'

The silenced hummed loud between them. The very air seemed to crackle as if there were a storm waiting to unleash.

'Do you even know what you are asking?' His voice had dropped to barely more than a husky whisper.

'Of course,' Phoebe lied. She remembered Elspeth's whispered warnings from so long ago and wished she had asked more. 'As you said, why else would I be here?' Her heart was thudding so loud she wondered that he could not hear it.

He stepped closer and stroked his fingers against her cheek, sliding them down to touch against her lips. Phoebe's breath shook. Her blood pounded all the harder.

'I am not sure that I believe you,' he said softly and let his hand fall away.

Her heart stuttered at his words—she knew just how close to the edge she was treading. Her father's life hung in the balance. She knew she had to persuade Hunter. Slowly she reached her face up to his and brushed her lips against his cheek.

His skin was rough with the stubbled growth of beard. The scent of him encompassed her, both familiar and enticing. It was such a very wicked thing to do, and Hunter must have thought so, too, for she heard his sudden intake of air and saw the sharpening of his gaze.

The candle in her hand began to tremble and she could not still it. He took it from her and set it down upon the chest of drawers, beside the looking glass.

'Miss Allardyce,' he said and his voice was so soft and so very sensual that it made her tremble all the more.

He lowered his face to hers, his mouth so close yet not quite touching. She felt the warmth of his breath caress her hair, her eyelids, the line of her cheek and everywhere that it touched her skin blossomed and tingled. His breath swept a kiss against her mouth and the sensation of it shimmered through her body, even though his lips had not yet touched to her own. The breath caught in her throat in anticipation.

'One last chance...' he whispered softly against her ear. A shiver stroked all the way down Phoebe's spine and the breath she had been holding rushed from her lungs. 'To change your mind...' His mouth hovered just above her own, so close she felt his words rather than heard them. She shivered again and felt her nipples tighten.

His eyes were dark in the candlelight, dark and dangerous and utterly beguiling.

'Miss Allardyce...' he whispered and his gaze swept slowly, sensually down to fix upon her lips. 'Phoebe...' and she quivered at the hunger in his voice.

She shook her head and reached her mouth towards his, and as Hunter finally claimed her lips she closed her eyes and gave herself up to him.

The kiss was more than Phoebe could ever have imagined a kiss to be. Gentle yet possessive. Enticing yet demanding. His lips courting hers to make her forget that anything else even existed. It seemed that she had waited all her life for this moment and this man. Nothing had ever felt so right, nothing ever so wonderful. She felt his arms around her, moulding her against his body, breast to breast, thigh to thigh, as his mouth worked its wonder upon her own. Phoebe yielded to him and all that he offered, splaying her hands against the hard muscle of his chest so she could feel the warmth of his skin through the fine linen of his shirt, pressing herself closer to feel the heat in his long muscular thighs.

She heard the rasp of Hunter's breath, a sound that mirrored her own. She was his, completely, utterly, just as he was hers. He deepened the kiss, his lips inviting hers to so much more, and she did not even think of not following. His tongue led hers in a dance that both fed and consumed, with such intimacy and passion as to scorch away all that was in its path. And the blood was rushing in her veins and desire was pounding in her soul, and everything was hot and reckless and overwhelmed with her need for Hunter. She felt she had known him for a thousand lifetimes, that he was her alpha and omega, that for her there would never be any other man.

He threaded his fingers through the length of her hair, teasing and mussing and stroking.

'Phoebe,' he whispered her name and she answered his call with everything that she was and everything that she would be.

The touch of his hand scorched through her nightdress, caressing her breast, her hip, her stomach, touching her as she had never been touched before, lighting a fire in her thighs and belly. She burned for him, ached for him, arched against him, wanting this and everything that could be between them. Then she felt his hand slip inside the nightdress, to the bare skin of her breast, his fingers teasing against its hardened sensitive peak, touching the very core of her being, rocking the world on its axis. She gave a moan and, as her legs buckled beneath her, stumbled back against the tall wooden bedpost even as Hunter caught her.

Phoebe glanced up, her gaze falling directly at the looking glass.

The woman she saw there was dark-eyed and flushed with passion, her hair long and wanton, her nightdress gaping to expose small pale breasts and she was in the arms of a tall dark-haired man. And even then it did not hit her, not until the man turned his face to follow her gaze and she saw that it was Hunter.

Hunter stared at the reflection and the shock of it cooled his ardour in an instant. Only then did he realise just what he was doing—ravishing Phoebe Allardyce with all the thoroughness of a rake. He stared, appalled at himself, and released her, stepping away to open up a space between them.

He saw the daze clear from her eyes, saw the sudden awareness and the shame and horror that followed in its stead. She looked as shocked as he felt, staring at him with great wide eyes as if she could not believe what had just passed between them. He could hear the raggedness of her breathing, see the tremble in her hands as she clutched her nightdress to cover herself.

'Phoebe—'

But she turned and fled, silent as a wraith.

Hunter made no move to stop her. Just stood where he was until he heard the quiet closing of the door. His heart was still thudding with a sickening speed. He raked a hand through his hair and wondered what the hell had just happened between him and Phoebe Allardyce. Such untutored passion, such connection and depth of desire. Hunter had never experienced anything like it before. And yet he had known she was an innocent from that very first tentative touch of her lips.

God help me, he thought. *God help me in truth.*

Her candle still sat upon his chest of drawers. Hunter lifted it, noting that his hand was not quite steady as he did so. His blood was still surging too hard, his heart beating too strong. He took a deep breath, and struggled to control himself. And then his eye caught the glint of something on the Turkey rug before his feet. He crouched to retrieve his diamond cravat pin, and by its side found the dark silken ribbon he had slid from Phoebe Allardyce's hair. He rose and surveyed the room.

Nothing was missing. Nothing else had been moved. He slipped the diamond pin into its place and threaded the ribbon through his fingers. And the look in his eyes was brooding, for he knew most assuredly that she had not come to his room to wait for him.

Miss Phoebe Allardyce had been searching through his jewellery casket...and had taken not one item.

Chapter Six

Phoebe stood by the window in her bedchamber, staring out over the walled garden and the still, dark water of the loch. The brightness of the morning sun hurt her eyes and she felt tired and groggy from a night devoid of sleep. Behind her the bed was a tumbled mess of sheets and blankets, where she had tossed and turned and worried through the hours of darkness.

The memory of what had happened between them, the clear knowledge of what she had done, made her cringe. She leaned her forehead against the glass and closed her eyes, knowing that the hours that had since passed relieved nothing of the fury of emotion that pulsed through her. Shame and embarrassment, guilt and desire.

She had led him to kiss her, to touch her in ways Phoebe could never have imagined. And the most terrible thing of all was the wickedness of her own feelings. That she had wanted his kiss, that in some deep instinctive way she had needed it. Hunter had awakened something within her that she had not even known existed, something she did not understand and that, standing here alone in the cold light of day, seemed very far away. She wondered how on earth she was going to be able to face him again, after what had passed between them, after what she had led him to believe. And yet if she was to hide the truth of what she had been doing in his bedchamber she knew she would have to do precisely that.

When she opened her eyes and looked out again the moor looked cold and bleak beneath the white-grey sky and the wind keened low through the panes of her window. And she seemed to hear again the echo of her father's words, *There are dark whisperings about him, evil rumours...* Phoebe shivered and forced her thoughts away from Hunter. There was the whole of Blackloch to be searched, and she could not balk from it. She turned and moved to face the day.

Phoebe and Mrs Hunter worked side by side on the tapestry. Each day they filled in a little more of the still-life vase and flowers sketched upon the canvas, their needles flashing fast in the sunlight of the drawing room. Mrs Hunter brought the roses to life with threads of dusky pink while Phoebe stitched at the freesias with a violet thread. They worked together in comfortable silence.

Mrs Hunter tied off her thread and searched in their thread basket for a skein.

'Oh, bother!'

'What is wrong?' Phoebe stopped stitching to glance round at Mrs Hunter.

'I am about to start the leaves and have left the pale green thread in my bedchamber. Would you be a dear and run and fetch it, Phoebe?'

'Of course.'

'I think it is on my bedside table,' she called as Phoebe exited the drawing door.

The green-coloured thread was not upon the bedside table. As Phoebe scanned around the room she realised the opportunity that had just presented itself. This was her chance to search the bedchamber, not for the thread, but for something else altogether.

It felt so wrong, so sordid, that she hated to do it, but one thought of her papa was enough to push such sensibilities aside. Phoebe began a systematic and speedy search. She started with Mrs Hunter's jewellery box, moved on to her trinket box and the drawers of her dressing table, then the drawers of the bedside cabinet. The minutes passed too quickly. She found the thread, a cool pale green reminiscent of Hunter's eyes, but nothing else that she was seeking, and knew that she could take no more time. Mrs Hunter was waiting. She gathered up the skein of thread and left.

'There you are, Miss Allardyce, or perhaps, as we are alone, I may call you Phoebe.' Hunter moved from his position leaning against the wall outside his mother's bedchamber. 'I thought you were never going to come back out of there. I believe my mother is in the drawing room if you are looking for her.'

Miss Allardyce gave a start and a tint of peaches coloured her cheeks. 'Mrs Hunter sent me to fetch some thread.' She handed him the skein as if offering her proof. 'It was not where it was supposed to be. I had to search for it and, well, it took an age in the finding.' Her voice was calm enough, but she was talking too much, revealing her nerves and, Hunter suspected, her guilt. 'If you will excuse me, sir, I fear I have kept Mrs Hunter waiting long enough.' He saw the calm determination slot back down over her ruffled poise.

He stayed her with a hand to her arm, and felt her jump beneath his touch. 'Only fifteen minutes, Phoebe, what are a few minutes more?'

'You were timing me?'

'In my eagerness to see you.' And it was only half a lie.

'Mr Hunter!' She sounded breathless.

'Sebastian,' he insisted, and told himself he was doing this for the sake of his mother's safety, and not because he had wanted Miss Allardyce since first setting eyes on her. Not that he would allow matters to progress anywhere near as far as taking her; unlike last night, now he was prepared. Hell, but the kiss had shaken him enough; he could not doubt what it had done to Phoebe Allardyce. What the hell was she looking for in the rooms of Blackloch? A little more pressure and she would reveal the truth in one way or another.

'Really, I must go.'

But Hunter slid his hand down her arm to take her hand in his. 'Are you forgetting our arrangement, Phoebe?'

'Arrangement?' Her expression was innocent and artless, her eyes filled with wariness she could not quite disguise.

'Surely you have not forgotten last night?' he murmured.

Her blush intensified. 'Last night…' And just for a moment something of the strength in her eyes faltered. Her hand slipped out of his and she backed away until the wall blocked her retreat. She dropped her gaze, hiding beneath the sweep of those tawny-red lashes so that he thought she would cease her pretence.

'Phoebe?' he said more gently.

She looked up at him then and he saw that he was wrong. They stared at one another across the width of the passageway and in her eyes was nothing of capitulation, only caution and, beneath it, a steadfast resolve that bordered on defiance. He wondered what she would do if he took her in his arms and kissed her as hard and thoroughly as he wanted to. What would it take to make her confess the truth of what she had been doing in his bedchamber last night, of what she had been searching for in his mother's rooms just now? Would she let him carry her into his bedchamber, throw her on bed and bury himself inside her? He made not one move, but something of his thoughts must have shown in his face for she paled, but she still did not back down.

'Sebastian…' The sound of his name upon her lips made his pulse kick. 'We will speak of this later. But for now I must not keep your mother waiting.' Her voice was all calmness and control. She turned to leave, but he caught hold of her elbow, preventing her departure. He felt her start beneath his touch, heard the slight catch of her breath, saw the frenzied leap of the pulse in her neck, and he knew she was not so unaffected as she was feigning. Her eyes locked with his, and in their depths he thought he saw the flash of guilt and fear and desire.

'I have already told you—'

He said not one word, just pressed the pale green thread into her hand and walked away.

Over the next few days Phoebe found it impossible to continue her search of Blackloch. Hunter was always around, brooding, silent and yet present. For all the animosity that existed between him and his mother, since the night she had gone to his bedchamber he had been spending more and more time in Mrs Hunter's company. And in his presence Phoebe felt a constant awareness of their 'arrangement' as he had called it. Every time their eyes met the memory of that night was between them, of his mouth possessing hers. The feel of his arms holding her close, of being pressed against the long hard length of his body. She denied the thoughts, pushed them away, knowing that she could not afford to let herself weaken, feeling a guilt at this unbidden attraction. Responsibility sat heavy on her shoulders. And the fear for her papa drove her on.

Beneath the shade of a crab apple tree in the walled garden Phoebe and Mrs Hunter sat reading.

'This was always my favourite spot,' Mrs Hunter told Phoebe, 'for it is nicely tucked away out of the wind.'

'Mother.' Hunter appeared through the arched gateway, making Phoebe start and lose her place in her book. He gave a grave bow. 'I am need of your company today to assist with the tenant visits.'

Mrs Hunter peered at him with irritation. 'I thought your steward, McEwan, did that.'

'The visits involve matters that would be better dealt with by a woman—the distribution of linens and such.'

Mrs Hunter frowned. 'What of Mrs Dawson?'

'Mrs Dawson left Blackloch shortly after you did.'

'And you did not replace her? It is little wonder the place is in such disarray without a housekeeper.'

Hunter said nothing, but it seemed to Phoebe, as mother and son stared at one another with expressions that boarded on glacial, the comfortable temperature within the sheltered garden spot seemed to drop a few degrees.

Mrs Hunter gave in first. 'It seems I have little option,' she complained with a scowl, which she then turned upon Phoebe. 'Come along, Phoebe, you may return the books to my room and ready yourself.'

'Ready myself?' Phoebe repeated and looked at her employer. 'But shall you not be attending with Mr Hunter alone?'

'No, I shall not,' snapped the lady. 'It is bad enough that I am being dragged around the countryside visiting one smelly peasant after another, but I am certainly not enduring the day alone.' And with a final glare at her son Mrs Hunter marched from the garden.

Phoebe met Hunter's gaze briefly, but a *frisson* of awareness tingled between them and she had a horrible suspicion as to the reason Hunter was suddenly desirous of his mother's company. She turned away before he could fathom anything of her thoughts and followed in Mrs Hunter's wake.

Hunter rode on his great black horse. Mrs Hunter and Phoebe sat in Hunter's fine coach, Mrs Hunter not wishing to ruin hers by trailing it through, as the lady put it, the mud of all the moor. The baskets of linens and food were fastened in the boot.

Within each farmstead Hunter spoke to the man of the house, he who was holding the tenancy to farm the land, and eke some measure of living from it. From what Phoebe could hear their conversations seemed to centre on breeds of sheep, trout in the lochs, deer and the maintenance of the farm buildings. While Hunter dealt with that side of it, Mrs Hunter was in her element bestowing sheets, blankets and great hampers of food on the wives. Between each farm she moaned incessantly about the mud dirtying her shoes and the wind ruining her hair. But once in the farms Phoebe could see that Mrs Hunter was secretly enjoying herself.

One of the farmsteads, the closest to Blackloch and located on a particularly bleak stretch of the moor, housed a family of eight children, all girls, the oldest of which looked to be only ten or eleven years of age. The younger girls, dressed in clothes that looked worn and shabby, were running about the yard when the carriage drew up. The older girls were helping their mother peg wet washing to a drying line. All activity ceased as the coach rolled into the yard.

The woman's husband, the tenant sheep farmer, was a thin, grey-haired man with a kind but work-worn face. He looked as if life on the moor was not an easy existence. Hunter and the man must have been talking of the barn for the pair of them were looking and pointing in that direction before walking off towards the small wooden building.

The small girls gathered round Mrs Hunter and Phoebe in silence, their little faces in awe of their visitors, their hands and fronts of their smocks revealing that they had been busy playing in the dirt.

'Oh, Mrs Hunter, ma'am.' The mother hastened to greet them, pink cheeked and breathless, and Phoebe saw the wash of embarrassment on Mrs Hunter's face as her gaze dropped to the woman's heavily swollen belly. Mrs Hunter glanced around almost as if checking that her son was not witnessing the woman's condition. And now Hunter's request for his mother's presence seemed to make sense and Phoebe felt ashamed at her thoughts over his motive.

'Such a pleasure, ma'am. I was just doing the washing for it is a fine drying day.'

'Indeed,' said Mrs Hunter and smiled as if she understood completely, even though Phoebe doubted whether Mrs Hunter had ever had to give a thought to the washing and drying of clothes in the whole of her life.

'Our Martha loves working in the big house. She cannae speak highly enough of you and Mr Hunter, ma'am,' the woman gushed.

Mrs Hunter smiled magnanimously and said to Phoebe, 'Martha Beattie is a maid of all at Blackloch.'

Phoebe thought of the freckle-faced young girl who lit the fires and drew the water and swept the stairs.

The footman carried over two baskets, setting them down upon a bench in the yard and opening the lids for the farmer's wife to see the linens in one and food in the other, before leaving to answer Hunter's summons.

'Oh, bless you, ma'am, bless you. I've never enough baby linens to go round. Rosie and Meg are still in nappies, and I didnae ken how I was gonnae manage wi' the other wee one on her way.' She patted her hugely rounded stomach.

The children's eyes lit up when they saw the hamper of food. Soon their curiosity overcame their awe and they edged closer.

'Can I offer you some water, or a little ale?' Mrs Beattie asked.

But Mrs Hunter declined graciously.

'Let me get this emptied so that you can take the baskets away back wi' you.' And the woman lifted both baskets.

Mrs Hunter frowned. 'Should you be…?'

Phoebe stepped forwards. 'Please allow me to help you with that, Mrs Beattie.'

'Ocht, they're no' heavy, no' next to a load of wet wash. Never be botherin' yoursel', miss.'

But Phoebe had taken hold of the baskets, which were, she could confirm, most definitely too heavy to be carried by a woman in Mrs Beattie's condition.

She carried the baskets into the cottage and set them down where Mrs Beattie directed, before helping the woman to unpack their contents. The cottage was clean, scrubbed and well swept, but the rooms were small and the bedroom in which they were piling the linens was tiny with barely room for more than the bed.

Phoebe and Mrs Beattie made their way back outside just in time to see toddler Rosie fall over beside Mrs Hunter. The toddler began to cry and tried to right herself, reaching with little muddy hands for the lady's fine silk skirt.

'No, Rosie!' shouted her mother, trying to rush forwards and prevent the calamity that everyone standing there in the yard could see unfolding before their eyes.

Phoebe reacted in an instant, sprinting and scooping the child up into her arms just in time, cuddling her in close so she would feel safe and secure. 'Oops a daisy, Rosie. Up you get.'

The little girl looked at her, fat tear drops balancing on the end of her lashes, her little nose all pink and wet.

'Have you been making some lovely mudpies?'

Rosie nodded.

Phoebe smiled at Rosie, 'And what's all this wet all over your face?' she asked.

Rosie sniffed back a sob.

'Shall we wipe it all nice and clean?' She set the little girl carefully on her feet out of reach of Mrs Hunter's dress; taking out her handkerchief, Phoebe wiped the child's nose and tucked the handkerchief in the pocket of the little mud-smeared smock. 'Just like a big girl,' she whispered.

Rosie patted her pocket. 'A big girl,' she said with a shy smile.

'I'm ever so sorry, ma'am, miss.' Mrs Beattie was looking from Mrs Hunter to Phoebe.

'There was no harm done,' said Mrs Hunter, but she lifted her skirts and started to make her way back to the carriage. 'And now we must be moving on. We are visiting quite a few of the farmsteads this afternoon.'

Phoebe smiled to reassure Mrs Beattie, who had taken a firm

hold of Rosie's hand. 'Good luck for the baby when it comes,' she said quietly.

'There's a month to wait yet, but thank you, miss.' Mrs Beattie smiled and then her eyes shifted to Phoebe's side. 'Mr Hunter, sir.' She bobbed a curtsy and hurried away to catch hold of another small child.

'Mrs Beattie.' Hunter nodded and Phoebe jumped at the sudden sound of his voice beside her. He leaned closer and said quietly to Phoebe, 'You will have no handkerchiefs left at this rate.' And she remembered their first meeting upon the moor when he had rescued her. Their eyes met just for the briefest of moments, but it was enough to send a myriad of shimmering sensations racing through her body just as if he had pulled her into his arms and lowered his mouth to take her own. She blushed and quickly averted her gaze.

'Phoebe!' called Mrs Hunter with impatience.

Fortunately for Mrs Hunter there was only one more tenant to be visited and he was without children, muddy or otherwise. He was an old man, tall and thin, but slightly bent, his hands large and ruddy, his knuckles enlarged with age and too many years of hard living. Dressed in his brown overalls and an old woollen work jacket patched at the elbows, he walked forwards to meet Hunter's horse, pulling a cloth cap from his head to reveal some sparse white hair as he did so.

Phoebe was surprised to see Hunter dismount and grip the man's hand in a warm greeting. The coldness had vanished from his face. Indeed, he was smiling so warmly and sincerely that it quite transformed his face, lighting all of the darkness to reveal something very different in its place. Phoebe stared and could not look away, shocked at the difference in him. And she felt a warmth steal over her heart.

She blushed at the feeling and at her staring, and glanced round at Mrs Hunter to see if she had noticed, but Mrs Hunter was also watching Hunter, and with a less-than-convivial expression. Her face was thoughtful, her mood sombre as if seeing him like this brought back memories that saddened her.

'I am sure Sebastian can manage this one by himself, Phoebe. McInnes lives alone so there can be no need here of female sensibilities. Besides, I am feeling a little tired.'

Hunter glanced round at the carriage at that moment, expecting to see his mother and Phoebe alighting.

Mrs Hunter looked away, but not before Phoebe had seen that the lady's eyes were blinking back the tears.

And when she looked at Hunter again he was making his way towards the carriage with a grim expression upon his face.

'Is there a problem?'

'I have a headache. I believe I shall return to Blackloch,' Mrs Hunter said without even looking round at Hunter.

'This is the last farmstead. We are for home after this.'

'I cannot wait; I am leaving now.'

'Will you not at least step out of the carriage and show your face to McInnes? He will be insulted if you do not.'

'What do I care for McInnes's thoughts?' Mrs Hunter glared at her son. 'He is a tenant. Little more than a peasant grubbing in the dirt with his sheep and his hens. Lord, Sebastian, you always did treat him better than your own fath—' She bit off the word but even to Phoebe it was obvious what she had intended to say. Mrs Hunter set her face straight ahead, stubbornness and fury was etched into its every line.

Hunter stilled. Phoebe saw the tightening in his jaw as if he was clenching his teeth, controlling some strong emotion.

'He is an old man.' Hunter said quietly so that McInnes would not hear. 'Put aside your personal grievances for me in this one instance. He has a mare not long foaled. Come, ask him about it.'

But Mrs Hunter's face remained front facing and stubbornly defiant as if she had heard not a word her son had spoken.

'He is ill,' Hunter said, and then added, 'Mother...please.' Phoebe could see what it cost him to plead.

'He is ill?' Mrs Hunter turned to him, anger and hurt blazing in her eyes. 'Your father was ill! What care had you about him?'

Hunter's face seemed to bleach while his eyes darkened. His lips pressed firm. He turned and walked away without another word.

Phoebe knew she had to act quickly. 'Ma'am, you are unwell, and little wonder when you have suffered a headache the day long and still undertaken all with a smile for the sake of those who admire and respect you.' She paused, knowing that she might be risking too much in what she was about to say, but she spoke the words anyway. 'I could make your apologies to Mr McInnes and see to the linen and the food...if you so wish.'

Mrs Hunter looked at her for a moment and Phoebe could see the anger and jealousy still simmering, and, behind that veil, the hurt and the grief.

'Thank you Phoebe, that is what I was about to ask.' Mrs Hunter looked away before the tears could betray her completely.

Phoebe nodded.

Hunter started to talk to McInnes, again, drawing the old man away from the carriage and his mother. McInnes was no fool—Hunter knew he would realise the truth. Then he saw the old man's gaze shift back to the carriage and he heard the crunch of footsteps; when he turned there was Phoebe Allardyce walking beside the footman and his hamper, carrying an armful of linen.

'Good afternoon, Mr McInnes. I am afraid that Mrs Hunter is quite unwell with a headache, but she has sent you some linen and some small extras, too, and she asked if I would be so kind as to enquire as to your mare. Mr Hunter was telling us that she recently foaled.' Miss Allardyce smiled a tremulous smile at the old man.

'Very kind of Mrs Hunter. Please be sure to thank her for me.' McInnes kneaded the cloth cap between his hands and gave a respectful nod and a tug of his forelock towards the shadowy figure of the woman within the carriage.

And Hunter watched with surprise as a gloved hand appeared through the carriage window in an acknowledging wave.

'This is Miss Allardyce, my mother's companion,' said Hunter, and his eyes met those of Phoebe Allardyce both in warning and question.

Then McInnes took the linen and the small hamper and disappeared with them into his tiny stone cottage, only to reappear in the doorway a minute later with a stone bottle in his hand. 'Will you be taking a dram, Mr Hunter?'

'Not today, thank you, McInnes. Mrs Hunter is unwell, I should be returning her to Blackloch. I will drop in when I am passing tomorrow.'

The old man nodded, then shifted his rheumy gaze to Miss Allardyce. 'Do you want to see the foal so that you might tell Mrs Hunter?'

'Could I?'

He had to admit that Miss Allardyce's acting skills were of the first order. She managed somehow to make her face glow with delight; her eyes were bright and her smile broad and warm as she looked at McInnes.

McInnes gave a chuckle. 'Just a quick peek, mind, so as no' to keep Mrs Hunter waitin'.'

And just like that, Alasdair McInnes was won over by the girl who was lying to her employer, and who was steadily working a search through Blackloch by stealth, no doubt with a view to theft. She was dangerous, Hunter thought. And not only with her lies and her subterfuge. She was dangerous enough to tempt a man, to make him forget what it was that drove him through every hour of every day. Even now he was too aware of her, of her slender neck with its soft velvet skin that he had nuzzled and mouthed, of the small dimple that appeared in the corner of her mouth when she smiled, and the sweep of her long dark-red eyelashes, and the depths in those clear brown eyes.

He watched her absorbed in what the old man was telling her, with her shabby plain blue dress and her prim pinned hair, and that most wonderful warm smile. Yes, Miss Phoebe Allardyce was definitely the most dangerous woman he had ever met. The sooner he discovered what she was up to and she was out of his house, the better.

Chapter Seven

The sunset had lit the moor in a fire of red hues but, for once, Sebastian Hunter was paying no attention. He had not seen Phoebe Allardyce since their return to Blackloch the previous day, yet he had been thinking of her and the mystery she presented without respite.

'You are sure that she met with no one either before or after her visit to the Tolbooth?' Hunter asked as he leaned against the mantel above the fireplace.

McEwan made himself comfortable in one of the winged chairs before the empty fireplace and sipped at his brandy. 'Quite sure. The only time she was out of my sight was when she entered the building of the gaol itself. There was no man.'

Hunter's thumb toyed absently with the cleft in his chin and his eyes narrowed in thought. 'How the hell are we going to find him?' he murmured almost to himself.

'How goes your side of the campaign? Has she searched any of the other rooms?'

'The bedchambers—mine and my mother's. Nothing was taken that I can see.'

'But if nothing was taken? You are certain she was searching the rooms?'

'Oh, I am sure of it,' said Hunter grimly.

'What can she be looking for?' McEwan frowned in puzzlement.

'I suspect the answer to that question is the key to solving the whole damn mystery.'

'And how are we to find the answer? Short of catching the girl in the act with the Hunter family silver in her pocket?'

'I suppose I will have to keep an even closer eye on Miss Allardyce than I have been doing.' Hunter made no mention of just how close an eye he had been keeping on his mother's companion, or of how the prospect both compelled and taunted him. 'My mother's safety is paramount.'

'Absolutely. We should stop at nothing to discover Miss Allardyce's scheme.'

The pounding of the wolf's-head knocker woke Phoebe in the night. Over the sound of heavy rain drumming against the peat land outside there was the sound of footsteps running up and down the stairs, of hushed voices, and small scrapes and bangs from Hunter's room as if he were opening and closing drawers or cupboards. Phoebe rose from her bed, pulled a shawl around her shoulders and peeped out into the hallway. A couple of wall sconce candles had been lit, casting the passageway in a dim flickering light.

And just at that same moment Hunter emerged from his bedchamber, pulling his great caped riding coat over his dark coat and breeches. His hair was ruffled and dark as a raven's wing, and over his cheeks and chin Phoebe could see the shadow of his beard's growth. He looked piratical, wicked and dangerously handsome. His gaze met hers and that same tremulous feeling fluttered right through her.

'A coach has come off the road. Assistance is required at the scene of the accident.'

'There may be ladies present amongst the passengers. I will come with you and help, if you will give me but a moment to dress.'

'You offer is appreciated, but unnecessary. The moor is difficult to negotiate in the dark and rain. As I said, I will deal with the matter. Go back to bed, Miss Allardyce.' He glanced towards his mother's door, which remained shut.

'Mrs Hunter has taken one of her sleeping draughts. I doubt the rumpus will wake her.'

A nod of the head and he was gone, his great coat swirling out behind him and only the sound of his booted steps running down the stairs. She heard the distant thump of the back door as she returned to her room to dress.

Downstairs a few servants were huddled in the hallway, discussing the possible severity of the coaching accident and what they should be doing.

'Oh, Miss Allardyce, Mr Hunter told us no' to waken you,' McCabe, the oldest of the group and Hunter's valet, said.

'Rest assured, you did not waken me,' she said with a smile, knowing that Hunter had no housekeeper and that his mother was in no fit state to oversee what needed to be done. 'Now, tell me, what instruction has Mr Hunter left?'

'He's no' left any instructions. The master went out in such a hurry, there wasnae time,' said Jamie. 'And Polly told us that Mrs Hunter's had her powder the night so there'll be no wakenin' her.'

'We thought we would wait up for the master to return,' added Polly.

'Where are the rest of the servants?'

'Most dinnae live in, miss, but come over fae Blackloch village in the morning,' said a dark-haired maid by the name of Annie, standing beside Martha Beattie.

'Well, I am sure we will manage as we are,' said Phoebe. 'Jamie and Gavin, fetch some more coal in and up to the guest bedchambers and then lay the fires ready to be lit. Lay the fire in my room, too, as I may need to move elsewhere if a large enough number of injured persons are brought to Blackloch. And light the fire in Mr Hunter's bedchamber.'

'Yes, miss.'

'Tam and Stewart, check the accommodation in the stables for extra horses and carriages and then return to your room above the stables. Get what sleep you can before Mr Hunter returns.'

'Polly and Annie, prepare a pile of the oldest linen that would be suitable to be used as dressings and bandages, and some drying cloths, too. Mr McCabe, are there any old clothes suitable for gentlemen and lady passengers to borrow?'

'I will check, miss.'

'And you had best set out some drying cloths and night clothes for Mr Hunter in his chambers; he will need them upon his return.' As if to emphasise her point the rain drummed harder against the great front door and the wind gave a howl as if moaning across the moor.

'Martha and Sally, come with me. We will boil up plenty of water. There may be wounds to be cleansed or baths required. And prepare a pot of soup for the simmer.' Phoebe began to roll up her sleeves.

'Cook doesnae come in until the mornin',' said Martha.

'I am sure we will manage between us.' Since the loss of Papa's money Phoebe had become adept at managing their household on the most meagre of coins. She could make a very palatable pot of soup, even if she did say so herself.

Phoebe and the servants worked hard, but when two hours later there was still no sign of Hunter she sent the servants back to bed, telling them to get some sleep and that she would wake them upon Mr Hunter's return. Phoebe wrapped her shawl around her shoulders and sat down in the night-porter's chair in the hallway to wait for Hunter.

* * *

The first hint of dawn was lighting the charcoal from the sky as Hunter and his men handed their horses and the gig across to the grooms in the stable. The rain was still falling, albeit lightly, and Hunter could feel the heavy ache of fatigue in his muscles as he entered Blackloch through the back door with the rest of his menservants.

The smell of the broth hit him as soon as he opened the door. His stomach growled its response. They peeled off their sodden coats and over-garments and left them to dry in the scullery. Not a single maid was in evidence so Hunter and his men helped themselves to the soup, ladling the broth into bowls, gulping down the warming liquid. The great pots of water were still warm to the touch although they had been moved off both the range and the open fire. On the long table at the side of the kitchen sat piles of linen sheets and some of his old clothes neatly folded. The big kitchen clock on the wall showed a little after four. All of Blackloch slept. Hunter left his men to find their quarters and went to seek his own bed.

He did not doubt that Miss Allardyce would have used his absence and his mother's sleeping draught to continue her search. Would he find her in his bedchamber again? Part of him hoped it would be so. And right at this moment he was too tired to be angry or to fight the temptation she embodied.

His boots made no noise upon the stairs up from the kitchen. But when he reached the hallway and glanced across at the porter's chair, he knew he had been mistaken. Phoebe Allardyce was not conducting a search of any room in Blackloch, for she was curled up fast asleep in the chair.

In the faint light of the dawn she looked very young, her face creamy pale and unlined in sleep, her lips pink and infinitely kissable, her auburn lashes long against the unblemished skin of her cheeks. She was dressed in the same blue muslin dress as ever, but her hair snaked over her shoulder in the long thick braid that she wore for bed. And from beneath the hem of her skirts, tucked up on the chair, peeped her stockinged toes, where she had curled her legs beneath her on the seat of the chair. His gaze dropped lower to the worn boots that sat neatly by the chair's wooden leg. He stepped closer, his own boots making a small noise against the stone flags of the floor and she stirred, her eyes fluttering open, yet still heavy-lidded with sleep.

'Mr Hunter,' she whispered sleepily, and the sound of his name on her lips was as if she had trailed her fingers teasingly down the length of his spine. She uncurled herself, yawned and stretched, the thin muslin stretched tight across her breasts. Hunter's mouth went dry.

'What happened with the accident?' She rose from the chair and stood in her stocking soles on the cold stone of the floor before him. 'Were there many injuries?' She looked up at him, her face filled with concern and he thought he had not realised just how much smaller than he she was. The top of her head barely reached his chin.

'Mr Hunter?' she prompted, and he realised he was staring.

'It was a town coach travelling too fast in the rain, the driver mis-judged the corner and overturned the coach across the road. There were two young gentlemen passengers, both shaken, but neither of them hurt.'

'Do they return to Blackloch with you?'

He shook his head. 'They were in a rush to reach Glasgow—one of them is the bridegroom in a wedding this morning. I sent them on in my coach.'

She met his eyes before her gaze shifted to take in the dirty wet state of his clothes. 'I thought you were wearing your greatcoat…'

'The coach had to be cleared from the road to prevent another accident.'

Her gaze dropped lower to take in the scrapes and cuts and dirt on his hands where he had been helping to lift the carriage and change the wheel.

'Your hands...' She took his hands into hers, her fingers small and slender beside his, her touch gentle as a caress. And when she looked up at him there was something in her eyes that made him think he had got Phoebe Allardyce all wrong.

'They should be cleansed.'

Her fingers felt chilled to his touch. He pulled his hands away, feeling suddenly confused.

'It is late, Miss Allardyce, go to bed,' he said and he knew that his voice was too hard.

He saw the small flicker of hurt before she masked it and walked away without a word, and he wished he could call back the harshness.

In his bedchamber, McCabe was snoozing in the corner chair.

'Mr Hunter, sir.' The valet wakened and got to his feet.

'What are you doing here, McCabe?'

'Beggin' your pardon, sir, but Miss Allardyce sent me.'

Hunter's eyes scanned the room that appeared so different to the one he had left earlier that night. The fire had been lit, casting a warm glow to cheer the darkness. A nightshirt was hanging over the second fireguard to warm and his bed had been neatly made.

McCabe saw the direction of his gaze. 'She thought as how you might be feeling the cold upon your return...wi' the weather and all.'

'Miss Allardyce organised this?' Hunter could not keep the sharpness from his voice.

'Aye, sir. She organised everything—the guest chambers, the linens in case there was a need for bandages and dressings, the hot water. On account o' Mrs Hunter havin' taken one of her pooders. She made the soup with Martha and Sally, too—in case there was a need for it.' McCabe removed a warming pan from the bed as he spoke.

Hunter could scarcely believe what he was hearing.

And later, after McCabe had gone and he finally found sleep, the thought on his mind was not the coaching accident or the moor, or the usual nightmare that haunted him, but Miss Allardyce…liar and would-be thief…who had held his household together for him this night.

In Mrs Hunter's dressing room Phoebe and the lady stood before the opened wardrobes trying to select a dress suitable for the rout that evening.

'Polly informed me there was something of an incident in the night.'

'Indeed.' Phoebe related the details of the carriage accident.

'I am surprised that Sebastian could drag himself from his slumber to attend the scene.'

'Ma'am, Mr Hunter not only relayed the gentlemen passengers to Glasgow in his own equipage, but personally participated in righting the damaged vehicle and removing it from blocking the road.' She thought of the cuts and scrapes upon his hands, of how wet his clothes had been and the fatigue that had shadowed beneath his eyes. And of the strange expression in his gaze before the dark pensive chill had returned.

Mrs Hunter waved away her words with an airy hand. 'Forgive me if I find that difficult to believe.'

'It is the truth, ma'am.' Whatever dark deeds Hunter had committed, his mother deserved to know that he had acted most honourably last night.

'And you would know this how precisely?' Mrs Hunter peered at her.

'I was wakened by the knocking at the front door of those who came to fetch Mr Hunter.' Phoebe hesitated over admitting her part in the night's proceedings.

Mrs Hunter peered more closely at her. 'Indeed, you look as if you have not slept a wink.'

'I did have some trouble finding sleep once more,' she offered and was saved from further explanation by Polly's arrival with Mrs Hunter's breakfast tray.

'Miss Allardyce, Cook was wondering if she might have a word with you in the kitchen,' said Polly.

Phoebe thought of the pot of soup that Cook must have come in to find this morning. She glanced at Mrs Hunter.

'Go on, girl, go and see what she wants,' said Mrs Hunter in a grumpy tone. 'And let us hope that I feel a deal better after my chocolate. I shall see you in the drawing room in an hour.'

Cook wished to know the recipe of the soup. Phoebe smiled and was only too happy to share. She was heading back up the stairs to her own chamber when she met Hunter coming down.

'Miss Allardyce.' He bowed.

'Mr Hunter.'

'I owe you thanks for all that you did last night,' he said stiffly. 'It was much appreciated.' He sounded ill at ease. He did not speak of their arrangement, nor did he try to take her hand or to kiss her. She wondered at the change in him.

Those pale haunting eyes held hers and there was something different in them this morning, as if he were looking at her for the first time. A footman passed in the hallway below. Hunter gave her a little nod of the head and carried on down the stairs, but a few steps later she glanced back at Hunter at exactly the same time as he looked back at her. A feeling of recognition and something shared, something binding, passed between them.

Hunter leafed through the pile of newly delivered letters.

The day was warm and sunny; the sky outside his window, blue and cloudless. There were two letters for his mother and all the rest were addressed to himself, all save the one at the bottom of the pile. The small neat handwriting on the front had directed it to Miss Phoebe Allardyce, care of Blackloch Hall. Both the handwriting and the slight scent of violet perfume indicated a female sender. He turned the letter over, and on the reverse written in small script at the top right-hand corner was the sender's name.

Hunter stilled. The shock kicked in his chest. The rest of the letters tumbled forgotten to the floor. He read the name again and again, and still the taste was bitter in his mouth and his stomach felt a small tight knot. *Miss Emma Northcote.* All he saw of the name was *Northcote*. It had been the start of the whole of this sorry mess. And the nightmare played again through his mind and he gripped so hard to the letter that his knuckles shone white. And then, quite deliberately, carefully, he set it down upon his desk. It sat there, a small pale square stark against the ebony; he reached for the brandy decanter and filled his glass, and with his eyes still fixed upon the letter, he drained it just as quickly. And outside the clouds moved across the sky to block the sun, and all of the darkness had returned.

Chapter Eight

'Damnation!' Mrs Hunter cursed. 'There is never a servant to be found in this wretched place when I need one. Should I have to run my own errands? Have I not reached the stage in my life when I warrant a little comfort and ease? And instead I find myself in this… this mausoleum of a house.' Mrs Hunter winced and rubbed her fingers against her forehead. 'Perhaps it is time that we went back to Charlotte Street, even if the decorating is not yet complete.'

'No!' Phoebe said a little too forcefully and found her employer peering round at her. She forced a smile and picking up Mrs Hunter's shawl draped it around the lady's shoulders. 'What I mean to say is, would it not be better to wait just a week or two more? You know how sensitive your head is to strong vapours. The smell of the paint would not be good for you, ma'am. Perhaps you should wait until it has dispelled somewhat before returning to Charlotte Street.'

Mrs Hunter nodded, but her face was all discontentment. 'You are probably right, Phoebe.'

'And Polly is preparing you a sleeping draught so you should rest well tonight.'

'For that, at least, I am thankful. Be a dear, Phoebe, and fetch my fashion journals from the drawing room. I left them in there earlier.'

'Of course.'

* * *

Phoebe was passing Hunter's study with the journals in her hand when he appeared in the doorway. She started, but then smothered the butterflies in her stomach to walk past him. He could not kiss her here in broad daylight where anyone might chance to see them.

'Miss Allardyce,' he said and her heart gave a little somersault. His face was paler than normal, his eyes glittered in the sunlight and there was something very cold and very dangerous in the way he was looking at her.

'I have a letter for you.'

'A letter?'

A movement of his hand and she saw the small folded parchment there. He held it out to her.

'Thank you.' The cool brush of his fingers against hers as she accepted the letter made all of the butterflies and tingles reappear. Her heart began to thud as ever it did when Hunter was around. She turned to hurry away, desperate to escape the madness of the feelings surging through her body.

'I could not help but notice the sender,' he said and beneath his usual coolness was an edge of something else. 'I did not know you are an acquaintance of the Northcote family?'

She glanced at the back of the letter and saw Emma's name. 'Miss Northcote is a friend of mine. We were at school together.' She folded the letter and slipped it into her pocket.

He stepped out into the corridor, walked closer until he was standing right before her, staring down into her eyes. 'So many things I do not know about you, Phoebe Allardyce.'

And there was something in his voice that sent a shiver down the full length of her body. She swallowed, feeling her stomach dance at his proximity, both wanting and dreading his kiss.

She grasped around for something to say. 'Are you acquainted with Miss Northcote, or perhaps one of her brothers?' She knew the moment the words were out of her mouth that she had chosen wrongly. Gone was the cool quiet intensity and in its place was pure and unadulterated anger. She saw the sudden tension that ran through Hunter's body, saw the tightening of his jaw, the sudden flare of fury that darkened his eyes. She edged away until her spine touched against the stone of the corridor wall. But Hunter saw the move, and in an instant his hands were leaning against the wall on either side of her head, his body so close to hers yet not touching, effectively trapping her where she stood.

'What manner of game are you playing with me, Miss Allardyce?' he demanded and his voice was low and guttural and tortured.

Her heart was racing in earnest now, thudding so hard she could feel the vibration of it throughout her body. She shook her head with the tiniest motion. 'I do not know what you mean.'

He leaned so close she could feel the warmth of his breath against her cheek and smell the sweet rich aroma of brandy. 'If you do not already know it, I give you fair warning, Phoebe.'

Her heart stuttered to a halt before racing off at full tilt again. He could not know, could he? She stared up into his eyes, and the intensity that was in them, the anger, and such tortured pain made her forget all about her own fears. 'Sebastian,' she said softly.

He squeezed his eyes closed as if aware he had inadvertently revealed too much, and when he opened them again the hurt was gone, hidden well away, and his anger was reined under some measure of control.

'Do you not know that you are playing with fire?' he said and his voice was harsh. 'If you are such good friends with Miss Northcote, you must know what I am.'

She shook her head. 'I…' she said, but something in his eyes stopped her.

He took her lips and this time there was nothing of gentleness, only of urgency and a need so overwhelming that it razed everything in its path. His mouth was hard and possessive as it claimed hers. He took her without mercy, his tongue plundering, his lips pillaging, ravishing her with his kiss as thoroughly as in the dreams that plagued her nights. It was a kiss that should have frightened, a kiss that should have punished, but in it she felt the measure of his desperation and hurt.

She knew she should have resisted, despite their 'arrangement'. All that was right and proper decreed that she should have made some excuse to escape him, but Phoebe reacted instinctively, responding to Hunter and the hurt in him. She wrapped her arms around his neck and gave herself up to his onslaught, salving his pain with her gentleness, meeting his passion with her own. Losing herself in the ecstasy and power of his kiss.

When he eventually raised his face from hers, he retreated, breathing heavy, leaning against the wall and staring at her with an unreadable expression upon his face. And Phoebe stared back, as aghast at what she had just done as Hunter looked. Her heart was thudding fit to burst. Her body felt molten from his touch. Everything was in tumult, everything, wild and overwhelming.

She picked up the journals from where they had fallen and walked away while she could, her head held high as if she were not trembling from the force of what had just exploded between her and Hunter. And not once did she look back at him.

'Phoebe, there you are. I was just about to send out the search party. What on earth took you so long?' Mrs Hunter demanded.

'Forgive me, ma'am, I…' Phoebe could not meet the lady's eyes. 'I had a little difficulty in locating them.' She set the fashion journals upon the table before Mrs Hunter and tried to mask the riot of emotion still pounding through her blood.

Mrs Hunter peered at her. 'Are you feeling quite yourself?'

No! she wanted to cry. *I have not been feeling myself since the moment I looked into your son's eyes.* She was still reeling from the hurt in Hunter's eyes and the fury that she had done nothing to provoke, still reeling from the wantonness of her response to him. She felt frightened by her feelings and how very little control she seemed to have over them. But Phoebe hid her fears and feelings and forced herself to look calmly at her employer.

'Perfectly,' she lied.

But Mrs Hunter was not convinced. 'Come and sit down beside me.' She patted the sofa seat by her side.

Phoebe had no choice but to obey.

'You look positively feverish, my girl, and breathless.' Mrs Hunter took Phoebe's hand in her own. 'And you are trembling.'

Phoebe quickly withdrew her traitorous hand from Mrs Hunter's, and felt the blush of guilt and embarrassment and turbulent emotion heat her cheeks all the hotter. 'I rushed up the stairs too fast so as not to keep you waiting any longer.'

'I should not need to remind you, Phoebe, that young ladies never run.'

'I am sorry, Mrs Hunter.'

Mrs Hunter gave a nod of conciliation. 'It is fatigue, Phoebe. I can see it in your eyes. And little wonder with having been awake half the night with the storm and the hullabaloo surrounding the coaching accident. I think I have been a little selfish in my demands of you today.'

'Not at all, ma'am,' said Phoebe.

'I am sending you to bed. You need to rest.'

'But it is Mrs Montgomery's rout this evening.' She thought of what Mrs Hunter's absence would mean—she would be alone at Blackloch with Hunter.

'Exactly—we both know what Amelia's routs are like. If it runs on as late as the last one, I shall stay overnight and travel back in the morning. Believe me, Phoebe, you are in no fit state for such an evening and I shall manage very well alone. And you need not fear to be left in Sebastian's company. My son will be gone to McEwan's house to dine with him and Mairi, so there will be no one here to disturb you.'

No one to disturb her.

All of her protestations died on her lips. Phoebe swallowed. She would be free to search Blackloch.

'Now, off with you, girl. I will not hear another word on the matter.'

The evening was still light, but the curtains were closed in Phoebe's bedchamber. Phoebe lay in the bed and listened to the faint chimes of the grandfather clock down in the hallway, and the crunch of Mrs Hunter's carriage as it rolled down the gravel of the driveway. Hunter was long gone, but Phoebe was thinking of him, just as she had been thinking of him all of the previous hours.

In all her three-and-twenty years no one had ever made her feel the way he did. She had never questioned her life. Not the loss of a mother so young, or the years spent keeping house and caring for a father who, for all his brilliant mind, had not the slightest notion of how to care for himself. Not the loss of a sister so beloved or the tragedy that went with it. Not even the loss of all their money and the gaoling of her father. She loved her papa, Mrs Hunter was more than kind and Phoebe had been content with her life. But now that she had met Hunter, everything up until that moment on the moor felt as if she had been existing rather than living.

He did not look at her as a daughter, a carer or a servant. Hunter looked at her as a woman. And no one had ever done that before. For the first time in her life she felt attractive and desirable and alive. He made her feel excited. He made her feel like she was glowing inside. And all of this while her papa was locked in gaol with a face beaten black and blue.

It was so wrong, for Phoebe loved her papa, and she could not understand the selfishness of her feelings, or how she could even be thinking of Hunter in such a way. And she wept with the guilt and confusion and she knew she could not allow this madness to continue. The Messenger wanted one thing. Phoebe knew she must focus only on that and her papa.

She dried her tears and slipped silently from the bed.

Hunter handed the reins of Ajax over to the groom and slipped into Blackloch. The dinner with McEwan and Mairi had been pleasant enough, but he could not dislodge the feeling of guilt over the way he had treated Phoebe Allardyce. He thought of last night, of her standing before him in the darkened hallway with that look of concern and tenderness in her eyes. The coaching accident had presented her with the perfect opportunity to continue her search of Blackloch, yet Miss Allardyce had forgone it in order to help him and his household. And he thought of how pale she had looked this morning, of the shadows that had pinched beneath those warm golden-brown eyes. Little wonder after everything she had done through the night. But all of Hunter's gratitude had been forgotten the moment he had seen that name upon the letter. Even if she had been sent here by the Northcotes to remind him of what he had done to them, or to exact some measure of revenge, she had not deserved the harshness of his treatment. And he thought of the passion of her response, of its gentleness and strength. Remorse moved over his heart.

Hunter did not go to his study, pour himself a brandy and sit staring out over the moor. Instead, he walked up the stairs and headed straight for Phoebe Allardyce's bedchamber.

Chapter Nine

Phoebe had almost finished searching the last of the guest bed-chambers when she heard the tread of feet upon the main staircase. Her first thought was that it was one of the servants taking advantage of the family's absence to use the main stairs. But even before she recognised the sound of the footsteps a shiver tingled through her body and her heart leapt—she knew it was Hunter. She quietly closed the cupboard door and stood where she was, listening. Her heart was galloping. If Hunter caught her in here, what feasible excuse could she give?

Hunter's bedchamber was at the end of the corridor. But the footsteps stopped short. She heard the nearby knock, the pause, the tread of his feet as he entered Phoebe's own bedchamber.

The room was empty. The covers on the bed were thrown back as if she had only just climbed from it.

Hunter moved forwards, pressed his hand to the sheets and found they were cool. He glanced around the room, seeing the curtains still drawn and Miss Allardyce's blue dress hanging over the door of the wardrobe.

His eyes narrowed and his mouth tightened. He crushed the tender feelings he had been harbouring, and strode out of the bed-chamber to discover just which part of Blackloch Phoebe Allardyce was engaged in searching, and found her standing, still in her night-dress, outside the door to the next guest chamber.

'There you are, Miss Allardyce.'

She stilled. 'Mr Hunter. I thought you were having dinner with Mr McEwan and his wife.'

'I was.' Hunter did not elaborate. 'I thought you were abed.'

She gave a nervous swallow. 'I…I have been in bed since this afternoon. I was merely stretching my legs.'

Hunter moved his gaze to the door of the guest chamber imme-diately behind her before shifting it back to the woman.

Her stance did not waver, but he saw the tiny flicker in her eyes, that moment of doubt, and the flush of guilt that coloured her cheeks. He was angry, partly at Miss Allardyce, but mainly at himself. He had had enough of women's games.

'Why are you and my mother really here at Blackloch?'

Her eyes widened slightly, but whether it was a response to the question or the cold demand in his voice he did not know, nor did he care.

'The town house is being decorated.'

'Forgive me if I find it difficult to believe that my mother's desire to change her wallpaper would bring her back here. She left Blackloch the day we buried my father and swore she would never return,' he said harshly. 'My mother loathes the very sight of me.'

'No!' Miss Allardyce took a small involuntary step towards him and shook her head. 'You are quite wrong. Mrs Hunter—' She caught herself back from saying what she would have, but the con-cern was still etched upon her face. She bit at her lower lip as if weighing up a decision. 'I am not supposed to tell you, but I think perhaps Mrs Hunter is wrong in keeping it from you.' She looked at him, her expression serious. 'If I confide in you, you must keep it secret.' She waited for his reassurance.

Hunter just looked at her. 'Miss Allardyce.'

'She would be very angry if she thought you knew. I could lose my position.'

Still Hunter would make no promise.

Phoebe Allardyce's eyes regarded him steadily. 'I would have your oath on this, sir, or I will tell you nothing.' And from the strength in her gaze Hunter knew it was no idle threat.

'Very well, you have my oath.'

Her eyes met his and he knew she would tell him. 'There have been two break-ins at the town house in Charlotte Street. The first was some months ago, not long after I first started as Mrs Hunter's companion, and the second was only a matter of weeks ago. Mrs Hunter would never admit to it, but the last break-in distressed her greatly. Nothing was left untouched. All of our most personal possessions were rifled through. She did not sleep well before the last break-in, and since then, well...' She raised her eyebrows and Hunter could only guess at how bad things had become. 'That is why she makes such use of sleeping powders. In answer to your question, Mr Hunter, I believe that your mother is here because she is frightened.'

Her words hit him hard. 'She should have told me,' he ground out.

She touched her fingers to his sleeve. 'Mrs Hunter is too proud. As I think are you,' she said softly.

His eyes met hers and he saw the sympathy that was there. It hardened his heart. He stepped back out of her reach.

'What was stolen?'

'That is the strange thing. Nothing was actually stolen, but they made something of a mess in their searching. I think that is why Mrs Hunter is having the house redecorated, that and, I suspect, as a way of wiping away the intruder's presence.'

The significance of what she was telling him slotted into place. 'There have been two break-ins at Blackloch since my father's death, both of which revealed nothing was taken.'

'How very peculiar.' She frowned.

'Break-ins in both properties in which nothing was taken, but the rooms turned over as if they have been searched most thoroughly… It sounds as if someone is looking for something very particular that they believe to be in my mother's or my possession.' He looked at Phoebe Allardyce.

She was staring not at him, but at some point in the far distance, a look of sudden realisation and horror in her eyes. The blood drained from her face so that she was pale as a ghost.

'What do you think, Phoebe?' he asked quietly.

She tried to mask her shock before she looked at him, but not very successfully. 'I do not know.' She swallowed and her gaze fluttered nervously around the corridor. 'It seems…unlikely. I mean, what on earth would such a person be looking for?'

'I was hoping you might be able to enlighten me as to that.'

Her eyes shot to his and he saw that they were filled with fear, more than just the fear of discovery. She was standing against the wall, holding her breath, her body rigid with dread. And Hunter had the sensation that something much more was going on here. He backed off a little.

'You witnessed the evidence of the break-ins in Charlotte Street so I am interested to hear your thoughts on the matter. Your insight could be valuable.'

She swallowed again and the small smile was forced. 'What are thieves normally after—money, plate, paintings…jewellery?' She gave a shrug. 'Anything of value, I would think.'

He nodded and came to stand opposite her, leaning back against the wall to mirror her stance. 'You know that I cannot stand by and allow a threat to my mother, Phoebe.'

She nodded and closed her eyes, but not before he had seen the unshed tears.

'Threats are such a terrible thing,' she said and her voice was barely more than a whisper. The clear brown eyes flickered open and how she managed to prevent the swell of tears from falling he did not know. 'And now if you will excuse me, sir, I must return to bed.'

She was so pale that Hunter thought she might swoon where she stood. But Phoebe Allardyce held her head high and walked the small distance to her bedchamber to disappear inside.

Phoebe could not sleep that night. The implication of what Hunter had said, that the Messenger was behind the break-ins and the violent ruthlessness of his search through Mrs Hunter's home and personal possessions, played in her mind. And for the first time she realised the significance of the Messenger having spoken of 'we' rather than 'I'. How many of them were involved in this and who were they that such a small seemingly inconsequential item could mean so much to them? Phoebe feared the strength and force of the men and what they could do to her papa. She feared she had allowed her attraction to Hunter and all that he made her feel distract her from the importance and urgency of what they had set her to do. And she knew that she must find what they wanted very soon.

She tossed and turned for hours, unable to find comfort, and had almost given up on sleep when a knock sounded on her bedchamber door. The maid Martha Beattie, who Phoebe had seen leave for home after dinner, slipped through the doorway wearing a dark shawl and with a lantern in her hand.

'Oh, Miss Allardyce, I'm so sorry to waken you.' The girl sounded breathless as if she had been running. Phoebe could smell the damp night air coming from her and see the girl's face was taut and pale and so filled with worry that it made Phoebe forget all of her own.

'Martha, what is wrong?'

'Oh, Miss Allardyce, it's my ma.' Martha began to sob and the lantern trembled in her hand.

'Take a deep breath, calm yourself and tell me what has happened.' Phoebe placed a steadying hand on the girl's arm.

'The baby is coming and my pa hasnae come back from Glasgow the day. I cannae run all the way to the village for the midwife and my ma says there's something wrong. I—I dinnae know what to do, miss.'

'Stay here, Martha, while I wake Mr Hunter. Then we will have someone fetch the midwife before we set off for your cottage.'

'Oh, miss...'

'We will do everything that we possibly can to help your mother.' She patted the girl's shoulder. 'Stout heart, Martha. I will be as quick as I can.' She lit her candle from Martha's lantern and hurried to fetch Hunter.

Hunter's face was not peaceful in repose. Whatever dreams he had did not look to be pleasant. He murmured and his head rolled against the pillow. In the flicker of the candlelight Phoebe could see the slight sheen of sweat upon his pale skin and the pain that racked his features and felt a surge of compassion for him. From the wall above the fireplace the dark-cowled man and the wolf looked down on her and this time when she looked at the monk, she had the strangest notion that he was not a monk at all, but something altogether more sinister. Such a painting could not help Hunter's nightmares. She turned her back on the twin watchers and touched a hand to Hunter's arm.

'Mr Hunter...Sebastian.'

His eyes were still drugged with sleep as he squinted into the lantern light. 'Phoebe?' And he reached for her, pulling her to him.

She placed a hand against his chest to restrain him and felt the warm firm muscle of bare skin. 'No, you must wake up. It is an emergency. Mrs Beattie's baby is coming, a month before it should. Martha is here for our help.'

Her words reached him and the drowsiness was gone in an instant.

'Mr Beattie has not returned from Glasgow and Martha has no means to reach the midwife.'

Hunter sat up and Phoebe saw that he wore no nightshirt. His chest, arms and stomach were pale and as defined with the taut lines of muscles as if he were a Greek god carved in marble.

'I will fetch the midwife and bring her to the Beatties' cottage.'

Phoebe dragged her eyes away from his nakedness, appalled that she could be staring at him, even at a time like this. 'If you are amenable I will have Jamie take Martha and me in one of the carriages back to her cottage while we wait for you to arrive. She ran all the way here, poor girl.'

'Take Jamie and the gig. It's easier to handle in the dark.'

She nodded and turned to leave.

'And, Phoebe…' he called after her.

She glanced back at him, and their gazes locked.

'Have a care.'

She nodded and hurried back to Martha.

When Hunter arrived at the Beatties' cottage with the midwife there was no sign of either Phoebe or Mr Beattie. A large pot of hot water was simmering over the fire. In the front parlour the children were red-eyed with tiredness and crying, their little faces streaked with tears and the smear of runny noses. The smallest one, Rosie, who was little more than a baby herself, had fallen asleep curled in a little ball on the floor. A terrible moaning was coming from the downstairs bedroom and every time it sounded the children's crying renewed. The midwife did not pause to remove her cloak, just disappeared into that bedroom. Hunter did not dare to even look through the door. He retreated into the hallway, feeling useless, not knowing what to do in this women's world.

Phoebe appeared from the bedroom, her sleeves rolled up, her cheeks pink from heat and exertion. 'Oh, Mr Hunter, thank goodness,' she whispered as her fingers brushed against his hand. Her relief at his presence was like a gentle touch against his heart.

'What can I do to help?'

'Look after the children.'

Hunter looked at her helplessly.

'Put your arm around them, cuddle them when they cry. Put a blanket over them when they are cold. Tell them that everything will be fine and that they must be good girls for their mother.' Then, to the young footman who was hovering ashen-faced by the kitchen door as if he would rather be outside, 'Into the kitchen, Jamie, scrub your hands, then fill another pail of water and set another pot on to boil. Once it has boiled, take it off the heat and let it cool.'

'Yes, miss,' Jamie mumbled dutifully.

And then she was gone, bustling towards the kitchen to return with a bowl of hot water and a pile of linen.

'Go,' she urged Hunter. 'You can do it.'

Hunter nodded, knowing that he had to help, and walked into the parlour of crying children.

The hours passed slowly, painfully, and still the baby had not been born. Mrs Beattie was in so much pain she did not know who was in the room with her and who was not. The low dull moan was now constant, and every so often she cried and wept for her husband. Phoebe closed off her emotions so that she could get through this night. She had seen this same scene before, and she knew how it would end. And yet even so, through those hours she mopped Mrs Beattie's brow and held her hand and willed the woman to keep going. And when the midwife went into her bag and brought out a large pair of metal spoon-shaped tongs, Phoebe understood.

'She's no' gonnae manage hersel', miss. We'll have to pull the babe out into this world.'

Phoebe nodded and went to scrub the tongs in hot water.

It was just like Elspeth, except that when the midwife handed her the baby, still warm from Mrs Beattie's body, the boy breathed and moved, a cry erupting from his little gummy mouth. Phoebe wiped him clean and swaddled the tiny body in fresh linen as his loud wails filled the air. And it seemed to Phoebe that she had never heard such a glorious noise.

Mrs Beattie raised her head from the pillow, looking for the baby.

'A boy, ma,' said Martha. 'A fine healthy boy.'

Phoebe rested the tiny bundle into the woman's outstretched arms.

Mrs Beattie smiled and tears of joy were streaming down her face. 'At last,' she whispered. 'And Malcolm not here to see it.'

Hunter stirred as Phoebe entered the parlour. Her eyes scanned the room, taking in the girls sleeping on the rug before the fire with Hunter's coat laid over them as a blanket. Hunter was on the sofa, a small girl snuggled into him on either side, and baby Rosie sprawled over his chest, his hand gently cradling the child. His hair was dishevelled and the shadow of beard growth darkened his cheeks and chin.

'Phoebe?' he whispered. 'I heard the babe's cries.'

'A boy, alive and well.'

'Beattie will be pleased.'

Together they carried the children upstairs into the bedroom and snuggled them into their beds, shooshing them with soft words when they stirred.

Phoebe spoke to Hunter in the little parlour. 'The midwife is almost finished, but someone needs to stay with Mrs Beattie and the baby. Martha is exhausted. She will be needed here tomorrow so I have sent her to bed and assured her that I will watch over her mother most carefully until the morning. There is nothing more that you can do here, Mr Hunter. You may as well go back to Blackloch and get some sleep.'

'Jamie can take the midwife back to the village. I will stay here—with you.'

'Mr Hunter—' But the look on his face was resolute and she did not have the energy to argue. Besides, she could not deny that she was glad of his presence. She felt the reassuring squeeze of his fingers against hers before she turned and walked away.

Malcolm Beattie returned some time in the wee small hours. His horse had thrown a shoe and the man had walked all the way home from Glasgow in the darkness. Hunter clapped Beattie on the back.

'Congratulations, Beattie, you have a fine son.'

'A son?' The tears were streaming down Beattie's cheeks, rolling unashamed, so incongruous a sight for the man. 'And Rena?'

'Your wife has had a night of it. She is tired, but the midwife assures us that she will be fine.'

'Thank God! Thank God!' wept Beattie.

Yet still Phoebe would not desert her post. She insisted Mr Beattie got a few hours sleep.

At eight o'clock two women from the village appeared at the cottage door armed with baskets of bread and eggs, cheese and ham and offers of help.

Only after speaking to them did Phoebe agree to leave.

Hunter took her arm in his and led her out to the phaeton, climbing up before her and then reaching down to help her up to sit beside him.

The early morning mist had not yet burned away. The moor seemed very still, a hushed quiet so that even the wind was but a breath upon his face.

'Jeanie and Alice from the village will take the girls to their own homes and care for them for a few days, and there will be others that will come later to help both Mr and Mrs Beattie,' she said.

'They are good people, all of them.'

'Yes.' Her face was pale, with blue shadows smudged beneath her eyes.

He twitched the reins and the two horses moved off slowly, the wheels crunching against the gravel and soil as they travelled along the narrow track.

Neither of them spoke, just sat in a silence that seemed comfortable to Hunter. There was only the song of the blackbird and the sparrows. He slowed the phaeton so that she would not be jarred with the roughness of the track and thought he saw a glimmer of moisture upon her cheeks.

'Phoebe?'

She turned her head away so that he would not see her face.

He stopped the carriage where it was and gently captured her face to bring it round to his. Her tears were wet beneath his fingers. It was the first time he had seen her cry and he felt moved by the sight of it.

'The night must have been difficult for you.'

She tried to turn away, but he did not release her.

'A birthing…when you are innocent of the knowledge of such matters…'

'No.' She gave a small choking sound, half-laughing, half-sobbing. She squeezed her eyes shut, but the tears leaked through to stream down her cheeks.

'Phoebe…'

'I am just tired, that is all. I will be fine once I have slept.' She sniffed and rummaged for her handkerchief.

Hunter was not sure he believed her. He passed her the clean one from his pocket. 'In settlement of my debt.'

She gave him a wobbly smile, took the handkerchief, dried her cheeks and blew her nose.

'You did magnificently,' he said quietly and stroked his thumb against her cheek.

She looked up at him and there was something in her eyes that mirrored what was in Hunter's soul: a sadness, a sense of loss that quite smote Hunter's heart. 'I did what had to be done,' she said. 'I always do what has to be done.' And he had the feeling that she was talking about so much more than the Beattie baby.

Tendrils of auburn hair had escaped to curl around her face; the long thick plait was messy as it snaked over her shoulder and down onto her breast. Her dress was stained with blood and other marks and her eyes were red-rimmed and glistening with tears. And Hunter did not know why there was such a tight warm feeling in his chest or why he had such a need to comfort her and take away her pain. He touched his lips to hers in the smallest and gentlest of kisses and when he drew away he knew that something had changed be-tween them, something from which there would be no going back. He wrapped his arm around her waist so that she was snug by his side, and gave a tug at the reins in his other hand. And he took her back to Blackloch.

Chapter Ten

'What on earth were you thinking of letting her attend a birthing, Sebastian?' his mother demanded the next day. She was seated on the sofa in the drawing room, staring at him imperiously and ignoring the plate of luncheon sandwiches on the table before her. Phoebe Allardyce, about whom they were talking, was upstairs fast asleep in her bedchamber.

Hunter was standing by the fireplace, leaning an arm against the mantel.

'Not only is she unmarried and a young gentlewoman…' And such was her agitation that she rose to her feet and came to stand before him that she might deliver the full weight of her displeasure all the better. 'Lord, Sebastian!' His mother's face crumpled. 'Phoebe's sister died in childbirth not two years since. Did she make no mention of the matter?'

He stared at his mother in horror. 'She spoke not a word of it.' And he thought of how hard Phoebe had fought to keep from weeping and he understood now that look in her eyes—it was grief, raw and unadulterated. It was as if a hand had reached into his chest and twisted his heart. 'Forgive me,' he uttered. 'I never would have let her go had I known.' But even as he said it he knew that he could not have stopped Phoebe from going to help Beattie's wife. The girl was as stubborn as himself. Stubborn, and damned courageous.

* * *

When Phoebe arrived in the drawing room later that day, ready to attend to Mrs Hunter's plans, she was surprised to find Hunter present. He was standing by the window, staring out over the moor, the usual brooding expression upon his face. Mrs Hunter was working on the tapestry. The room was in silence, but there was not the same chilled tension in the air between them that had been there in those early days of their arrival at Blackloch.

'Ah, Phoebe, my dear.' Mrs Hunter smiled and patted the sofa next to her. 'Come and sit by me and tell me how you are feeling.'

'I am well, ma'am, thank you. How was Mrs Montgomery's rout?'

'It was as we expected, Phoebe.' Mrs Hunter sniffed in a superior way, but her eyes were kind. 'I have been hearing of last night's events.'

Phoebe glanced over at Hunter, unsure of just how much he had told his mother. His eyes met hers.

'News of Mrs Beattie's emergency is all round the village. Mrs Fraser, the local busybody, called upon my mother this morning,' he said.

'She is wife to Sir Hamish Fraser of Newmilns,' corrected Mrs Hunter in an irritated tone, 'although I will admit to her being a bothersome woman.'

Hunter moved from his stance at the window to take the seat furthest from Phoebe and his mother.

Mrs Hunter frowned at him, but there was nothing of malice in it. Her face softened again as she turned to Phoebe. 'Now, you are not to worry, Phoebe. I soon set Eliza Fraser straight once Sebastian had explained the whole of it to me.'

Phoebe stared in amazement. Her gaze shifted from Mrs Hunter to her son and back again. 'Thank you.'

'I never did like that woman,' Mrs Hunter confided.

* * *

Hunter stayed for the next hour, and in truth, although Phoebe was glad to see the thaw in relations between him and his mother, she was relieved when he left. She was too aware of last night, and the emotion that still echoed from it. Too aware that Hunter had not left her, but stayed with her until the end at the Beattie cottage, too aware of the tenderness in his eyes at the weakness of her tears. The gentle brush of his lips had meant more than either of their previous passionate exchanges. That one small kiss had somehow shifted what lay between them, deepening it, calling to her all the more. And Phoebe was afraid that she might betray something of her feelings for him before Mrs Hunter.

The maid had brought Phoebe's freshly laundered blue dress to her chamber the next morning.

'Most of it came out in the cold-water soak, but there is still some staining, miss,' the maid's voice sounded beside Phoebe.

The two women stared at the bodice as Phoebe held it up to the light. The brownish marks sat like dark islands within a sea of faded blue muslin.

'Some ribbon and lace might hide the marks. I could sew some pieces across,' Phoebe said.

The maid chewed at her lip. 'It'll need a fair old length of ribbon but, aye, I think you're right. Do you want me to do it, miss?'

Phoebe smiled and shook her head. 'I will manage myself, but thank you for the offer.'

The maid bobbed a curtsy and turned to leave. 'Oh, miss.' She stopped, turned back to Phoebe and produced a letter from within her apron. 'I checked your pockets before I put your dress through the wash and found this.'

'Thank you, Agnes,' she said, but the maid had already left.

It was the letter Hunter had given her the day before yesterday—

Emma's letter about which he had been so angry. The scene in the corridor outside his study seemed a lifetime ago.

Her fingers broke the sealing wax, unfolding the paper and even before she began to read a shiver of foreboding had rippled down her spine. And the words that Emma had written upon the paper made her sit down hard upon the bed.

I am much worried by the news that you are to accompany Mrs Hunter on her visit to Blackloch and her son, for there is something that you should know of Mr Sebastian Hunter. An ominous feeling was forming in the pit of Phoebe's stomach. Her eyes raced on, skimming Emma's neatly penned words.

You are already aware of the great folly that Kit perpetrated and thus the current most unfortunate circumstances in which my family finds itself. Kit, Emma's brother, had bankrupted the family at the gaming tables so that Emma and her family had lost their home, their money and their reputation. Their lives had been ruined.

Sebastian Hunter was chief amongst the pack of rakes who beguiled Kit into their gang. Kit looked up to Hunter, admired him, as if there was anything about the man to be admired, hung on his every word. It was Hunter who took Kit to that gaming den the night he lost our fortune and Hunter who goaded him to such recklessness. He cares nothing for anyone other than his own selfish pleasure. Indeed, my dear friend, Hunter would ruin you without so much as a second thought. Thus, I implore you, Phoebe, with all my heart, to heed my warning and guard yourself most carefully from Hunter.

A cold shadow moved over her heart. Phoebe stared at the words that Emma had written, words so similar in vein to the ones her papa had spoken. The same warning issued from the two people that she loved and trusted the most. A warning that so contrasted with all she had seen of Hunter. She thought of the man who had cared enough about his tenants to visit them in person, gifting money and food and linens. The man who had ridden out in the dead of night in the driving rain to help those involved in a carriage accident. He had saved her from the highwaymen, fetched the midwife for Rena Beattie, and she did not think she would ever forget the sight of him in the parlour with the Beattie children snuggled all around. But most of all she thought of the small tender touch of his lips against hers when the memory of Elspeth had threatened to overwhelm her.

She moved to stand by her bedchamber window, staring out over the moor and the darkness of the loch. The day was cool and grey as if summer had already left. She closed her eyes, not knowing what to believe.

Hunter had to wait until that morning to follow Phoebe down to the scullery, where she was mixing up a pot of face cream.

He chased out the maid who was washing dishes and closed the door behind her.

'Sebastian!' Phoebe whispered in a scandalised tone. 'You will have the staff gossiping.'

'It is the only way that I may speak to you alone.'

'You should not be down here.' She turned away and resumed her pounding of the pestle against the mortar.

'You should have told me of your sister, Phoebe.'

She stilled, the pestle loose within her fingers.

'If I had known…' The words petered out. 'The night before must have been a torture for you.'

She shook her head, but still did not look at him.

He moved to her, taking the mortar and pestle from her hands and pulling her gently round to face him.

'The birthing itself was not so bad,' she said. 'I did not let myself think of anything save Mrs Beattie and the baby.'

'And on the moor afterwards, when all the clamour was over and all of the thoughts were there in your head?'

'That was hard,' she admitted.

'Why did you not tell me, Phoebe, when we were alone? I would have understood.'

'I have never spoken of Elspeth or the baby. It distressed my papa so much when she died that he would not hear her name mentioned in the house again. It was…terrible.' She pressed her hands to her face, covering her eyes. 'I must not speak of it, I must not even think of it, for I cannot start weeping, not here, not like this.'

He took her in his arms and held her to him, stroking a hand over her hair.

'I am here if you wish to speak of it. You may come to me, Phoebe, and you may speak of it and think of it and weep about it as much as you will. There is no wrong in that. I understand your pain, Phoebe, I know what it is like to feel such grief.'

'Your father,' she whispered.

'Yes.'

'Of whom you do not speak either.'

'No.'

'We are a fine pair.'

'We are, Phoebe Allardyce, a fine pair indeed.' He traced a finger over the line of her cheek.

'You should go now,' she said. 'I promised Mrs Hunter that I would make up this beautifying lotion for her.' She gestured to the mortar and pestle and the recipe in the opened fashion journal on the table top before it. 'She is waiting.'

'Let her wait a little longer.' And he lowered his mouth to hers and he kissed her, tenderly, gently, to salve the hurt that was in her heart.

Hunter and McEwan began installation of the new drainage system at the lower end of the moorland the next day. It was an important event, for the land was in a sheltered spot close to McInnes's farmstead and, if the operation proved successful, the land might be used for crops instead of lying as useless bog for most of the year. Phoebe was thankful that Hunter's attention was engaged elsewhere for it was Tuesday and she feared he would have insisted upon driving her to Glasgow, and she could not face lying to him over her father. But when she had gone to leave for Kingswell, she had discovered that Hunter had left instructions for Jamie to both take her to Glasgow and bring her back again in the gig. She had the young footman let her out at the Royal Infirmary and told him to spend the next hour down at the Green while she pretended to enter the hospital. Then she ran all the way down to the Tolbooth.

'Phoebe. You are pink-cheeked and puffing. Come and sit down.'

She sat in the chair across the table from her father in his prison cell.

'The day is warm.' She smiled as she gave the excuse, but her gaze was busy studying his face, checking that his bruises were fading and that he had taken no new hurts.

'You look radiant, child,' he observed. 'Just like your mother when she was young and in love.' He smiled and his eyes took on a faraway look as he remembered her mama from across the years. 'Something of the moor air must be agreeing with you.'

Phoebe's heart gave a little flutter as she thought of Hunter and realised that her father was not so very far away from the truth. She glanced away so that he would not see it in her eyes.

'How are you enjoying Blackloch Hall?' he asked.

'Very well, indeed.' Phoebe relayed something of her days at Blackloch, rambling on, telling her papa all the small details of the farmsteads and the tenants and the coaching accident that she knew he would be interested to hear. She made no mention of Mrs Beattie or the baby.

'So Hunter went to the gentlemen's assistance?'

She nodded. 'He cleared the road of the damaged vehicle and had the shaken passengers transported to Glasgow in his own coach.'

Her papa looked at her with such an expression of surprise on his face that she wondered if she had said too much of Hunter.

Her gaze dropped, moving over the sheets of paper strewn in piles across the table's surface between them. Her papa's writing was small and cramped and he had filled the sheets one way, before turning the paper at a right angle and writing across the lines of words already there, making a lattice of words that utilised every available space on the paper.

'I am sorry that I could not bring more paper with me today,' she said to change the subject from Hunter. Indeed, there had barely been enough to pay to the turnkey.

'You are here, and that is all that matters to me. To see your face, Phoebe, it gladdens my heart.'

'Dearest Papa,' she whispered and felt the emotion sweep over her. 'How does your book come along?'

Sir Henry nodded. 'Nicely enough, although I have had a new thought concerning one of my hypotheses.' A distant look came into his eyes. Phoebe recognised it well. Her father was thinking of his chemistry. 'I might need to write to young Davy on the matter. I wonder…'

She felt a measure of reassurance that her papa must be feeling his old self if he was so absorbed in his science.

'Mmm…' And it was some minutes later before Sir Henry remembered that she was sitting there before him.

She laughed aloud; so did he and the sound of his laughter eased the worry from her heart.

'I did not tell you, did I, my dear? I am to have a new cellmate.'

The laughter died upon her lips. 'A new cellmate?'

'Before the week is out. Wonderful news, is it not? I do like some company.' He stopped, staring at her with eyes laden with concern. 'What is wrong, child? You look as if you have just heard a death knell. Is it something I said?'

'No. No, of course not. Nothing is wrong.' She shook her head and forced a smile. 'It is wonderful news indeed, Papa.' And all of the danger and the threat was back in the space of a moment, all that she had not thought of in these past days with Hunter. 'Now tell me all about your book,' she asked to distract him.

Her father smiled and began to tell her all about his latest theory.

If her visit to the Tolbooth had not been enough to remind Phoebe that the Messenger meant what he said, there was no room for doubt the following morning. When Phoebe met with Mrs Hunter in her little sitting room at ten o'clock, the lady was positively beaming, a sight that in Mrs Hunter was rare indeed.

'We are going to Glasgow today to order ourselves some new dresses.'

'New dresses, but—' Phoebe thought of the few coins in her purse.

But Mrs Hunter rushed on. 'For London. Caroline Edingham, Lady Willaston, has written to me, insisting that I visit her at the start of next month, and do you know, Phoebe, I am going to go. It is exactly what I need.' Mrs Hunter flicked a finger at Polly to pass her the fashion journals from the table in the corner. 'And, of course, it goes without speaking that, as my companion, you will be coming with me.'

Phoebe stared at Mrs Hunter, speechless as the memory of the Messenger's words ran through her head: *At the start of September Mrs Hunter'll be travelling down to London to visit a friend, no doubt taking her trusty companion with her.*

'I know,' said Mrs Hunter, quite misinterpreting Phoebe's shock. 'Is it not just too too good? And I am sure that your papa, even with his current state of health, would not wish you to miss such an opportunity.'

'I am not sure,' said Phoebe weakly. The Messenger was setting everything in motion just as he had promised.

'Well, I mean to convince him, even if I have to go up to that hospital and tell him myself.' Mrs Hunter smiled.

Phoebe could barely keep the horror from her face. It was the nightmare come true.

'La, I declare I have not felt so excited in an age. In two weeks, Phoebe, we shall be in London,' she said. 'Only two weeks. And there is so much to be done.'

'So much indeed,' murmured Phoebe. Two weeks to find what she sought. Two weeks to evade Hunter and her feelings for him. Two weeks to save her papa's life.

Hunter made his way towards the drawing room. A week had passed since his mother's announcement of her trip to London, during which Phoebe had successfully avoided him thanks largely to his mother spending all day every day shopping in Glasgow.

'A strong box is a splendid idea for the town house, Phoebe,' Hunter heard his mother saying as he approached the half-opened door. 'At least I know my jewellery would be safe.'

'Maybe you should use one here. Does Blackloch Hall possess such a thing?' She was trying to sound casual, but he could hear the slight tension beneath the façade. Hunter's eyes narrowed. He stopped where he was and listened in.

'Not as far as I know.' His mother did not seem to notice anything amiss with the question. 'My husband had one in our town house in London, but never here. I believe Edward never thought Blackloch at risk of break-ins.'

'He was most probably right,' he heard Phoebe say in a reassuring tone. 'Blackloch is a most secure place.' He felt a small measure of relief that at least she had not frightened his mother by revealing her knowledge of Blackloch's burglaries. There was a pause and then she said, 'Mrs Hunter, I could not help but notice the preponderance of wolves in the decoration of Blackloch. It is most unusual.'

'And quite frightful, I know, my dear, but the wolf is the Hunter family emblem. I believe it stems from some play on the name; the original Hunters must have been hunters in the true sense of the word, just as much as the wolf. Men and their silly games!' His mother gave a small laugh. 'But enough of this talk, Phoebe. We have more important matters to discuss, such as your stubborn refusal to permit me to buy you more than one new dress.'

'Your offer was most kind and I thank you for it, but I have more than enough serviceable dresses.' Hunter thought of the bloodstains that had marred the bodice of her dress the night he had brought her back to Blackloch. 'And you have already been more than generous to me.'

He turned and quietly retraced his steps away from the drawing room.

The day grew more dismal as it progressed. There was a dampness in the air, a dull grey oppression that brought on one of Mrs Hunter's headaches and lowered everyone's spirits. At three o'clock the lady took a tisane of feverfew and went to lie down, leaving Phoebe to brood alone in her bedchamber.

Phoebe paced the room. She could not rest, could not even sit still. And she dared not go down to the drawing room, for Hunter was about and she had no wish to let him see her, not when she felt so worried and anxious and desperately ill at ease. She did not doubt that he would fathom something of her distress, and what could she tell him when he asked the reason?

Events were slotting into place, all of them engineered by the Messenger. He would be waiting for her in London, waiting for what she was supposed to have found, except that she had searched everywhere in Blackloch that she could think of and discovered nothing. And when she arrived in London he would find her and learn that truth. She knew what the consequences would be for her papa. Her palms grew clammy and she felt queasy. She had not found what the Messenger wanted. And she knew she was falling in love with Hunter. It was all of it a mess, a terrible dangerous mess.

Phoebe stood by the window and stared out at the black water of the loch, and the great dark heavy sky, and the wild bleakness of the moor, and felt something of its dark beauty touch her spirit. She leaned her forehead against the window pane so that its coolness soothed the heat from her head, and let the moor calm her.

'So we are no closer to solving the mystery of Miss Allardyce?' McEwan asked as he stood by the fireplace of Hunter's study, watching the golden lick of flames devour the coal.

'Further investigation is required,' said Hunter. He did not look round at McEwan, just stood by the window staring out over the moor. It was dark today beneath an ominous leaden sky. Not a breath of breeze to stir the slow creeping stillness. He did not want to tell McEwan how much he had learned of Phoebe Allardyce in these few short weeks and how much he had come to feel for her. None of it mattered. She was still a would-be thief. He had not yet discovered what she was looking for.

'The man has never shown for any of her prison visits. I followed her each time. There has been no one. And your contact in Glasgow could turn up no further information upon her. Perhaps you were mistaken, Hunter. Perhaps you should just let it be.'

'No.'

'You are spending much time with Miss Allardyce.'

'It is a necessary part of my investigation.' Hunter turned to look at McEwan.

'People are beginning to notice.'

Hunter narrowed his eyes ever so slightly. 'She is a would-be thief.'

'She is also your mother's companion, a lady and a young and comely one at that.'

'And what is that supposed to mean?'

'That you should be careful if you do not wish to find yourself having to offer for her.'

'I am intent on discovering the truth, not bedding her.' Yet the thought of bedding Phoebe Allardyce was dangerously arousing. 'I have not had a woman these nine months past. I have not gambled. I am not a damned rake.' He was keeping the promises he had sworn.

'I know, Sebastian.' McEwan clapped a hand against his shoulder. 'Just have a care, that is all I am saying.' And McEwan left, leaving Hunter sitting alone.

The wind tapped against his window, moaning softly, stirring the deep red of the curtains. He thought of Phoebe and all he had not said to McEwan: that he wanted her, that he cared for her, even knowing that she was a liar and had searched his home. He stroked at his chin, his fingers toying with its cleft. She had even quizzed his mother. And now he was sure she was avoiding him. Hunter pushed aside his emotions, deadened them, just as he had all of the months past. This was about a threat to his mother's safety. He could not afford to let his feelings for Phoebe sway him.

He rang the bell for a footman, and summoned Miss Allardyce.

Chapter Eleven

'You wished to see me, Mr Hunter.' Phoebe was determined to keep matters on a formal footing. She faced him with a feigned serenity, showing nothing of her worries, nothing of the feelings that roared in such turmoil. Behind her the study door remained open as was only appropriate for a single lady alone in a room with a gentleman.

'Close the door and come and sit down.'

'I do not think that is—'

'Just do it, Phoebe.' The tone of his voice was almost weary.

She turned to close the door and there it was. Facing her. On the wall beside the door. A portrait of a man with the same brilliant green eyes as Hunter, a man whose face had the same classical features, but aged by the years. Instead of the dark ruffle of ebony hair, the man's hair in the painting was a dark peppered silver. But upon his face was the same brooding expression that Hunter wore. She saw all these things in a second, but none of them was why she was staring at the painting. Her heart began to beat very fast.

'Phoebe?'

She knew she should turn away and answer Hunter, but she could not. She walked closer to the painting, peering up at its every detail as the tension coursed through her body.

'My father,' he said and she could hear the slight change in his voice.

All was quiet in the room. She heard the spit of logs on the fire, as the flames licked around the wood to release the subtle scent of pine throughout the study, and the slow ticking of the clock. Phoebe knew how difficult this might be for Hunter. She did not want to hurt him, but she had to ask the question.

'The ring he is wearing…'

She did not hear Hunter move, but felt his sudden close presence. The words she spoke were calm and quiet, a stark contrast to the roar of tension through her body. 'A silver wolf's head with emerald eyes.' It matched precisely the description the Messenger had given her. 'A most unusual design,' she said and did not dare to look round at him.

'One of a kind, so my father told me.' Hunter answered, his voice so close behind her she felt the nape of her neck and shoulder tingle.

'I wonder what became of the ring…?' There did not seem to be enough air in the room. The clamminess prickled upon her palms.

'It was my father's,' said Hunter, 'and now it is mine.'

'You must consider it to be the most precious of keepsakes.'

'I do. It was the last thing my father gave to me, the last tangible link between us.'

His words made her falter—she remembered how very much it had hurt to part with Elspeth's possessions. And it seemed that from across the years she heard again the sound of her father's grief, sobbing in the depth of the night when he thought there was none to hear. Papa. The thought of him was enough to push her to the task. The quiver of her nerves stilled.

'The ring,' she said quietly, and her eyes never left the portrait. 'Where is it now?'

She felt Hunter's hand rest upon her right shoulder and schooled herself not to react. He moved, turning her as he did so, so that they were standing face to face. She kept her eyes trained upon his cravat, on the knot he had used to tie it. The minutes stretched and still Hunter was waiting and she knew she must meet him head on over this. She raised her gaze to meet his.

They looked at one another across that tiny divide and the very air seemed to crackle between them.

'Guarded most carefully,' he said, 'close to my heart.'

Phoebe's focus dropped to Hunter's chest.

The wind howled across the moor and the branches of the old clambering rose tapped against the study window.

Slowly she reached her hand out to lay it very gently against his black superfine lapel. Through all the layers of shirt and waistcoat and coat Phoebe could feel the strong steady beat of his heart. Inch by tiny inch, as if dragged by a will that was not her own, Phoebe raised her eyes to look into Hunter's, and they were the colour of a Hebridean sea. As they stared into one another's eyes the distance between them seemed to shrink.

She knew she should look away, drop her fingers from where they touched him, change the subject to talk of small trivial matters. She knew all of that, yet she did none of them. And when Hunter took her mouth with his own she met his lips with a passion that flared through the entirety of her being. Her hand slid up his lapel to the nape of his neck. She felt his arms close around her, felt him pull her so that their bodies stood snug together, her breasts crushed against the hard muscle of his chest. She kissed him with all the need that was in her soul.

There was a slight tap at the door as it swung fully open. Hunter and Phoebe jumped apart.

'Forgot to leave these—' McEwan stopped, the shock evident upon his face. 'I do beg your pardon,' he said and retreated as quickly as he had entered, the thin pile of papers still gripped within his hand. The door closed firmly behind him.

Phoebe stared, horrified at what she had just done. She glanced at Hunter. His normally pale cheeks held a faint touch of colour. His hair was dishevelled where she had threaded her fingers, and there was a slight elevation in his breathing. And in his eyes was shock and desire and anger. She said not a word, just turned and fled.

McEwan did not let the matter lie.

'What the hell are you thinking of, Hunter?' His steward ceased his pacing, raked a hand through his hair and stared across the study at Hunter in disbelief. 'You were supposed to be keeping an eye on her, not seducing the girl.'

'I was not seducing her,' Hunter said stiffly and wondered if he had not set out to seduce Phoebe Allardyce from the very start.

'Then she was seducing you? To get her hands on whatever it is that she is supposed to be seeking?'

Hunter's jaw tightened.

'Or is all of this just an excuse that you might have her?'

'Be careful, McEwan. You go too far.' His voice was cold and hard-edged.

McEwan stopped pacing and came to stand before him. 'I am sorry, Sebastian, but I am worried for you. I thought at first this business with Phoebe Allardyce was a blessing in disguise. It drew you out of your megrims, gave you a purpose, a task on which to focus.'

'No.' Hunter shook his head in denial.

'Yes, Hunter,' McEwan affirmed. 'When was the last time you sat in this study the whole night through? When was the last time you drank a bottle of brandy in one sitting? Do you observe no correlation with Miss Allardyce's arrival?'

McEwan was right, Hunter realised, but he was not about to admit it.

'But in the space of a few weeks that has changed. You are obsessed with the girl.'

'Hardly,' murmured Hunter and knew it was a lie.

'Do you deny that you want her?'

'I make no denial,' said Hunter coldly. 'I have wanted Phoebe Allardyce since the moment I set eyes on her.'

McEwan gave a nod as if Hunter was confirming all that he knew.

'But it does not mean that I will act upon it,' finished Hunter.

McEwan gave a cynical laugh. 'If you were not acting upon it, what then was it that I interrupted this evening?'

'It is not as you think, McEwan. Everything is under control,' he lied. 'I know what I am doing.'

'Whatever else you suspect her of, whatever else you think her, she is still your mother's companion. Think what would happen had it been Mrs Hunter who had walked in that door instead of me.'

'My mother never comes in here. Besides, the whole reason I am doing this is to protect my mother.'

'Are you certain of that, Sebastian?' McEwan said softly.

Hunter did not answer the question. Instead he walked away to stand by the window and stare out over the moor. The clock marked the passing seconds. 'I know what Phoebe Allardyce is searching for.'

Hunter heard the change in McEwan's tone. 'What is it that she means to steal?'

'My father's ring.' He turned and gestured towards the portrait of his father on the wall.

McEwan walked right up to the painting and studied the artist's rendition of the wolf's-head ring upon his father's finger. Then he shook his head and when he looked round at Hunter his face was crinkled in puzzlement. 'Of all the possibilities... It is not even gold. Why on earth would she want it?'

'I do not yet know.'

McEwan came to stand before him. 'You will have a care over how you do this, won't you, Sebastian? You know if this goes wrong that it will touch your mother's reputation as well as your own.'

'It will not go wrong.' He saw the concern on his friend's face. 'I know what I am doing, Jed,' he said again quietly.

'I pray that you do, Sebastian. You have been through enough these past months. I do not wish matters to go worse.' He struck the top of Hunter's arm in a manly gesture of support and then left.

Hunter stood there alone, but he did not turn back round to the window and the moor. Instead he walked up to where McEwan had stood, and Phoebe before him. Hunter stood in the same spot and looked up at the portrait. His eyes focused on the ring in the painting and he felt the same strong sweep of emotion as ever he did when he looked at it. If it had been any other item in the whole of this house... Hunter wished with all his heart that it were so. For Phoebe Allardyce was trying to steal the one thing he had sworn to guard with his very life. A shiver rippled down his spine as he remembered his father's words—tenacious and insistent, even when Edward Hunter was dying. And Hunter could not suppress the feeling that something sinister was at work here. He moved his gaze up to his father's face, so sober and serious.

'What is the significance of the ring, Father, that she will risk all to steal it?' he whispered quietly.

But his father just stared down at him with the same disapproval that had been there every time he looked at Hunter. And the room was silent save for the beat of Hunter's heart.

Phoebe was not surprised to find Hunter's coach, rather than Jamie and the gig, waiting when she exited the front door the next morning. The sky was a thick lilac-grey blanket of cloud, imbuing the light with a peculiar acute clarity and washing the landscape with that same translucent purple hue. For once, perhaps the only time since Phoebe had arrived at Blackloch, there was not a breath of wind. The air hung heavy and still and the atmosphere seemed pregnant with foreboding, but whether that was just a figment of Phoebe's own guilty conscience she did not know. Hunter's coach, a deep glossy black, luxurious and sleek, sat before her. Jamie in his black-and-silver livery pulled the step down into place. She could see the coachman already up on his seat at the front.

'Miss Allardyce.' She heard the crunch of Hunter's boots across the gravel and her pulse leapt.

'Mr Hunter.' She hoped that nothing of the flurry of emotion showed upon her face. In the strange light of this day the contrast of his pale skin, dark dark hair and clear emerald eyes was striking. To Phoebe, Hunter had never looked more handsome or his eyes more intriguingly beautiful. Nor had he looked so worryingly dark and brooding. His gaze met hers and she felt a shiver of sensation touch her very core.

He gestured towards the waiting coach, but did not make the excuse of attending some meeting in Glasgow or the dangers of highwaymen upon the road. Neither did Phoebe make any attempt to decline his invitation. They both knew that matters were beyond that. She climbed in without a word.

Her head was thick from lack of sleep. Her eyes stung with it. The hours of the night had been filled not with rest, but with worry—over the wolf's-head ring and her papa and Hunter.

She knew that they needed to talk, but she did not know what she could say. *Give me the ring so that the villains will not kill my papa?* Hardly. She could tell no one, least of all Hunter. And she was afraid that she might have roused his suspicions, that he might question her interest in the ring. She was afraid, too, of what might happen between them closed together and alone in the coach all the way to Glasgow. But Hunter did not mention the ring. Indeed, he hardly spoke at all. He spent his time staring out of the window, although she had the impression that he was not seeing anything of the passing countryside, but wrestling with some great problem that tortured him. He appeared to have such a weight of worrisome thought to dwell upon that she tried to draw him into light conversation, but Hunter would not be drawn and when he looked at her it seemed to Phoebe that he could see too much, of her, of her lies, and her feelings for him. She could not risk him seeing the truth so she left him to his brooding and turned her gaze to the other window.

There was the sound of the wheels rumbling along the road, and the horses' hooves pounding in their rhythm…and the strange heavy silence that hung in the air. The moorland passed in a blur of colours, all grey sky and purples and earthy browns. And with every mile that passed Phoebe grew more conscious of the tension within Hunter. He had not spoken, had not moved, other than to cast the odd intense glance in her direction.

By the time the coach crossed over the River Clyde and made its way along Argyle Street the rain was drumming softly against the roof, and Phoebe could only be relieved that she would soon be at her destination. But as they reached the Trongate Hunter banged his cane on the roof and stuck his head out of the window to say something to his coachman. Reminding the man to follow up High Street to the Royal Infirmary, or so Phoebe thought. But a matter of minutes later the coach did not turn left as it should have done, but stopped directly outside the Tolbooth.

Phoebe's heart stuttered before thundering off a reckless pace. Her blood ran cold. Deep in the pit of her stomach was a horrible feeling of dread. Through the window of the coach she could see the great sandstone blocks of the building, the rows of windows and the steps that led up to the portico over the front door. She turned her gaze to Hunter's, trying to hide the truth from her face.

'Why have we stopped here?'

'Because you have come to visit your father.'

She gave a small laugh as if this was some jest he were playing. 'My father is in the Royal Infirmary.'

'Sir Henry Allardyce has been a prisoner in the Tolbooth gaol these past seven months,' Hunter said.

'You know?' she said in a low voice from which she could not keep the horror.

'Of course I know.'

'For how long have you known?'

'Long enough,' he said.

She closed her eyes as if that could block out the nightmare of what was happening.

'Why did you not tell me, Phoebe?'

She opened her eyes and stared at him. 'Why do you think?' she demanded, incredulous that he even needed to ask the question, then shook her head. 'I did not want to lose my position as your mother's companion.' She turned her head to stare out at the gaol building, raising her eyes to the tiny barred window of the third floor room in which she knew her papa waited. 'Does Mrs Hunter know, too?'

'She does not.'

Her gaze jumped to his.

'Fifteen hundred pounds on a failed medicinal chemistry company…'

She balked at how much of the detail he knew.

'Your father's debt is nothing of your doing, Phoebe. Do you not already suffer enough for it?'

She stared at him. 'You cannot mean that you do not intend to tell your mother the truth about me?' she said carefully, not sure that she had understood what he was saying.

'That is precisely what I mean, Phoebe.'

There was a dangerous swell of emotion around her heart, and then the penny dropped and she realised what he really meant.

'Oh…I understand,' she said and there was an ache in her heart. 'Because of our arrangement. You wish to—'

Hunter's eyes flashed a vivid green with anger. In one swift fluid movement he had their hands entwined and their faces barely two inches apart.

'There is no arrangement. There was never any arrangement.'

'But…'

'If I were the rake you think me, you would have been in my bed the very first day that we met.'

She sucked in her breath.

'We both know it is the truth.' They were so close she could see each and every black lash that lined his eyes, and all of the tiny hairs that made up the dark line of his brows. Some strange force seemed to be pulling them together.

Phoebe fought against it.

'What other secrets are you hiding, Phoebe?' he whispered, and his breath was warm against her mouth, his lips so close yet not touching.

She stared into his eyes and she wanted to tell him, indeed, longed to tell him. To share that terrible burden that had weighed on her all of the weeks she had been at Blackloch Hall. For a moment the temptation almost overcame her, but at the back of her mind were the words the Messenger had spoken, words that haunted her every hour of every day, *One word to Hunter or his mother and you know what'll happen… I'll hear if you've talked.* Phoebe did not doubt that the villain would hear, for he had already more than proven the extent of his knowledge. Much as she wanted to tell Hunter, she knew she could not risk her father's life.

She gave the tiniest shake of her head. 'None that I can share,' she said softly, and with a will of iron and a heavy heart she turned her face away.

Hunter did not move. She felt the weight of his eyes upon her for minutes that were too long. Until finally, at last, he turned away and opened the door and would have climbed out had she not stopped him.

'Do not! I mean, it would be better if you are not seen here… outside the prison…with me.' Her gaze darted to the street beyond, checking the passing bodies for a sight of the Messenger and feeling relief that he was nowhere to be seen.

She saw his eyes shift to follow where she had scanned before coming back to hers. She saw, too, the speculation in them and the hard edge of anger.

'The visiting time is already waning. If I am to see my papa…'

He gave a nod. 'I will wait here for you, Phoebe.'

Hunter stood with McEwan at the study window, watching the thick sheet of rain that had shrouded the moor for the last few hours since he had brought Phoebe back to Blackloch. The light was so dim that the room was grey and shadowed as if night were already falling, even though it was only six o'clock.

'The roads will flood if this does not ease soon,' Hunter said.

'Most of the servants elected to leave early,' said McEwan, 'just as you said.'

'They will need to work fast to gather in the livestock and secure their houses. The storm will hit tonight.'

'Cook has left a cold collation.' McEwan looked worried as the intensity of the rain seemed to increase as they stood there. 'Mrs Hunter is not yet returned from her visiting,' he noted with concern.

'My mother is not fool enough to travel in such weather. She will stay overnight with the Fraser woman in Newmilns.'

There was a pause before McEwan said, 'I could take Miss Allardyce to stay with me and Mairi tonight.'

'And why should you do that?'

'You know fine well why, Hunter,' said McEwan softly.

Hunter looked steadily at McEwan. 'Mairi will be worrying about you, McEwan. You should be heading back to her.'

Blue gaze held green as McEwan challenged what he was saying. The seconds passed, until at last Hunter raked a hand through his hair and glanced away.

'I have...' He tried again. 'I feel...' But he could not form the words. 'It is none of it as you think, McEwan. I would not hurt her. I...' Again the words tailed off.

Hunter felt his friend's eyes scrutinising him, seeing too much. He turned his gaze away, but it was too late.

'Lord, Hunter,' McEwan said softly. 'I had no idea...' He paused, seemingly absorbing the magnitude of what Hunter had just revealed, then he met Hunter's gaze once more. 'I'll leave you alone with Miss Allardyce, then.'

Hunter gave a nod and watched his friend leave.

Chapter Twelve

Phoebe was not asleep when the first clap of thunder resonated in the dark hours of the night. Indeed, she had not slept since climbing into the bed despite the fatigue that hung heavy upon her. Her mind was too active, running with images of her papa and of Hunter, and her legs were so restless that it was a discomfort to lie still.

She slipped from the bed and parted her curtains to look out over the garden and the loch and the moor. But the rain was so heavy and the darkness so complete that she could see nothing at all, not even her own reflection. She stood for a while and listened as the thunder rolled closer, its crash exploding through the air louder each time it sounded, shaking the very foundations of the moor and Blackloch and Phoebe herself.

Using the red glow of the fire ashes, she found the remains of her candle and lit it from the embers. Her dinner tray still sat on the table by the door, her single plate with its remnants of cold ham and chicken upon it. And she thought of Hunter eating alone in his study while she ate alone up here, while all of Blackloch was empty save for the two of them. And as the thunder crashed and rolled around the heavens, Phoebe pulled her shawl around her and, with her candle in her hand, moved quietly towards the door.

Hunter was not in his bedchamber. His bed had not been slept in. She made her way down the stairs and knocked lightly against the study door before letting herself in.

Hunter was standing by the window, a glass of brandy in his hand, watching the storm. The room was warm. The remains of a fire glowed on the hearth.

'Phoebe.' He turned to her, and she saw that he was wearing only his buckskin breeches and shirt pulled loose and open at the neck.

A fork of lightning struck out on the moor, the flash flickering momentarily to illuminate the study and Hunter in its stark white light. His hair was dark and dishevelled, and his chin and jaw shadowed with beard stubble. She walked to stand by his side.

Hunter sat his glass down on the windowsill and did not touch it again.

The curtains stirred where they hung on either side of the window. The chill of the draught that slipped through the edges of the panes prickled her skin. The candle guttered and extinguished. Between the peals of thunder the rain drummed loud and hard, and the soft moan of the wind sounded.

Phoebe and Hunter stood side by side, not touching, not looking at the other, but only out over the moor at the storm. The lightning forked, blinding and white against the darkness of the sky, stabbing down into the land. And the thunder crashed as if the gods were smashing boulders in the heavens.

'It is magnificent,' she breathed. 'The storm, the moor…'

'Truly,' he replied.

And neither moved their gaze from the view beyond the window.

Another strike of lightning. Another roll of thunder. And Phoebe began to speak. Her voice was quiet. She did not look at Hunter, only at the moor.

'My father is a scientist. His interest lies in medicinal chemistry, the discovery of compounds that may be used to cure or relieve disease states. He has had a small laboratory within our house for as long as I can remember and is never happier than when he is working at his research. A year or so ago, he met a man who said he could take one of his ideas, an antimonial compound for the treatment of various toxic conditions, and manufacture it in large quantities in the factory that he owned, that they should start a company. My papa is a clever man, but his head is full of science, and when it comes to business…' She let the words peter out. 'The gentleman said he would look after all of that side of matters. The antimony was a great success. But the company was not. The gentleman took the monies and ran off to the East Indies, leaving all of the debts and no money to pay them. In the paperwork it all came down to my papa. There was nothing we could do.'

'And so your father was sent to the Tolbooth,' Hunter said.

'To stay there until the debts can be paid.'

'I am sorry, Phoebe.' She felt his hand take hers, but neither of them shifted their stance or their gaze.

'An old friend of my papa has a sister who heard that Mrs Hunter was seeking a companion. There was nowhere for me to go and no money to keep me. Your mother's position seemed the ideal solution. We had to lie, of course, for no lady would wish to take on a companion with the hint of scandal, let alone a papa imprisoned.'

'I am afraid that my mother has been sensitised through the years to gossip and scandal. All of it my fault.' His fingers were warm and supportive. 'You must miss your father.'

'Very much indeed. He worries about me out here without him, and I worry about him inside the Tolbooth gaol.'

'You are fortunate indeed to have his love.' She heard the pain in his voice and her heart went out to him.

'Mrs Hunter…' Phoebe hesitated, aware of the sensitivity around the issue. 'Relations between you and Mrs Hunter seem a little improved of late.'

'I do not delude myself. My mother will never forgive me, nor do I ask her to.'

And she remembered Mrs Hunter's words from across the weeks. *If you knew what he had done...* She brushed her thumb against his. 'For what crime must you seek her forgiveness?'

Outside a crash of thunder rolled across the sky.

He turned to her, looking down into her face through the darkness. The thunder was fading as he gave his answer. 'She believes that I killed my father.'

A gasp of breath escaped her. Whatever dark family secret she had imagined it was not this. All of the warnings came flooding back. All of the whispers and gossip to which her papa had alluded. 'And did you?' she asked.

Another fork of lightning flickered across the sky, revealing Hunter's face in flashes of bleaching light. And upon his face was such an agony of grief and of guilt that she knew what his answer would be even before he uttered the words.

'Yes.'

'I do not believe you,' she whispered.

He pulled her to him with nothing of gentleness, his hands angling her head so that their faces were almost touching. 'I killed him, Phoebe,' he said and his voice was raw. 'And I must live with that knowledge for every day of the rest of my life.' He backed away and she could see the horror in his eyes before he looked away.

Phoebe moved quickly, taking hold of his arms and guiding him down into his chair. 'Tell me,' she said. 'Tell me all, from the very beginning.'

And Hunter did. He told her the story of how he had been a rake and a dissolute in London, running with a crowd that included one of Emma Northcote's brothers. Of how Northcote had ruined himself and his whole family, and Hunter had been blamed, chief amongst his friends, for leading the boy astray.

'He was too young,' said Hunter. 'I did not realise my influence upon him. I had no idea he would go so far. It was the tipping point for my father. When he heard of the Northcotes' ruin he cut off my allowance, called me back to Blackloch, said I was hedonistic, selfish, immature, indulged by my mother and a disappointment to him. All of it was true, of course. But my father was an exacting man and I never felt that I could live up to his expectations. I gave up trying when I was still a boy. I turned to McInnes, spent much of my youth hanging about his farmstead.' Hunter smiled a little at the memory of his time with the old man.

Phoebe understood what she had seen on the moor that day when Hunter and his mother had visited McInness on the moor. 'And your father's death?' she urged.

'It was here in this study. We argued, my father and I, over Northcote. Everything he said was the truth, but I did not want him to see how much his words flayed me. I walked away from him, even knowing that he had been feeling unwell for those few days. I am ashamed to even think about it.'

She sat on the arm of the chair and took his hand in her own. 'Go on.'

'He hauled me back, gave me the rollicking I deserved. But the strain of it, the physical exertion, was too much. He collapsed. It was his heart, you see. As he lay dying he ordered me to change my ways, to take responsibility for the family.' The lightning flickered and Hunter seemed to hear again the echo of those disjointed words that his father had struggled so hard to speak: *...order...wolf...take responsibility for...* 'Ten minutes later he was dead.'

'Oh, Sebastian,' she whispered and leaned down to take him in her arms.

'It was all my fault, Phoebe, both Northcote's ruin and my father's death.'

'No,' she said, but he would not look at her. 'Sebastian,' she said more firmly, and took his face in her hands and forced him to do so. 'You made mistakes, heaven knows, we all do. You might have been selfish and imbued with all of those vices which you admit, but what occurred was not your fault. Emma's brother made his own choices. And as for your father, you said yourself that his heart was weak.' Her thumbs stroked against his jaw line. 'You are a good man, Sebastian Hunter.'

Their eyes clung together and in the flash of lightning she saw that his glistened with unshed tears. 'You are grieving. Your mother is grieving. You feel enraged and lost and despairing all at the same time. I felt the same for my sister. I still feel it. A soul can bear such grief, but guilt and blame and bitterness—these are what destroy a heart. You must stop blaming yourself, Sebastian.' She felt his tears wet against her fingers.

'Oh, Sebastian.' She slipped from the chair arm to kneel astride him and pull him to her and she held him against her breast while he silently wept.

She held him until the thunder was just the faintest rumble in the distance and the lightning no longer flared across the sky. And when he moved to look into her face it seemed the most natural thing in the world to kiss him. Gently. Tenderly. As if her lips could mend the wound that was in his soul.

'Phoebe,' he whispered, and there was such a heartfelt plea in that one word. She kissed him with all the love that was in her heart. And Hunter kissed her back. There was no need for words. They needed one another. And when he unfastened the ribbon of her nightdress and let it slip low to uncover her breasts she revelled in his gentle touch. His fingers stroked and caressed, and when his mouth replaced his fingers, so that he was tasting her, kissing her, laving her, she clutched his head to her and wanted him all the more. He lifted her slightly, adjusted her position upon him, moving her nightdress to bare her before settling her down to straddle his groin. She could feel the soft buckskin of his breeches against her most intimate of places.

'Sebastian,' she breathed. And then he began to rock her, in a steady easy pace, so it seemed as if she were riding him. She could feel the press of his manhood straining through his breeches, could feel herself rubbing against it. And all she knew was that she needed him and he needed her. And the need was in the white-hot heat in her thighs and the slick moisture between her legs, and the ache of her breasts; all feelings that Phoebe did not understand, just as she did not understand what was happening between them except that it was right, except that there was such a warmth and love and understanding that it almost overwhelmed her.

She groaned aloud at the glorious sensation that was growing in her. Such pleasure, such need. She wanted it never to stop and yet she was poised on a knife edge of passion, reaching for something more. She rode him harder, faster and when his mouth closed over her breast to suckle her nipple an explosion of sensation burst throughout the whole of Phoebe. Such a flood of exquisite delight as if she and Hunter were lifted from the dark storminess of Blackloch and the moor to a place of golden sunlight and paradise.

She collapsed onto him, planting a myriad of butterfly kisses over his temple and eyes and cheeks. She kissed his mouth and whispered his name a thousand times over. And all she felt for him was love, pure and complete. He rolled her round so that they lay together upon the chair, her back snug against his chest, his arms around her stomach, and now that the thunder had subsided there was only the steady drum of the rain against the moorland. Hunter pulled his coat to cover them and kissed her hair and her ear and the edge of her forehead. They slept and when the slow grey dawn came they watched together while it crept across the moor.

Hunter watched his mother and Phoebe across the drawing room as Phoebe poured the tea the maid had just delivered.

'Apparently Eliza Fraser was down in London for the Season and delighted in telling me all of the latest *on dit*. She was talking down to me as if I were some country bumpkin. Indeed! Well, I can tell you that the wind soon dropped from her sails when I told her that I was for London this very weekend. "Oh, but London will be quiet this time of year. 'Tis such a shame you missed the Season."' His mother impersonated Mrs Fraser's patronising tone. 'On the contrary, says I, only the best of the families will have returned for the Little Season. That quieted her.'

'I am sure it did.' Phoebe smiled and passed the first cup to his mother. He noted how careful she was not to look at him today and he could not blame her. It was only months of practice that enabled Hunter to sit there and show nothing of the fury of conflicting emotions that were vying in his breast.

'She has a new wardrobe of gowns from Mrs Thomas of Fleet Street and insisted on telling me the vast sums that each had cost. So not the done thing!' His mother sipped at her tea. 'I told her I prefer Rae and Rhind of Glasgow for my dresses. When one finds a talented dressmaker I always feel it is important to retain them and not float on a whim to another.'

'Absolutely,' agreed Phoebe, who managed to pass the next cup of tea to Hunter without meeting his eye.

'Talking of which, we are for Glasgow tomorrow to try on and collect our new dresses.' His mother smiled broadly, the first time in over a year that he had seen such a sight. 'I simply cannot wait to reach London. You have not visited the city before, have you, Phoebe? You must be in a veritable frenzy of excitement over our little trip.'

'Quite,' said Phoebe, but to Hunter's eye she seemed to pale and there was a look of pure dread in her eyes before she masked it. He was quite certain he had not imagined it.

His mother peered closer at Phoebe. 'You are looking a little pale and tired, my dear. I expect you did not sleep well because of the thunder.'

'The thunder did waken me,' Phoebe admitted and a faint peach blush washed her cheeks. She added a lump of sugar to her tea and concentrated on stirring it.

'It is always worse out here on the moor.' And fortunately his mother began talking of her plans for London again.

'I thought I might come with you to London, Mother.' Hunter nonchalantly dropped the news into the conversation.

He heard the quiet rattle of china of Phoebe's cup against its saucer before she set them down upon the table.

His mother frowned. 'I do not think that is a good idea, Sebastian.'

'On the contrary, I am quite convinced of its merit.'

'I see,' said his mother, tight-mouthed. All of her animation had vanished. The cold haughty demeanour was resumed. 'I had intended staying in the town house, but if you mean to—'

'I shall stay with Arlesford if it suits you better,' he said, cutting off her protestation.

She sniffed. 'I suppose London is a big enough place.'

'I am sure that it is.' As Hunter rose to leave, Phoebe's eyes came at last to his for just the smallest moment. All that was between them seemed to roar across the room before she looked away again.

The worst of the weather had passed by Thursday when Phoebe travelled with Mrs Hunter to collect their new dresses from Glasgow. The day was mild, with grey-white skies and a stiff breeze, but at least it was not raining, and the puddles still remaining from Tuesday's storm soon dried.

They had spent an hour with the dressmaker and left with the promise to return later that same afternoon as there were only two small alterations to be made to an evening gown and a walking dress for Mrs Hunter. There were so many shops to be visited, shoes to be collected, stockings and reticules to be bought, fascinators, feathers and ribbons to be perused, soaps and perfumes to be selected. And Mrs Hunter's full set of luggage to be sent down to Blackloch ready to be packed.

Phoebe had been glad of the activity; at least then she could not dwell and worry over her papa and Hunter…and the ring. Her feet had been aching by the time Mrs Hunter's heavily laden carriage was making its way back towards the moor. Mrs Hunter had been tired, too. She had closed the curtains and laid her head back on the squabs and, lulled by the rocking of the carriage, dozed. And then there was nothing to distract Phoebe from the confusion of worries and fears that crowded her mind.

They had not long turned onto the road beyond Kingswell that would take them across the moor to Blackloch when the carriage came to a halt.

'Stand and deliver!'

The voice was rough and horribly familiar.

Mrs Hunter's head rolled and she came to her senses. 'Phoebe? Are we home?'

Phoebe reached across the carriage and took the lady's hand in her own. 'We have not yet reached Blackloch, Mrs Hunter. I fear that we are being held up by highwaymen.'

'Be away with you, you fiends!' roared John Coachman and then there was the crack of pistol fire, and yells and shouting and an ominous thud upon the ground outside as if something heavy had fallen upon it.

'Oh, my word!' Mrs Hunter clutched instinctively to the locket that Phoebe knew lay beneath all of the layers of her clothing.

'Stay calm, ma'am. I will not let them harm you.'

'Phoebe!' Mrs Hunter's face drained of all colour as the door was wrenched open and Phoebe saw the same masked highwaymen that she had met on a journey from a lifetime ago.

Chapter Thirteen

'Out you come, ladies. Just a brief interruption of your journey. Heading over to the big house, are yous? All nicely laden up.'

Black Kerchief grabbed first for Mrs Hunter. Phoebe swatted his hand away. 'We need no assistance, thank you, sir. I will help the lady.' The highwaymen stood back and watched while Phoebe jumped down, kicked the step into place and helped Mrs Hunter down onto the road.

'Well, well, well, Jim,' Black Kerchief said when he saw Phoebe in the full light of day and she knew that he recognised her just as readily as she had recognised him. 'If it's no' the lassie that escaped without payment the last time. This here bit of the road is dead. No passing coaches or carts. No horsemen or walkers. There's no gent to come galloping down the road to save you this time.'

'What is he talking about, Phoebe?' Mrs Hunter turned to her.

'Oh, now that's interesting. You didnae tell her of our wee encounter the other week.'

'The first day I came to Blackloch these men tried to rob me. Mr Hunter arrived and saved me. That was why he had the bruising upon his face that first night at dinner.'

'Hunter himself, was it?' said Red Kerchief Jim. 'Hell, I would have wet m'breeks if I'd known.'

'Why did you not tell me, Phoebe?' demanded Mrs Hunter. 'Why did he let me think—?'

'Save the questions and explanations for later, ladies,' interrupted Black Kerchief. 'For now, there are other more pressing matters to be dealt with.'

'Such as relieving yous of your purses and jewels,' said his accomplice and slammed the door of the carriage shut.

Only once the door was closed did Phoebe realise the full magnitude of their situation, for on the ground ahead lay John Coachman groaning faintly, a bullet in his shoulder. Jamie lay trussed on the ground, blood trickling from a gash on his forehead.

Mrs Hunter clutched a trembling hand to her mouth. 'Oh, my good lord! You have killed him!'

'Not quite, but that's what happens when you dinnae do as you're asked,' said Black Kerchief.

'Aye,' said Jim and aimed a pistol at Mrs Hunter. 'You've been asked for certain items and I dinnae see you doing much to deliver them. Purses and jewels, now, if you please!'

Mrs Hunter was so white Phoebe thought she would faint.

'Jim, such impatience. Have I no' told you before that there are better ways of persuading ladies?' Black Kerchief said.

But Mrs Hunter had already extracted her purse and lady's watch from her reticule and was passing them to the black-masked highwayman. She slipped the pearl earrings from the lobes of her ears and the rings from her fingers, hesitating only over her wedding band.

'Come on,' growled Jim as he took the jewellery from her. 'All of it.'

'For pity's sake! She is a widow. Will you not even leave her her wedding ring?' demanded Phoebe.

'A nice weighty piece of gold like that? I dinnae think so, miss.'

Mrs Hunter pressed her lips together and Phoebe knew it was to control their tremble. She eased the ring from her finger and handed it to the fair-haired highwayman. 'That is all I have with me.' Her fingers fluttered fleetingly to touch her dress where the locket lay hidden.

Jim checked the purse for its contents and, satisfied with what he saw, threw it to Black Kerchief, who was standing a little back.

'Now we move to you, miss, and you better have something with which to pay the price this time.' Jim moved towards her.

'No' so fast.' The taller highwayman came to stand before Mrs Hunter. 'You're hiding something, lady.'

'I have given you all that I have,' Mrs Hunter affirmed again.

Black Kerchief's eyes dropped to the exact spot on her chest against which her fingers had strayed. 'Give me it willingly, lady, or I will take it from you.'

Whatever was within the locket must be precious to Mrs Hunter. Indeed, Phoebe had long suspected it to be a miniature of her husband. She moved to distract the highwayman.

'She has nothing more to give you. Leave her be.'

But Black Kerchief ignored her and levelled his pistol at Mrs Hunter's face.

Mrs Hunter swallowed and with fingers that were visibly shaking unfastened the gold chain at the back of her neck to slip the locket from its hiding place. The chain coiled like a snake into the highwayman's open palm and she laid the large golden oval body on top of it.

He opened the locket.

Mrs Hunter squeezed her eyes shut as the villain looked upon her most precious of secrets.

'Looks rather familiar, wouldn't you say, miss?' Black Kerchief held the locket up to show Phoebe its contents, so that she learned at last Mrs Hunter's secret. Inside were two miniature portraits, a dark-haired handsome man with pale emerald eyes, and a boy that could only be the man's son. For a moment Phoebe thought she was looking at Sebastian and his son, then she realized that Sebastian was the boy and the man was the same one she had looked upon in the large stern portrait within Hunter's study—Hunter's father. The two people Mrs Hunter loved best in the world—her husband and her son. And Phoebe knew in that moment that for all her accusations, for all that she had said, Mrs Hunter had never stopped loving Sebastian.

'You have everything else. Will you not leave her this one thing at least?' Phoebe asked the highwayman.

He gave a callous laugh. 'What do you think?' And he closed the locket body with a snap and threw it to his accomplice.

'And now for you, miss. What have you got to offer me? A coin or two?' He pushed her hard against the polished burgundy-gloss body of Mrs Hunter's carriage and pulled the mask down from his face to dangle around his neck. She recognised too well his face and the lust that was in it. He grabbed hold of her wrists, holding them above her head with one of his hands while the other found the pocket of her dress and rummaged. He dropped the two small plain white handkerchiefs that he found there onto the road and spat in disgust.

'No purse.'

His fingers raked roughly against her own. 'No rings.'

His large bulky body crowded against hers and his hand roved boldly over her bodice and down farther over the tops of her thighs, licking his lips as he did so. 'Nothing concealed.' Phoebe struggled against him, but he just smiled.

'What payment are you going to offer me? I'll have you know the price has gone up since the last time.'

'You are a villain, sir!' she hissed through her teeth. 'A veritable villain. Unhand me this instant!'

'Oh, little Miss Vixen, I'm nowhere near to unhanding you just yet.' And his mouth descended hard upon her own. His kiss was nothing like Hunter's. He tasted of tobacco and ale. He reeked of horses and sweat. She kicked out at his shins, tried to bite the thick furred tongue that invaded her mouth.

Black Kerchief drew back, releasing his grip on her wrists to dab at the trickle of blood over his lips. 'You shouldnae have done that, lassie.' And his hand gripped hard to her throat, pinioning her in place against the coach door so that she could not move, could not scream, could barely breathe.

Mrs Hunter began to sob. 'Please do not hurt her, I beg of you.'

'Tie the old lady up, strip the luggage of anything valuable and check the inside of the coach.'

Jim's eyes flickered towards Phoebe. 'We havenae the time for this. Bring the lassie wi' us. We can both hae our fun o' her then.'

'I'm havin' her and I'm havin' her now. So get on and do as I say, Jim. This'll no' take me long.' Black Kerchief slipped the pistol into his pocket with his free hand and produced a knife in its stead. The blade was short but wicked as he held it pointed straight at Phoebe's heart.

Phoebe said nothing, just looked directly into the highwayman's evil black eyes and thought it ridiculous that he could just extinguish her life so easily upon the moor. He leaned closer, then slashed the length of Phoebe's bodice.

Mrs Hunter screamed at the top of her lungs.

'Hell, Jim, gag her before they hear her in Blackloch.'

'No!' yelled Phoebe. 'Leave her be, you fiend! She paid what you asked.'

But Black Kerchief released her and landed her a blow across the face, so that her head cracked against the door of the carriage. The moor breeze was cool against her skin as the highwayman ripped the remaining material open, and his hands were rough and calloused against her breasts. His mouth fastened upon hers once more, his rancid breath filling her nose so it was all she could do not to gag. The knife dropped, its handle bouncing against Phoebe's boot, but Black Kerchief had other things on his mind. She ceased her struggle, let him think that he had cowed her, as her fingers crept into the pocket of his jacket and fastened upon the pistol. She extracted it quick as a flash, wrenched her mouth from his and pressed the muzzle hard against his belly.

'Stand away, sir, or I will shoot.'

Black Kerchief's eyes narrowed. 'I bet you havenae the first idea of how to fire a pistol,' he sneered.

'Shall I just pull back the cock, squeeze the trigger and see what happens?' She did not take her eyes from his as her thumb pulled back the cock lever as far as it would go.

Black Kerchief felt the motion and backed away, raising his hands, palms up in a gesture of submission. 'Easy, lass, no need to get excited.'

'Leave the locket, then get on your horses and ride away while you still can.'

He laughed, but there was nothing in his eyes save wariness and malice. 'Jim'll have a bullet through you before you can pull the trigger.'

From the corner of her eye she could see Red Kerchief with his pistol aimed right at her. He started to move towards her.

'Stop where you are, sir, or I will shoot your friend,' she shouted to him without taking her eyes off Black Kerchief.

'And I'll shoot you and then the old lady.' The pistol was in his right hand. With his left he produced a knife from the leather bag slung across his chest. 'You might no' have a care for your own life, but I could make a right mess of her before I finally put a bullet between her eyes.'

Phoebe did not doubt that he would do it, too. Black Kerchief's eyes were waiting and watchful. She knew she had no choice. She lowered the pistol and the highwayman snatched it from her, the victory plain on his face.

'Now where were we?' He grabbed her and threw her onto the ground; standing over her, he unfastened the fall on his breeches.

Hunter's big black stallion came flying over the road.

His first pistol killed the red-masked highwayman outright. Black Kerchief ducked towards the carriage and fired, the ball catching the top of Hunter's arm as he charged up to them. But Hunter kept on coming, his second pistol's shot hitting Black Kerchief in the chest. The highwayman tried to stagger away before crumpling to his knees and slumping face first onto the ground.

Hunter leapt from his horse, shrugging out of his coat as he ran towards Phoebe. The blood was stark against the white of his shirt, a dense crimson stain spread across his left arm and shoulder.

Phoebe gave a little cry and ran to him.

He swirled his coat around her to cover her nakedness.

'Sebastian! There is so much blood!' The oozing wound clearly visible through the tear in the sleeve of his shirt. Her eyes widened in terror.

'The bullet has scratched my skin only, not torn through the muscle. It does not signify.'

His hands gripped the sides of her upper arms. 'Phoebe,' he whispered and there was such anguish upon his face. 'My God, I thought…'

'I am unharmed. But they have shot John Coachman,' she said, 'and tied up Mrs Hunter and Jamie.' She gestured towards where his mother lay bound and terrified. 'Go to her. I will free Jamie.' She stooped and picked up Black Kerchief's knife where it still lay upon the soil and when she stood with the knife in her hand, she saw the sudden uncertainty on Hunter's face.

'I will see to Jamie. My mother will want you, Phoebe.'

'No, you are wron—' she started to say, but he was already gone, walking away to help the young footman.

Phoebe hurried to Mrs Hunter and dislodged the gag from the older woman's mouth, then cut away the ropes that bit into her wrists and ankles.

'Mrs Hunter,' she began, but the lady was not even looking at

Phoebe. Her eyes were trained on a spot beyond where Phoebe was kneeling.

'Sebastian is bleeding,' Mrs Hunter said. 'Oh, Phoebe, he is hurt.'

'The bullet grazed him. There is much blood, but he is not badly wounded,' Phoebe tried to reassure Mrs Hunter, but it seemed that the lady could not hear her. Her face was ashen, her eyes wide and staring.

'He is hurt,' she said again.

And then Phoebe felt Hunter by her shoulder.

'Mother,' he said and the bag of jewellery and money was in his hand.

'Oh, Sebastian!' Mrs Hunter sobbed and she clutched him to her. 'My son,' she cried. 'My son!'

Phoebe took the loot bag from him and recovered the locket. 'Mrs Hunter has worn this locket day and night for all the months that I have known her.' Phoebe opened the locket and showed the paintings within to Hunter. 'She has never stopped loving you,' she whispered, and, pressing the locket into his hand, she rose and went to help Jamie.

'Should you not be sitting down, Hunter? Come take a seat.'

Hunter glanced round at his friend from where he stood by the study window and gestured to the black arm sling he was wearing. 'You saw the wound, McEwan; it is a scratch. I am only wearing the damn thing to pacify my mother.' Two days had passed since the incident on the moor and in that time his mother had given him little peace.

'She is most concerned over your health.'

'She has not stopped fussing over me since we returned to Blackloch. She has even postponed her trip to London.'

'At least matters seem resolved between the two of you.'

'I am glad of it, McEwan, truly I am, but she is taking such an interest in my affairs that it has proven nigh on impossible to speak to Phoebe alone.'

'Hunter, should you be…?'

'When I saw that villain strike her…' Hunter shook his head.

'Your reaction is understandable,' said McEwan.

'I should have killed him the last time and none of this would have happened.'

'You could not have known, Sebastian.'

'She has no one to protect her, Jed. Her mother and sister are dead. Her father is imprisoned through a mess of debts that were no fault of his own. She is three-and-twenty years of age and alone.'

'How is Miss Allardyce subsequent to the attack?'

'As far as I can tell she is bruised, but otherwise uninjured. The bastard meant to rape her, McEwan.'

'Hell,' muttered McEwan.

'I will speak with her.'

'And say what?' McEwan laid his hand upon Hunter's good shoulder. 'Hunter, no matter what has happened, she is your mother's companion and there is this other business of your father's ring to consider.'

'There is an enemy at work here, Jed, but I cannot believe that it is Phoebe.' He met McEwan's eyes. 'There has to be some other explanation behind it.'

'Maybe,' said McEwan but he did not sound convinced.

'I mean to confront her over it, to hear her side of the story.'

Phoebe came down the stairs and was about to cross the hallway on her way to the drawing room when she saw Hunter walking towards the bottom of the stairs. A week had passed since the highwaymen's attack on Mrs Hunter's carriage, a week in which Phoebe's love for Hunter had grown. Her eyes scanned over him, noting that he was no longer wearing the black arm sling and she gave a little sigh of relief that his arm was healing so well. He looked so strong and devastatingly handsome and her heart swelled with love and warmth when she saw him.

He stopped where he was on seeing her, and such a determined look came over his face that Phoebe's heart turned over. There was no way she could avoid him.

'Mr Hunter.' She gave a polite nod and made to pass him, but he captured her and pulled her into the shadows of the servants' corridor at the side of the hallway.

'Phoebe, we need to talk.' His hands were gently around her waist, his body close to hers as he stared down into her face.

'Mrs Hunter is waiting.' She tried to break away, but Hunter did not yield.

'Meet me tonight. Come to my study once my mother is in bed.'

'I cannot,' she whispered.

'Why not?' His green gaze bored down into hers.

Because I love you. Because if I let myself be alone with you I do not think that I can hide that truth from you, and they will kill my papa. Because if you were to learn what I am, what I would do to you, you will hate me. But Phoebe spoke none of those truths.

'I have duties to which I must attend.'

'Tomorrow morning then, first thing, before breakfast.'

'No, Sebastian. We cannot meet alone, not then or any other time.'

She saw the muscle flicker in his jaw.

'Why not?'

'I…I have my position to consider. And you have yours.'

There was a flash of fierce green fire in his eyes. 'Damn it, Phoebe, this is nothing of positions. You know there are matters of which we must speak.'

'No,' she forced herself to say. 'I do not.' She could not let herself conduct an affair with him. She had to find the ring and steal it, to save her papa. But she loved Hunter. And she had not found the ring. And she did not know what she was going to do.

Their eyes clung together, her heart was aching, but she could not let herself weaken. The distance between them seemed to shrink. His face was only inches from hers. She could smell his scent, feel his warmth. The little hairs on the back of her neck stood up at the feel of his breath against her cheek. She ached for his kiss, longed to wrap her arms around his neck and press her lips to those of this kind, strong, glorious man whom she loved.

'You must let me go,' she whispered.

'For now,' he said and pressed a fierce kiss to her lips. It was a kiss of possession, a kiss that seemed to seal all that was between them. And then he released her.

Phoebe walked across the stone flags of the hallway just as a maid appeared on the stairs leading from the kitchen and scullery.

'Mrs Hunter rang from the drawing room,' the girl said.

'I am on my way to her at this very moment.' Phoebe smiled and hoped that nothing of Hunter's kiss showed upon her lips. But the maid did not seem to notice anything awry. Phoebe tucked a loose strand of hair into her chignon, and accompanied the girl towards the drawing room.

Hunter had not moved. She did not need to look back to know that he was still standing there in the shadows watching her.

A few days later Hunter was sitting opposite his mother and Phoebe in the breakfast room, sipping at his coffee and thinking. The day was bright, a last throw of summer. Sunlight filled the room, lighting Phoebe's face and showing too well the shadows beneath her eyes. She looked as if she were sleeping badly, and when she thought that no one was watching there was a worry in her eyes. And she had been avoiding him most successfully.

A footman brought the mail in, setting the silver salver down by Hunter's elbow.

Two letters for himself. One from his tailor, the other with Dominic's writing on the front. Three for his mother. And one for Phoebe, not from Emma Northcote; indeed the handwriting looked masculine and simplistic as if someone had taken pains to disguise their hand—the sender's details were not recorded upon the back of the letter.

He passed them across, threw the tailor's letter aside unopened and broke the wax on Dominic's note. Hunter's eyes scanned over Dominic's words. He smiled at the news.

'Be a dear and run and fetch my reading glasses will you, Phoebe.' Hunter felt a pang of irritation at the way his mother treated Phoebe.

'We have servants for that sort of thing,' he said drily and set Dominic's letter upon the table before him.

His mother looked up at him in surprise.

A hint of colour washed Phoebe's cheeks. 'It is no inconvenience, I assure you, sir.' And she slipped away before he could reach for the bell.

There was the cracking of wax and rustle of paper as his mother unfolded her letters. She picked up the first and held it at arm's length, peering at it with screwed-up eyes. 'Writing the size of an ant. Cannot see a word of it. Read it to me, Sebastian.'

'Hawkins writes to inform you that the decorators have finished at the town house in Charlotte Street. And that all is order for your return.'

Phoebe came back into the breakfast room just as he was reading the words. He saw her stiffen, saw that she understood the implication of that news just as well as he. But she did not look at him, just smiled at his mother and delivered the spectacles.

'So soon.' His mother seemed surprised.

'You do not have to leave,' he said. 'Indeed, I insist that you stay.' He thought of what Phoebe had told him of the break-ins at Charlotte Street and of his mother's fears. And he thought, too, of Phoebe.

'You are a young man, Sebastian.' His mother smiled. 'You are already burdened with an old woman's overlong visit.'

'You are neither old nor a burden. And I insist that you stay.'

'I will not hear of it,' his mother said, but she laughed and there was a sparkle in her eye that he had not seen since before his father's death.

From the corner of his eye, where he was surreptitiously watching Phoebe open her mail, he saw her fold the letter away almost as soon as she had opened it. Hunter glanced across at her, just as she looked up and met his gaze, and what he saw in her eyes was a fleeting glimpse of fear before she glanced down, and when she looked up again all of that was hidden and she was quite herself again.

'Good news?' his mother enquired and gestured to the letter clutched tight in Phoebe's hand.

Phoebe's smile was almost convincing. 'Nothing important,' she said. 'Now, what plans do you have for today, ma'am?'

Hunter rode Ajax hard across the moor. The wind was harsh against his cheeks, the sky a bright white-grey, lighting all of the moor with that clarity that he loved. In the distance he could see a pair of eagles soaring high in the sky, the birds huge and majestic. Hunter noticed it all, even though his mind was fixed most firmly on Phoebe Allardyce.

The letter had to be linked in some way with her search for his father's ring, its address penned by a male hand. And he thought of the man he had seen her meet outside of the Tolbooth, and the fear that flashed in her eyes as she saw the letter's contents. He had no intention of just letting her walk out of Blackloch, out of his life. There was too much that he still did not know. He needed answers. He needed her.

Hunter rode faster, harder, longer. And by the time he walked Ajax into Blackloch's stables he knew what he would do.

Chapter Fourteen

In the privacy of her bedchamber Phoebe stared again at the letter that had been delivered that morning. A letter that comprised only three words: *We are waiting.*

And whatever she might have been hoping, that the postponed trip to London might have in some way meant that the nightmare had vanished, those three words told her that she was wrong. Whether she went to London or not, whether she was here at Blackloch, or in Mrs Hunter's house in Charlotte Street, the Messenger would find a way to reach her…and, more importantly, her papa. She did not have the ring. Indeed, she was no closer to finding it now than she had been the first day she had arrived at Blackloch. Hunter had it, guarded most carefully as he had said. Maybe not even in Blackloch. Maybe in a bank or safety deposit box. Wherever it was, Phoebe had almost given up hope of finding it. And when she thought of what that meant she wanted to weep.

The clock had just chimed five when she heard Mrs Hunter's bedchamber door open and the lady's slippered steps across the passageway.

Phoebe screwed the letter to a ball and threw it onto the fire, watching the flames consume the paper and burn it to a cinder. Then she straightened her back, held her head up and went to follow Mrs Hunter down for dinner.

Hunter waited until both his mother and Phoebe were seated before he took his own seat. Hunter was at the head of the table, Mrs Hunter at the foot; Phoebe sat in between the two, her back to the windows and facing the door.

'Such fine salmon,' commented Mrs Hunter. 'I must compliment Cook.' Phoebe watched her clearing her plate. Such a marked change for the lady who, in all the months that Phoebe had worked for her, had only ever picked at her food. The lines of Mrs Hunter's face were no longer gaunt and sharp looking; she looked softer, happier, more agreeable. In contrast, Phoebe was feeling tense and worried. She had not the slightest appetite and there was a tinge of nausea in her stomach. She poked her salmon around her plate to make it look as if she were eating it, and cut her beef into small pieces, only one of which passed her lips.

'Indeed,' agreed Hunter.

The conversation passed on around her. Phoebe made small noises of agreement, but otherwise said little. Plates were delivered and removed. All she could think of was her papa.

'But you are not recovered enough to endure the rigours of such a journey, Sebastian.' Mrs Hunter's exclamation brought her from her reverie. Phoebe noticed that the last of the plates had been removed.

'Mother, I am perfectly recovered and the injury was the merest scratch in the first place.'

'I am not sure.' Mrs Hunter sounded doubtful.

'Besides, Arlesford has written to me. He is expecting an addition to his nursery. He and Arabella are planning a ball to celebrate the good news and we are invited.'

Hunter rose from his seat and walked down the side of the table opposite to Phoebe, pausing just past her. He produced a letter from the pocket of his dark tailcoat and passed it to his mother with his right hand. His left hand leaned flat upon the table as he did so.

Mrs Hunter slipped her spectacles from around her neck onto her nose and read the opened letter. 'How delightful! And I suppose it would be such a shame to disappoint Lady Willaston. It was so kind of her to invite me and she was to have thrown a card rout in my honour.' Her eyes moved to Phoebe and they were filled with concern. 'What say you, my dear? Given what happened upon the moor, I would understand perfectly if you do not wish to travel to London.'

Phoebe barely heard the question. She was too busy staring at Hunter's hand leaning upon the crisp white tablecloth, at his long, square tipped fingers. Her heart began to race. She bit her lip and slowly raised her gaze to his.

Hunter's eyes glittered as green and intense as the emeralds in the silver wolf's-head ring that he wore.

'Phoebe?' Mrs Hunter prompted.

She drew her gaze away from Hunter's. 'London sounds delightful. It is exactly what we need at this moment in time.' She did not know how she managed to keep her voice so calm and level when everything of her emotions was in such chaos.

'I am so glad that you think so, my dear.' Mrs Hunter smiled and returned the letter to her son. 'When shall we leave?'

'As soon as possible,' said Hunter as he slipped the letter into his pocket. 'Unless Miss Allardyce has any objection.'

'I have no objection whatsoever.' She tried to feign a smile, but could not do it. The relief was sour, tainted by deep sickening dread. In her ears she heard only the whisper of betrayal and in her heart felt a deep pulsating ache.

'In that case, come along, Phoebe, we shall leave Sebastian to his port and organise the maids to our packing.'

As she followed Mrs Hunter out of the dining room Phoebe could not help glancing back at Hunter. He was still watching her, his gaze intense. And Phoebe shivered at the prospect of all that lay ahead.

* * *

They travelled to London in Hunter's sleek black travelling coach, after Phoebe had visited the Tolbooth gaol to bid her papa farewell. Hunter himself insisted upon riding, despite all of his mother's protestations, and, although she worried about whether his arm was healed enough, Phoebe was glad. There was such a tension of feelings between them; she feared that, once they were enclosed within such a small space, his mother would be aware of it.

They broke the journey twice, staying in expensive and comfortable inns, Phoebe and Mrs Hunter sharing a room, Hunter in his own. And with every hour that passed, and every mile that took them closer to London, Phoebe felt as if she were travelling to some sort of inevitability that could not be stopped. Hunter treated her just as a gentleman should treat his mother's companion, nothing more, but when he drew near, when his glance met hers, her whole body flared its response and her heart glowed with love. And from the look in his eyes she knew that he felt it, too.

Every day her eyes scanned his fingers for the ring: she saw it only once more and then thereafter, when he removed his gloves, his hands were bare. And even if he were to wear it, there was only one way she could think of to glean it from him and she could not bear the thought of tricking him, of seducing him, of stealing from him. Soon they would be in London, and soon the Messenger would make contact. Phoebe tried not to think of what was coming.

The town house, in Grosvenor Street, held many memories for Hunter. The smart terraced house of golden sandstone had belonged to his father the last time Sebastian had stayed here, and now it belonged to Sebastian. The paintwork around the door and Palladian windows still appeared a fresh glossy black, the window panes sparkled and the steps were scrubbed and clean, just as if the house had not lain empty for almost a year. Even the door knocker had been replaced for their arrival by Trenton, Hunter's caretaker butler, and Mrs Trenton, his housekeeper-wife.

They had been in London for four days. Four days of shopping and excursions, routs and musicales, none of which had seen Hunter alone with Phoebe.

He stood in the empty echoing hallway. The black-and-white chequered marble floor gleamed a reflection of the crystal-and-obsidian-tiered chandelier that hung suspended from the high ceiling. To the right-hand side, close to the door that led into the drawing room, stood a circular table inlaid with mother of pearl and obsidian, and upon which was a silvered glass vase containing a huge bloom of white flowers. On the wall on the left, above the black chinoiserie chairs lined with their backs to the wallpaper, was a large elaborate gold-framed mirror. The décor of the house, in all rooms save for the study, was elegant, sophisticated and in stark contrast to the sturdy old comfort of Blackloch. The smell of the place filled his nostrils, Mrs Trenton's own beeswax polish mix and the echoes of his father and the years he had spent here.

He stood there in the silence, absorbing it all, letting the memories of last year and all that had been wash over him. There was still a sadness, but the terrible eroding guilt had lessened since the night of the thunderstorm with Phoebe. She believed in him. She did not blame him.

From the drawing room came the tinkling of women's laughter: his mother and her friends…and Phoebe. A vision of Phoebe played in his head. For all that they had not been alone, that was not due to Phoebe. She was no longer avoiding him. She had seen the ring. It was just a matter of time before she came to his room.

He lifted his hat, gloves and cane and went off to spend another afternoon at the home of his friend, Dominic Furneaux, the Duke of Arlesford.

'So let me get this straight. This Miss Allardyce has ignored rolls of bank notes and bags of sovereigns, your mother's diamonds and the priceless paintings hung in your drawing room to search exclusively for a ring.'

Hunter could see the way Arlesford was looking at him across the library. He glanced away so that his friend would glean nothing of the depth of his feelings over the matter.

'Most peculiar.' Arlesford frowned as he thought. 'And there is nothing in particular about this ring?' The Duke picked up the brandy decanter and poured a measure into each of two glasses, passing one to Hunter before sipping from the other himself. 'Aside from the fact it was your father's and thus has significance to you,' he added more gently.

'The ring is indeed precious to me, more so than you can imagine, but why it should be so to any other is a mystery. There is nothing exceptional about it apart from its unusual design. I have only seen its like once before, on a cane belonging to our favourite viscount.'

Arlesford's frown deepened.

'But quite what that means I do not know. Silver and chip emeralds are hardly worth a mint.' Hunter took the brandy with a murmur of thanks. He took a single sip and then set it down on the occasional table. 'And then there was the man she met with outside the gaol.'

'He might have been a lover, rather than an accomplice.' Arlesford arched an eyebrow. 'Or maybe even both.'

Hunter felt himself tense. The muscle flickered in his jaw. 'He was not her lover.'

'How can you be so sure?'

'Just a gut instinct,' he said, keeping his voice flat and without emotion so that Arlesford would not guess the truth.

'And the letter she recently received?'

'Whatever was written within it frightened her for all that she tried to hide it.'

'What are you thinking?' Arlesford sipped at his brandy.

'Intimidation.'

'Not that some collector with an eye for the unusual, perhaps even Linwood himself, has found himself a little thief willing to steal for him?'

'She is not like that.'

'She certainly has you on her side.' Arlesford smiled in a suggestive way. 'Pretty little thing, is she? Captured your fancy?'

Hunter's eyes narrowed. He stopped pacing and came to stand directly before Arlesford in a warning stance. 'Have a care over how you speak of Miss Allardyce.'

'What aren't you telling me, Hunter?'

'There is nothing else you need to know.'

Arlesford's eyes were too perceptive as he looked down into Hunter's face. 'She is a thief and your mother's companion,' he said.

'My mother's companion maybe, but Phoebe is no thief.'

'Phoebe?' Arlesford arched an eyebrow.

'Damn it, Dominic,' snapped Hunter.

A knock sounded at the door and Arlesford's wife, Arabella, entered. She smiled a radiant smile at her husband, before speaking to Hunter.

'I thought I heard your voice, Sebastian.'

'Arabella.' Hunter bowed.

'So glad to see you again. Now, tell me, are you and your mother attending Lady Routledge's ball this evening?'

'We are.' He thought of Phoebe.

'How lovely. Please tell her I am so looking forward to seeing her again.'

'I will.' Hunter nodded. 'If you will excuse me, I must head back to Grosvenor Street.'

As Hunter made his way down the stone steps outside Arlesford House, the Duke and Duchess of Arlesford stood by the library window and watched him. Arabella leaned back against her husband as he wrapped his arms around her.

'He is more changed than I realised, Dominic. He seems a man with something pressing upon his mind.'

'Indeed he is, my love,' said the Duke. 'And from the looks of it, a deal more than he is willing to admit.'

At Lady Routledge's ball that evening Phoebe sat with Mrs Hunter and a group of her friends, two of whom were accompanied by their own companions. She was only half-listening to the chatter going on around her; she was too aware of Hunter leaning against a nearby Doric column, of the brooding expression upon his face and the way his gaze came too often to rest upon her face.

'Is that not so, Miss Allardyce?' Mrs Hunter asked.

'Indeed, yes, ma'am,' she answered as if she had been following the conversation most carefully. And when she slid a surreptitious glance across at Hunter again he was still watching her.

She turned her gaze away and looked longingly at the dance floor, where Hunter's friend the Duke of Arlesford was dancing with his wife. Arabella Furneaux, Arlesford's duchess, was by far the most beautiful woman in the whole ballroom. Tall and elegant, she wore her hair piled in a mass of golden shining curls high at the back of her head, several of which had escaped to trail artlessly around her perfect throat. The dove-grey silk dress overset with silver gossamer must have cost a small fortune if its cut and fit and richness of material were anything to judge by. Next to Arabella, Phoebe felt drab and old-fashioned in her old green-silk evening gown. But the duchess was also kind and warm and had included Phoebe completely in her conversations with Mrs Hunter. And when the dance was over, and Arlesford delivered her back to the seat she had taken beside Phoebe and Mrs Hunter, Phoebe saw Mrs Hunter glow with pride at her favour with a duchess. And soon the ladies were all of a-chatter again.

* * *

Across the ballroom behind the pillars, Hunter was standing beside Arlesford, talking to Bullford and feeling ashamed of his shoddy treatment of his old friend at their last meeting in Glasgow.

'Think nothing of it, old man,' Bullford waved away Hunter's apology. 'Just glad to see you are feeling better.'

Hunter nodded. 'You enjoyed your visit with Kelvin?' Over Bullford's shoulder he had a good view of Phoebe. Arabella was sitting by her side and the three ladies seemed deep in conversation.

'Grand to see the old boy again. Had a splendid time. Even if it was m'father that forced me to make the trip. Can't upset the old man.'

'Quite,' said Hunter curtly.

'Sorry, didn't mean to…' Bullford blushed. Hunter relaxed a bit, knowing that it was his own sensitivity and not Bullford that was causing the problem.

'I know, Bullford.'

'Damned good at putting my foot in it these days.'

Hunter shook his head. 'My fault, not yours.'

Bullford gave a nod and smiled in his usual good-natured way. 'Your mother in good health, Hunter?' Bullford turned to look across at Mrs Hunter.

'She is.' The three men's gazes moved across the room to where Mrs Hunter was sitting. But Hunter was not looking at his mother.

'Who is the pretty girl with Mrs H.?'

Hunter frowned. 'That is Miss Phoebe Allardyce, my mother's companion.'

'Looking at the dance floor as if she'd like to be up there. Mind if I ask her to dance, Hunter?'

Mind? Hunter felt a burst of fury just at the thought. He did not think that he could very well ask Phoebe to dance without raising a few eyebrows, notably those of his mother. But he would be damned if he'd see her being handled around the dance floor by some other man.

'She is here to accompany my mother, not to spend the evening dancing,' he said stiffly.

'You're dashed hard on the girl, Hunter. Mrs H. seems to have plenty of company at the minute, but naturally I would ask the lady's permission first before stealing her companion onto the floor.'

Arlesford drew Hunter a meaningful look.

Hunter remained stubbornly tight-lipped.

Arlesford trod on his toe.

'When you put it like that, Bullford…' Hunter said grudgingly.

'Knew you wouldn't be so unreasonable as to see the poor girl sat in a ballroom full of dancers and music the whole night, without so much as a chance to take a turn upon the floor for herself. Girls do so enjoy a dance. Should ask her up yourself, old man.'

Hunter resisted the urge to plant Bullford a facer right there and then, and had to stand and watch as Bullford made his way around the edge of the dance floor towards Phoebe.

'Damnable rake!' muttered Hunter. 'He need not think to get any of his ideas about her.'

'Bullford has cooled his heels much as you, Hunter. He is behaving himself these days. Besides, he is right; she has been looking at the dance floor as if she would care to take a spin upon it.'

Hunter clenched his jaw to stopper the reply he would have made.

Arlesford appeared oblivious. 'Linwood is here.'

Arlesford did not make one movement, yet Hunter felt the tension emanate from his friend just at the mention of the viscount's name. For all intents and purposes it appeared that Arlesford's gaze was fixed on Bullford handling Phoebe up onto the dance floor, but Hunter knew that his friend's attention was elsewhere.

'Left-hand corner, opposite side of the room,' said the duke quietly.

Hunter's eyes sought out Linwood and found him standing behind the chairs where his mother and sister were seated. 'He was with Bullford when I met him in Glasgow.'

'I did not know the two of them were on such good terms,' said Arlesford.

'I believe their fathers are old friends.'

'Then more pity Bullford.'

Hunter did not give a damn about Linwood right at this moment. He was staring at Phoebe and Bullford and wondering how he was going to endure the rest of the night.

By one o'clock in the morning Phoebe and Mrs Hunter were making their way down the stone steps outside Lady Routledge's house towards the carriage. Arlesford had called Hunter back into the hallway to say something to him.

For all of the tension between herself and Hunter, Phoebe had still enjoyed the evening. Not only had she made a new friend of Arlesford's duchess, Arabella, but she had actually danced three times; once with the Duke of Arlesford and twice with another of Hunter's friends, Lord Bullford. And for all that she had longed for it, Hunter had not asked her and she knew that he was right not to have done. Indeed, he had barely spoken a word to her all night, just watched her with that same intense brooding expression and more than a hint of anger in his eyes.

They were almost halfway down the steps when Phoebe's reticule slipped from her fingers. She turned to lift it, but someone else was there before her: a gentleman, dark-haired, olive-skinned and handsome.

'Your reticule, miss.' He handed it to her.

Phoebe's heart began to beat too fast. Her eyes met his that were black as the night that surrounded them.

He lingered for only the briefest of moments, then bowed and walked away into the night.

Mrs Hunter had almost reached the carriage, but Phoebe stood, staring after the gentleman, not at the lithe confident way that he moved, or even at the dark eyes as they glanced back at her.

'Come along, Phoebe, stop wool gathering, girl,' Mrs Hunter called.

Phoebe made her way towards her employer, but her mind was still filled with an image of the gentleman's walking cane—an ebony stick, mounted with a silver wolf's head handle in which she had seen the glow of two emerald eyes.

Chapter Fifteen

$\mathbf{M}$rs Hunter slept late the next day. And Hunter had taken Ajax out into Hyde Park for a gallop with Arlesford. Phoebe realized that this might be the opportunity she needed. She tried not to think about what it was she was doing, stealing from the man she loved, and concentrated on the technicalities of performing the act itself.

She broke her fast alone in her bedchamber with a tray of coffee and a bread roll spread with marmalade. When the maid came to remove the tray Phoebe waited until she heard the girl disappear down the servants' stairs, then crept out into the corridor. As she passed Mrs Hunter's room, the one through the wall from her own, she paused and listened, but from inside came only silence. Hunter's room was across on the other side of the main staircase. Phoebe made her way quietly towards it. She was just crossing the landing when, ahead of her, the door to Hunter's bedchamber opened and a maid carrying an armful of bed linen appeared. Through the open door Phoebe could see another maid still within the room.

'Beggin' your pardon, ma'am.' The maid bobbed a curtsy and hurried away with her load, towards the servants' stairs at the far end of the corridor.

'Good morning, Betsy.' Phoebe forced a smile and made her way down the main staircase as if that had been where she was headed all along. She went into the drawing room to worry and to wait and to wonder how, amidst this carousel of balls and routs and visits, she could keep on pretending that everything was normal.

Only twelve hours later and Phoebe was sitting by Mrs Hunter's side at Lady Willaston's card party. The ladies were all playing in one room and the gentlemen in another. Phoebe partnered Mrs Hunter, and played against Arabella and Mrs Forbes, and then the forthright Lady Misbourne who bossed her daughter, the Honourable Miss Winslow, terribly, and who was exceptionally skilled at the game, much to Mrs Hunter's annoyance. Phoebe was relieved the game was over and Mrs Hunter, having realised that if she was to progress anywhere in the evening she would require a partner more talented in the whist stakes than Phoebe, had allied herself with Mrs Dobson. Phoebe watched for a while, then wandered off to the ladies' withdrawing room to powder her nose. She made her way back, thinking of the wretched wolf's-head ring, and wondering if she dared feign a headache to return to the town house in Grosvenor Street and search Sebastian's bedchamber. As she rounded the corner just past the stairs, heading into the foyer between the two card rooms, she walked right into a gentleman.

His hands closed around her arms, steadying her, but drew back as soon as he knew that she would not stumble.

'I beg your pardon, miss.'

She looked up into the dark eyes of the gentleman who had returned her reticule the previous evening.

'Miss Allardyce, I believe.'

'I…' Her gaze dropped to the walking cane in his right hand, to its silver wolf's-head embedded with emerald chips, before returning once more to that dark, handsome face. And her heart was pounding and she felt the cold hand of fear touch to her blood. 'We have not been introduced, sir,' she said primly and made to walk on.

But he shifted his stance ever so slightly to block her path. 'Then permit me to introduce myself. I am Linwood. You played cards with my mother and sister earlier this evening, I believe—Lady Misbourne and Miss Winslow.'

'They are most talented players,' she said carefully and glanced again at his walking cane, which was identical in every detail to the ring that she had seen upon Hunter's finger. It could be no coincidence. If the wolf's-head symbol held some significance for him, it might well explain why a man would go to such lengths to possess the ring.

She waited for the question that would follow, tried to frame her explanation within her mind as to why she did not have the ring in her possession.

'They are much practiced. It is my mother's favourite pastime.'

She gave a nod and looked away. Knowing the power that this man held over her father made her feel sick to her stomach and desperately afraid.

'Miss Allardyce?' He leaned closer, a folly of concern across his face.

She stepped back to keep a distance between them and felt her spine bump against the plaster of Lady Willaston's wall.

'You appear to be a little unwell, Miss Allardyce. Perhaps I should fetch Mrs Hunter to you.' He turned away to leave.

'Please do not, sir,' she said quickly and placed a hand upon his arm to stop him. 'I am quite well, I assure you.' She hesitated, 'And able to answer any questions you may wish to ask of me…'

He shook his head and took her hand from his sleeve, holding it before him as if he would kiss it. 'I fear you are under a misapprehension as to—'

'What the hell do you think you are playing at, Linwood?' Hunter's low growl interrupted whatever the viscount had been about to say.

Phoebe jumped at Sebastian's sudden appearance.

'Hunter,' Linwood inclined his head '…always a pleasure to see you.' But the smile on his face was one of sarcasm. 'Thought you would be busy keeping Arlesford company.' Linwood's face was filled with such a burning contempt that Phoebe felt shocked to see it.

'Take your hands off her.' Sebastian spoke quietly, slowly, every word controlled, but it did not disguise the menace of the threat that lay beneath that harsh control. His skin was white as marble beside the dark looks of the viscount, his eyes a clear cold green... and deadly.

Linwood released her hand and said silkily, 'I had no idea you had such an interest in Miss Allardyce.'

Sebastian stepped right up to Linwood until they were too close. As he towered over the slighter man he stared down into Linwood's face. 'Miss Allardyce is my mother's companion and, as such, I consider any insult dealt her an insult against my family. Do not think to start your games with me or mine.'

The word 'mine' seemed to hang in the air. Linwood's gaze shifted to Phoebe's face and she felt herself blush before he turned back to Sebastian.

Linwood smiled a dark mocking smile. 'Is it true?' he asked. 'What they say about you and your father's death?'

There was a roaring silence.

She saw the tiny telltale flicker in Sebastian's jaw, saw the sudden change in his eyes.

'Mr Hunter.' She stepped quickly between Sebastian and Linwood. And then more softly, 'Sebastian.' His whole body hummed with violence. She knew she had to stop him before it was too late. She laid her hand against Sebastian's lapel. 'Please...do not do this, I beg of you.'

And then Arlesford was there beside Sebastian.

'Miss Allardyce.' Linwood bowed at her as if they had just conducted a civilised and polite conversation.

Bullford appeared at the other side and murmured something to both Sebastian and Arlesford so that the three men walked off into the Marquis of Willaston's library.

Phoebe glanced up to find Mrs Hunter standing not ten feet away in the doorway of the ladies' card-playing room, and from her pale shaken face she knew that the lady had heard Viscount Linwood's question.

'I seem to have developed something of a headache. I wonder if you would mind, Mrs Hunter, if we were to leave a little early this evening.'

'Not at all, my dear,' said Mrs Hunter, and she allowed Phoebe to lead her away in the direction of the front door. Phoebe did not look back towards the library.

It was not surprising that Mrs Hunter slept late the next morning. And, according to Trenton, Sebastian had gone out, although the hour of the morning was so early that Phoebe rather suspected, perhaps, that that meant he had not come back to the house at all. Knowing how Sebastian blamed himself for his father's death Phoebe could only guess at just how very deeply Linwood's words must have cut. She felt his pain, and felt a rage that Linwood could deal such an underhand barb.

Supposing he had gone after Lord Linwood. Supposing the two of them had fought, or, worse still, duelled. Sebastian might at this very minute be lying wounded on a common. He might even be dead. Phoebe pressed her palm to her mouth, trying to quell the unbearable thought. And her heart was swollen and aching, for she knew that she loved him. Utterly. Completely.

She paced the drawing room, knowing she would not rest until she was certain Sebastian was safe. And she thought of his veiled claim on her. *Do not start your games with me or mine.* Of course people would expect him to have an interest in the reputation of his mother's companion—should she lose it Mrs Hunter would be affected. But Phoebe knew there was so much more to it than that.

Linwood guessed it, too, if that look upon his face had been anything to go by. And she worried all the more about the ring and why he had not asked her for it, and what that might mean for her papa.

She paced and she worried—about the ring, and her papa, and Sebastian. The thoughts were running round and round, until she thought her head might explode.

She could not settle to her needlework. She read the same page of her book three times before abandoning it upon the sofa and toyed with the jet-and-ivory carved chess pieces neatly lined up upon their board in the corner, before abandoning them to stand by the window and look out on to the street. The road was quiet; only one carriage passed and a milkmaid carrying her wooden churns across her shoulders. Phoebe raised her eyes to the sky, the same white-blue sky that Blackloch sat beneath.

A flock of starlings flew by and she thought of the great black crows that cawed and the golden eagles that soared over the moor. She closed her eyes and in her mind she could see that wind-ravaged land with its bleak hills and its hardy sheep and the black curve of the narrow road that snaked across it. Standing there in the drawing room of the London town house, Phoebe thought she could smell the clear fresh scent of the wind and the sweetness of the heather and the tangy pungent peat smoke that curled from the farmstead chimneys. The storm of thoughts calmed to settle as still and cool as the deep dark water of the Black Loch itself.

She could not steal from Hunter. She loved him. And she was sure that he harboured some measure of affection towards her. There was no right or wrong answer. No simple black and white, only a world washed in tones of grey. But now that she had made the decision Phoebe felt strangely calm. She sat down upon the sofa, picked up her embroidery and settled back to wait for Hunter's return.

In the morning room of Arlesford House Hunter rubbed at his head and accepted the coffee that Dominic offered. The two men sat alone. The servants had been dismissed and Arabella had not yet woken.

'I should have called him out.'

'Maybe,' said Arlesford. 'Lord knows the bastard deserves it. But you have more than your own reputation to consider in this, Hunter.'

'My mother does not remain unaffected by the insult dealt.' Hunter sipped at the coffee and tried to shake the brandy-induced ache from his head.

'I was not referring to your mother.'

Hunter glanced up from his cup.

'Miss Allardyce…' said Arlesford.

'Miss Allardyce has no bearing on this.'

'On the contrary, Hunter, your mother's companion may have prevented you and Linwood brawling in possibly the worst of places, but at some cost to her own reputation.'

Hunter thought of Phoebe's hand in Linwood's and frowned, making the pain ache all the more in his head. 'She did nothing untoward.'

'Hunter, London does not know what Linwood did to Arabella. They do not understand why you and I should despise him so. Last night they saw only you cutting in on his conversation with Miss Allardyce. She called you by your given name, Hunter, and restrained you in a way that suggested a degree of familiarity between the two of you.'

Hunter winced. 'I would not have her reputation sullied.'

'Even though she would thieve from you?'

Hunter said nothing, but his jaw was clenched and stubborn.

'Is she your mistress?'

'Certainly not! Hell's teeth, Dominic, I would not… I am not… Not any more!'

'Then what is between the two of you?'

Hunter shook his head as if to deny the question.

'Hell, Sebastian, any fool with eyes in his head can see the way you look at each other. You love her.'

Hunter dropped his head into his hands.

'You love a woman who has lied to both you and your mother, who has abused her position and is intent upon stealing from you,' said Arlesford.

'Phoebe Allardyce is courageous and warm of heart. She is compassionate and kind.' Hunter did not say that she had suffered as he had suffered, that she understood him, that she forgave him. 'I cannot bear that she should suffer, Dominic. I would take her every hurt upon myself to free her from it. My mind longs for her. My heart aches for her. And, yes, my body wants her, all of her, in every way possible. Knowing that she lied, knowing that she would steal the ring—it makes no difference to any of it. If that is love, then I am guilty of it.'

Arlesford gave a gruff reassuring pat against Hunter's shoulder. Then the two friends sat in silence for a few minutes.

'What do you mean to do about it?'

'I mean to discover why she is trying to steal the ring.'

'And the rest of it?'

'One step at a time, my friend.'

Phoebe was alone in the drawing room when Hunter returned to Grosvenor Street. He dismissed Trenton and closed the door behind him.

She came to her feet, hurried to stand before him, her eyes scanning his body before rising to search his face. 'You are unhurt?'

'Quite unhurt. Why would you think otherwise?'

'Last night with Lord Linwood, and then it seemed this morning that you had not come home and I thought… I have been so filled with worry that he might…that you would be…'

And he knew exactly what she thought and her concern touched his heart. He took her hands in his. 'Phoebe.' He stroked a hand to her cheek. 'I stayed the night at Arlesford House. I was angry after my encounter with Linwood and wished to cool my temper before returning here. I am sorry, I did not think you would be worried about me.'

She glanced away, embarrassed.

'You have my gratitude for preventing me from brawling with Linwood last night. I dread to think what it would have descended into had you not acted so promptly.'

She gave a little nod.

'When I saw you with Linwood…you were white as a sheet. What did he say to you to frighten you so?' His thumbs moved over the backs of her hands where he held her.

She shook her head. 'Not what I thought he would say. In truth, I do not even know if—' Then she stopped herself, and looked up into his eyes. 'Sebastian, there is a matter on which I would like to seek your help, but…' She bit at her lip.

'Phoebe, you must know that you can come to me with anything, anything at all, and I will do all within my power to help you.'

'Even if it is something you do not like or a matter that is most dishonourable?'

'I will help you, Phoebe. I give you my most solemn word.'

She nodded and moved her hands within his. 'I pray you can understand the difficulty of the position I find myself in. I cannot do as they ask, yet nor can I not do it.'

From the hallway came the sound of Mrs Hunter's voice quizzing Trenton, then her footsteps treading towards the drawing room.

Phoebe glanced nervously at the door. A furrow of worry marred her brow.

Hunter kissed the furrow away. 'Meet me here in the drawing room, at eight o'clock tomorrow morning. We will speak then.'

She nodded and hurried back to the sofa to pick up her embroidery. By the time his mother entered the room, Phoebe was calmly stitching and Hunter was standing braced by the window, watching the world go by.

And as to the events of the previous evening, his mother said not one word.

Phoebe and Mrs Hunter spent the afternoon shopping, while Sebastian went to his club to meet with Arlesford and Bullford, only returning to Grosvenor Street at half past four.

'I am going for a nap, Phoebe, and I recommend that you do likewise. Remember that we have the theatre at seven.'

Phoebe gave a nod.

Then Mrs Hunter spoke to the butler hovering discreetly in the background. 'Trenton, has m'son returned yet?'

'He has not, madam.'

Then back to Phoebe. 'I do hope he remembers that he is supposed to be accompanying us.'

'I am sure that Mr Hunter will return in time.'

'We do have to make a stand after last night.'

Phoebe nodded.

'And if we see Lord Linwood tonight, Phoebe, you had best hold me back as well.' Mrs Hunter smiled and then retired to her bedchamber, leaving Phoebe alone in the drawing room.

She had only been sewing for a few minutes when a knock sounded on the drawing room door and Trenton, appeared. 'A message for you, Miss Allardyce.' He handed her the sealed note. 'Delivered by hand, miss—the lad did not wait for a reply.'

She recognised the carefully formed handwriting in which her name upon the letter's front had been written and a wave of nausea swept through her. She dismissed the butler before sliding a finger along the edge of the paper to break the sealing wax. On the note within the instructions were concise:

Head towards Davies Street on foot immediately. Come alone. Tell no one. Bring what is required.

There was no signature, but Phoebe did not need one to know who the letter was from—the Messenger.

She shivered and moved quickly to the window, knowing that whoever had sent this must be watching the house to know that she was alone and able to leave this house at this moment. A gentleman rode past on his horse. A cart carrying coal rumbled over the cobbles and a carriage was almost out of sight in the opposite direction. An old man hobbled along the pavement and a couple of urchins were cheeking the coachman of the chaise waiting outside the house three doors down. No sign of the Messenger...or of Lord Linwood.

She moved away again, folding the letter into the pocket of her new fawn day dress. A chill seemed to touch to her blood and a shadow cloud over all of her hopes. She shivered again and hurried to fetch her bonnet.

'Shall you be requiring the carriage, miss?' enquired Trenton as she stood in the hall with her bonnet tied in place.

'No, thank you, Mr Trenton.' Phoebe fitted the gloves onto her fingers. 'If Mrs Hunter should enquire, please tell her that I have gone for a short walk. It is such a fine day.' She smiled, but the smile felt stiff upon her lips and more like a grimace. She did not have the ring. Hunter was gone from home. And she dare not ignore the summons.

Chapter Sixteen

She had been walking in the direction of Davies Street for only some five minutes when the black closed carriage stopped beside her. The door opened and the Messenger jumped down, pulling the door shut again behind him.

'Miss Allardyce, we meet again, just as I promised.'

'Sir.' She looked at him and felt fear and that same overwhelming sense of dislike and anger.

He waved his hand towards the coach. 'Your carriage awaits, miss.'

'I am not getting in there with you. We may discuss what you will out here just as well.'

'May be, miss, but there's someone who wants to meet you.'

A vision of Lord Linwood appeared in her mind.

The Messenger added, 'I must insist, Miss Allardyce. Or maybe you've forgotten all about your pa since you've been down here in fair old London town?'

Phoebe met the Messenger's sly gaze squarely. 'The carriage it is then, sir.'

He opened the door, kicked down the step and bundled her inside before following. The door slammed shut and, before her eyes could adjust to the dim light of the interior, a dark hood was thrust over her head. She fought to free herself, but rough hands clasped hers, wrenching them behind her back and holding her tight.

'Unhand me, you villain!' she demanded, the hood muffling her words.

'Calm yourself, Miss Allardyce. I have a mind to speak with you without revealing my identity, that is all.' The voice, which came from the seat directly opposite, was not that of Lord Linwood. It sounded like that of an older gentleman and there was something vaguely familiar about it, although she could not place it.

The Messenger's grip tightened unbearably and Phoebe ceased her struggles.

'That is better.' The gentleman took a breath. 'Now, let us not prevaricate, Miss Allardyce. Do you have the ring?'

'I…' Her stomach clenched at the thought of revealing the truth to this man. She knew he must be very powerful. She knew just what he could do to her father. 'It is not yet in my possession.' The hood was a thick heavy black material that smelled faintly of sweet tobacco and sandalwood. It not only rendered her effectively blind, but made it hot and difficult to breathe.

'Not yet, you say?' the gentleman said. 'And yet you have had ample time in which to recover it, Miss Allardyce. Perhaps you do not have so much care for your father as we had thought?'

'I have every care for my father, but it has been difficult. At first I could not find the ring at Blackloch Hall—'

'At first, implies that you have now discovered its location.'

'I…' To admit it felt like a betrayal of Hunter.

'Miss Allardyce.' The man's voice was harsh with warning.

'The ring is in Mr Hunter's possession.'

'You have seen it?'

'I have, sir.'

'Where precisely, Miss Allardyce?'

'It was upon Mr Hunter's finger.'

'He wore it?' The man sounded shocked.

'He did, sir.'

There was a small cogitative silence.

'Does he have it with him here in London?'

Phoebe was loathe to tell them.

The silence within the carriage seemed very loud.

'Your father is in danger and yet still you hesitate to co-operate.'

'Sir, I am co-operating fully. Have I not searched every last room in Blackloch Hall for you? I…I am not certain as to the ring's precise whereabouts since we have come to London.'

Another loaded silence stretched between them, in which Phoebe could only hear the sound of her own breath loud within the hood.

'I have heard a whisper that you harbour tender feelings for Hunter,' he said at last.

'No.'

'And from what I saw of Hunter's little display last night he is certainly not indifferent to you.'

'You are wrong, sir.'

'Having an affair with his mother's companion while pretending to us all that he has reformed his rakish tendencies after a year spent brooding upon his lonely moor.'

'Such scurrilous accusations are false! There is nothing between Mr Hunter and myself.'

The man laughed at her protestations. 'That is why you do not have the ring, is it not, Miss Allardyce? You cannot bear to steal from him.'

'No!' she lied. 'I have already told you the reason I do not yet have it.'

'That was no doubt true at first, before Hunter seduced you.'

'He did not seduce me, sir. I will not hear you say it of him.'

The man let another silence open up so that Phoebe did not know whether he believed what she said or not. The seconds stretched to minutes.

'If you have a notion to confide in Hunter, or anyone else for that matter, Miss Allardyce, I will arrange for him to follow the same fate as your father.'

'You would not dare to threaten him.'

'Oh, I assure you, Miss Allardyce, we will do more than threaten. We are very powerful. There is no one who can hide from us.'

'Who are you?' she whispered.

'No one that a young lady should concern herself with.'

'Do not hurt him. I have told him nothing.'

'Then let us keep it that way. I will know if you tell him. Nothing escapes me, Miss Allardyce. Believe me when I tell you I have eyes and ears everywhere.' She could hear the smile in his voice. 'And so now to the ring once more, my dear. My patience wears thin with the wait. I require that the matter be concluded by the end of this week.'

'Impossible, sir,' Phoebe protested.

'If the ring is not within your possession by then, Miss Allardyce, I shall make arrangements for Hunter to be relieved of it by violent means. And, of course, then there is the little matter of your papa to be dealt with... Both their lives will be extinguished.'

'No! I beg of you, sir!'

'The end of the week, Miss Allardyce. Not a day longer. When you have secured it, wear this red shawl and stand by a front window of Hunter's town house. We will then send you instructions of how to proceed.' He passed her a small thin red shawl. 'Go now, my... associate...will assist you out of the carriage.'

She heard the slide of a window. 'All clear, gov,' said the Messenger and then he manhandled her to what she presumed must be the door, standing behind her and pulling the hood from her head as he opened the door and tipped her out onto the footpath. The door slammed and the carriage pulled away at a brisk pace, leaving Phoebe blinking in the sudden strong sunlight.

* * *

Hunter had arrived in the drawing room of his town house in Grosvenor Street at five minutes before eight the next morning. The curtains were open and the early autumn sunlight filled the room. He was still waiting at nine o'clock when he enquired of Trenton as to his mother and Miss Allardyce, and was told they were both not yet risen for the day. He took Ajax for a gallop in Hyde Park, and returned two hours later to find both ladies in the drawing room entertaining Lady Chilcotte and her daughters. He had endured an hour of Lady Chilcotte thrusting her eldest daughter beneath his nose in far too obvious a manner, but Phoebe did not once meet his eye.

After luncheon, when his mother had decided to go shopping, again, Hunter accompanied them, carrying parcels once the footman's arms became full. And again Phoebe would not meet his eye, even when she had perforce to take his hand when he assisted the ladies into and out of the coach. At the fashionable hour of five o'clock his mother expressed a desire to take a drive in Hyde Park. And again Hunter accompanied them. And still everything of Phoebe was closed against him, almost as if their conversation of the previous day had never occurred, so that he grew increasingly convinced that something had happened between then and now, something to make her change her mind.

At dinner in the town house Hunter gave up waiting and addressed her directly.

'You seem a little preoccupied today, Miss Allardyce. Is all well with you?'

'Everything is fine, thank you, sir,' she answered and it seemed she had to force herself to look at him. Her eyes were dark and troubled, her face pale with a haunted expression she could not quite hide. Hunter resolved to speak to Trenton to discover if Miss Allardyce had received any new letters.

'Then you will be accompanying my mother to Arlesford's ball tonight?'

'I...um...' She hesitated. 'I do have something of a headache.'

'A headache, Phoebe?' asked his mother.

'Perhaps I would be better to stay at home tonight—that is, if you could manage without me tonight, ma'am.' Phoebe looked at his mother and not once at him. But Hunter knew exactly what she was doing. She knew this was the ball to which both his mother and himself had been especially invited. She wanted to be alone in the town house, and Hunter had a good idea as to the reason.

'How very peculiar,' he said. 'I feel the stirrings of an ache in my own head.' Hunter touched a hand to his forehead. 'Perhaps it is a contagious headache, Miss Allardyce.'

'Well, I cannot very well go alone,' said his mother, 'and if both of you are struck down with it, perhaps it is only a matter of time before I, too, am likewise affected. And I was so looking forward to the night. I have my new grey-silk ball gown especially for the occasion.'

'Now, ma'am, we cannot have that,' said Phoebe quickly. 'If you will excuse me, I will go and lie down for half an hour and I am sure that will help diminish the headache.'

'Very well, Phoebe,' said his mother.

Phoebe sat by Mrs Hunter's side at the Duke of Arlesford's ball and tried not to look at Hunter. She had successfully eluded him the whole day through, but the strain of it had frayed her nerves and she was feeling tense and miserable. Her eyes roved through the throng of people, remembering the man in the carriage's words that he had eyes and ears everywhere. Was the man here himself, watching her and Hunter even now?

On the other side of the ballroom she saw Emma Northcote, but Emma's eyes moved to where Hunter was standing behind Phoebe's chair and when she looked at Phoebe again she gave a small shake of her head as if to tell her that there could be no friendship while Phoebe was allied with the Hunters. Emma turned her attention back to her mother. Phoebe glanced round and saw that Hunter had seen the interaction between Emma and herself.

He waited until his mother was fully engaged in conversation before leaning forwards and saying quietly, 'Phoebe—'

'Ah, there you are Hunter, old man, and Miss Allardyce, too.' She was mercifully saved by Lord Bullford's interruption. Hunter shot his friend a look of irritation. And then, after speaking to Mrs Hunter, Lord Bullford had her up on the dance floor for the next two dances, and by the time he returned her to her seat Hunter was over talking to Arlesford.

'You are sure about this?' Arlesford asked.

Hunter nodded. 'I know it is a big favour to ask of you, but it is the only way that I can see of getting her alone.'

'Very well,' Arlesford gave a nod. 'Only do not cause a scandal at Arabella's ball.'

'I will guard against it most carefully. Thank you, Dominic. You know I would not ask were it not important.'

'I am well aware of the importance of Miss Allardyce to you.'

Hunter turned to leave.

'Sebastian,' his friend said softly.

Hunter glanced back.

'Good luck.'

Hunter gave a grave nod, then made his way nonchalantly from the ballroom.

Phoebe was making her way back from the ladies' withdrawing room as the Duke's footman approached her.

'Miss Allardyce?'

'Yes?'

She saw the letter as he slipped it from his pocket and her heart began to race. She thought of the Messenger and his master in the carriage. 'I was asked to deliver this note to you, miss.' He slipped it to her surreptitiously and, with a bow, was gone.

She hid it in her pocket and headed a little farther up the corridor, away from the withdrawing room and ballroom, before ducking in to an alcove to read it. The hand in which her name was written was none that she recognised. It was not in the careful font of the Messenger, but the wax seal had been smudged just like those on his notes. Nor was it in the strong black spikes of Hunter's writing. She broke the seal and opened out the letter to find one short message written in the centre of the paper:

Come alone to the Duke's rose conservatory. There have been further developments since yesterday.

There could only be one person who would write such a message. He was here, watching her. She crumpled the paper and pressed a hand to her head. The end of the week, he had said. There were still two more days to go. What could possibly have happened? She drew a deep breath and smoothed the letter out before folding it neatly and placing it in her pocket. Then she braced her shoulders and went to find Arlesford's rose conservatory.

The footman led her down an unlit narrow corridor lined its length with closed mahogany doors. The man ignored every door and kept on walking. The farther they walked from the ballroom the darker it became. Darker and darker until Phoebe had to strain her eyes to see what was before them.

Phoebe knocked once upon the door and then she pushed it slowly open to reveal a room illuminated by soft silver moonlight. The sweet perfume of roses seeped from within. She stepped inside.

There was no messenger waiting to pounce and slip a hood over her head this time. Indeed, on first impressions the room seemed empty. Three sides of the conservatory and the roof were part constructed from glass. The silver moonlight flooded through the wall of windows to light the collection of beautiful blooms housed within. The perfume of the roses was more intense in here; it seemed heady and intoxicating. She walked into the centre of the room. There was no one…and then she heard the door close behind her and her heart stuttered as she turned to face the villain once more. It was not the Messenger who was standing there leaning back against the door, but Sebastian.

'You?' The moonlight revealed him in full.

'Who were you expecting, Phoebe?'

'I…' She shook her head. 'I have to go. I cannot leave Mrs Hunter waiting.'

'Not yet, Phoebe.' He walked slowly towards her.

Her eyes measured the distance to the door, but he seemed to take up all the space and she knew she would not make it past him without capture.

'You did not keep the meeting we had arranged for this morning.'

'I…' The music floated through from the ballroom, faint but still audible. 'I could not.'

'And all day you have avoided me most studiously.'

'You are mistaken.'

'I am sure that I am not.'

She swallowed hard and her heart was thudding so loud she was sure Sebastian must hear it in the quietness of the room.

'Yesterday you asked for my help.'

'The matter has resolved. I have no need of your help.'

'If it had, you would have simply told me such. What changed between our last meeting and this morning?'

'Nothing changed.'

'Save the letter you received.'

'I received no letter.'

'Hand-delivered by an urchin paid a copper to do so, or so Trenton informs me.'

'Oh, *that* letter.' She wetted her suddenly dry lips. 'I had quite forgotten about it.'

'Who was its sender, Phoebe?'

'Sir!' she exclaimed pretending to be shocked.

'Phoebe,' and his voice was something of a growl.

'A…friend.'

'The same friend whom you left almost immediately to meet.'

'I met with no one. I went for a walk, that is all.'

'In the evening and alone?' he persisted.

'It was not so late.'

'Late enough that when you returned some half an hour later your hair was in disarray.'

'Trenton exaggerates. The wind coupled with the vigour of my walking may have loosened a few of my pins.'

'Who is he, Phoebe?'

'I do not know what you are talking about.'

'The man you met last night.'

'I told you, I met no one.' She set a determined look upon her face and tried to walk right past him. 'If you will excuse me, I must attend to Mrs Hunter. She will be wondering where I have got to.' But he caught her arm and pulled her to him.

'Why will you not trust me, Phoebe?' he whispered and the underlying pain in his voice echoed that in her heart.

'I trust you, Sebastian. You must know that.' She stared up into his eyes.

'Then tell me what is going on.'

She glanced away in despair. 'I cannot.'

'Cannot or will not?' he demanded.

She looked up at him, took his face between her hands. 'Sebastian, I trust you with my very life, truly I do. But this matter of which we speak, this is the one thing I cannot tell. Please believe me, were there any other way…'

'You do not have to do this, Phoebe. I can help you. I can keep you safe, if that is what you fear.'

She dropped her hands and tried to turn away, knowing the irony of the situation. 'This has nothing to do with my safety.'

But he would not let her go. 'Who are you protecting?'

You, she wanted to cry. *My papa.* But she said nothing, just shook her head.

'Phoebe.' His fingers stroked soothingly against her cheek. 'Do you not know I would lay down my life for you?'

She turned her head to kiss the tips of his fingers. 'And I, for you.'

'But still you will not tell me?'

She shook her head sadly. 'Forgive me, Sebastian,' she whispered and reached up to touch her lips briefly against his.

'Phoebe...' She could hear the torture in his voice.

They stared into one another's eyes. And when his mouth moved slowly to hers she kissed him with all the love and all the tenderness that was in her heart. Telling him with her actions what she could not tell him in words. She threaded her hands through his hair, pulling him closer, pressing herself to him, needing his strength, needing his passion.

She shivered in delight as his hands swept over her body, stroking over the swell of her hips, her buttocks, up over her ribcage. Their bodies clung together. They breathed the same breath. They kissed until she no longer knew where she ended and he began. And Phoebe knew she would never love anyone the way she loved Hunter.

A knock sounded. By the time the door opened, Hunter had thrust Phoebe behind him and turned to face the door.

'So sorry to intrude, old man.' Lord Bullford was glancing away in obvious embarrassment. 'Came to warn you that Mrs H. has noticed her companion is missing.' He cleared his throat several times and did not look once in Phoebe's direction.

Hunter scowled at his friend, but his words when uttered were civil enough. 'Thank you, Bullford.'

Lord Bullford disappeared into the darkness of the corridor, his footsteps fading to merge with the low lilt of the music.

'I must go,' she said.

Hunter nodded. 'I will follow in a while so it is not apparent we have been together.'

She walked away and left him, to follow down the dark corridor all the way back to the ballroom.

The morning after the ball Phoebe and Mrs Hunter sat in the morning room, drinking coffee and eating toast. Sebastian had not yet emerged from his bedchamber.

'And how is your head this morning, Phoebe?' enquired Mrs Hunter.

'Much recovered, thank you, ma'am.' Phoebe sipped at her coffee and ignored the slice of toast that lay on her plate.

'You should have told me you were taken unwell with it last night. I was quite worried when you disappeared for such a while.'

'I am sorry to have worried you. I thought only to step away from the heat and bright lights and music for a while.'

'Well, as long as you are recovered now.'

'Completely,' said Phoebe. She drank some more coffee to try to dispel the thick blanket of fatigue that seemed to cloak her brain this morning. She had slept little. All the thoughts in her head were of Sebastian and her papa, of the Messenger and the gentleman in the carriage. And the words that kept running through her head were Sebastian's: *Do you not know I would lay down my life for you.*

'I plan a day of rest and recovery today, so that we will be fresh for tomorrow. I thought an afternoon visit to Mrs Stanebridge, then an early night,' said Mrs Hunter.

'A good idea, ma'am.' Yet, in truth, Phoebe knew that she could settle to nothing. Her nerves felt frayed, her mind in turmoil; her body ached for a sleep that would not come no matter how long she lay upon a bed. Time was running out. Phoebe had only one more day to steal the ring.

Hunter did not leave the house, yet he stayed away from Phoebe and his mother, seeking instead the comfort of his father's library. Trenton had been given instructions to deliver any letters that might arrive addressed to Miss Allardyce to Hunter himself. And when the ladies went visiting in the afternoon, he sent two footmen to follow discreetly to guard their safety. He stared out onto the London street that was so different from his moor and he waited for the day to pass and the night to come.

He sensed the flare of emotion in Phoebe when she saw him enter the drawing room after the ladies' return, but she hid it well. Her attention stayed fixed on his mother and the stories she relayed of their afternoon at Mrs Stanebridge's. She smiled in all the right places, made the right agreements and nodded frequently, yet beneath the façade of normality there was such an air of tension about her that he did not know how his mother could fail to notice it.

'I am having dinner with Fallingham tonight and will probably stay there overnight.'

His mother gave a nod. 'But you will be back tomorrow to take Miss Allardyce and me to Colonel and Mrs Morely's as you promised?'

'Of course.' Hunter smiled, then toyed with the wolf's-head ring, twisting it in small rotations around his finger in an abstract manner.

His mother did not miss the movement. She peered across at his hand. 'Is that your father's ring you are wearing?'

He glanced down at the ring, and the wolf's eyes stared back up at him. 'It is. I had forgotten that I was wearing it,' he lied. He rang the bell, then twisted the ring from his finger and held it upon the flat of his palm for a moment.

'I never did like it,' said his mother, 'but Edward would not be without it.'

When Trenton arrived Hunter handed him the ring. 'Please see that it is placed in the jewel casket in my bedchamber.'

'Very good, sir.'

'I will see you tomorrow, Mother.' He gave her a small bow and then turned to Phoebe, who was sitting as still and pale as a statue, her eyes trained on the ring. 'Miss Allardyce.' Her eyes moved to meet his, and there was such a look in them that Hunter's resolve almost broke—relief, disbelief, sorrow and guilt.

'Mr Hunter,' she said softly and gave him a curtsy.

Chapter Seventeen

By midnight the last of the servants had retired for the night. Mrs Hunter had long since been abed and Phoebe was standing fully dressed in her faded blue muslin by the window of the guest bedchamber. The night sky was clear, the moon waning, shrinking towards the crescent it would soon become, and the street lamps still burned, their orange glow lighting the darkness. The opportunity for which she had prayed and hoped and waited all of these weeks past was finally here. And the moment was bittersweet. She both dreaded and longed to hold the ring in her hand, to slip it into her pocket and walk away. Tomorrow she would wear the red shawl by the window and await the Messenger's instructions. And finally she would give him the ring. It would be done. She would be a thief and a traitor, and Sebastian and her papa would be safe.

She knew she could not stay as Mrs Hunter's companion after that, not when she had abused her trust, and not with all that lay between her and Sebastian. To face him knowing what she had done would be a torture she did not think she could bear. She would give notice, travel back to Glasgow, find some other way to survive. She had her health. She was fit and strong and not afraid to work, even as a maid if needs be.

With trembling fingers she struck the tinderbox and lit her candle, then quietly made her way to Sebastian's bedchamber.

The curtains had been closed so the room was in darkness. Her heart was beating in a fast thudding fury as the door clicked shut behind her. The room still held Sebastian's scent, his cologne and soap and the smell of the man himself. She stopped where she was, allowed herself to breathe in that familiar scent and felt her heart and her body tingle in response. She bit her lip as the sensations washed over her, and she heard again the whisper of his voice: *Do you not know I would lay down my life for you?* She forced herself to the task. Holding the candle aloft, she surveyed the dim shadowed room by its tiny flickering light.

It was not so large a room, indeed barely larger than the guest room in which she was ensconced and very much smaller than the lady's room in which Mrs Hunter now slept. She wondered why Sebastian had not taken the room designated for the master of the house. But maybe this had been his room as a boy, and maybe there were too many associations with the room that had been his father's. On the right-hand side of the room a large four-poster bed faced out from the wall. Even in the candlelight she could see the undisturbed bedding was a deep rich claret to match the curtains that covered the window. She let her gaze linger a moment there, imagining Hunter's dark head against the pillow, and his body naked beneath the sheets. She felt her heart swell with love for him.

There was a small bedside cabinet to the left of the bed and, on the right, a dressing screen. On the wall to her immediate left-hand side, the mahogany-framed fireplace was dark and empty. Ahead of her, on top of the chest of drawers, sat the same ebony wooden casket that she had searched at Blackloch, not hidden away this time but sitting proudly on display. She took a deep breath, moved forwards and set her candlestick down by its side.

The lid raised easily and without a single sound; she searched the top black velvet-lined tray. There was Sebastian's diamond cravat pin and his signet ring. She lifted the tray out and sat it down beside her candlestick while she returned to the casket. Beneath where the tray had lain were the two saucily painted snuffboxes she had seen before and Sebastian's gold pocket watch. But the wolf's-head ring was not there. She began to rake again through the items of the tray. And then she heard the noise. She glanced around and the diamond pin fell from her fingers as she gasped and backed away, for there in front of the dressing screen stood Sebastian.

'I thought that you had...' she whispered.

'I know what you thought, Phoebe,' he said softly as he came to stand before her.

'I...' There was nothing she could say, not a single explanation that would excuse her presence in his bedchamber, rummaging through his jewellery casket. She stared at him in horror, knowing what this meant for both him and her papa.

'You will not find it in there.' He slipped his fingers to the watch pocket of his waistcoat. At the end of the chain dangled not a watch, but the wolf's-head ring. He freed it from its anchoring and sat it upon his palm before holding his hand out before her. 'As I said, I keep it close to my heart.'

She looked from the ring to Sebastian's face. 'How could you know?'

'From the time you looked upon my father's portrait in the study at Blackloch I have known, Phoebe,' he said with such gentleness that it made her want to weep.

'I'm so sorry, Sebastian.' She placed her hands over her face, covering her eyes, knowing that all was lost.

'You may as well tell me about it now.'

'I cannot,' she whispered, frightened that if she did it would only make matters worse for both Sebastian and her father.

There was a small silence and then she heard him move, felt him take her in his arms. 'You know that I love you, Phoebe.'

'You must not love me.'

'It is too late,' he said softly against her ear. 'My heart is already yours as yours is mine. Do you deny it?'

She shook her head.

'Then tell me what this is all about.'

'Please do not ask me.' She touched her fingers to his mouth to stop his words.

He kissed them before drawing them away. 'You know I cannot do that.' And there was such a determination in his eyes that she feared her own resolve. 'What power has this man over you?'

But she just shook her head and spoke with a certainty she did not feel. 'I will not tell you, Sebastian, no matter how many times you ask me.'

'Then you leave me no alternative, Phoebe.' He stared down into her eyes. 'I will wear my father's ring to Lady Faversham's rout to-morrow. Flaunt it to whomsoever it is that is pulling your strings. And set the whisper that you have told me all.'

'No! Please Sebastian, I beg of you, do not!' Phoebe felt the blood drain from her face. She stared at him in horror and mounting panic.

'But I must, Phoebe…if you will not tell me.' And the look on his face was so adamant that she knew that he would do it.

'They will kill you, if you do,' she said in a voice that was all of despair. And she could not stop the tears that leaked from her eyes. 'And they will kill my papa, too.'

'They threatened your father.' Sebastian placed his hands upon her upper arms and she could see the concern and the anger on his face. 'I should have realised.'

She nodded.

'But he is in the Tolbooth.'

'They have already beaten him and I do not doubt their threats to take the matter further. They are very powerful, Sebastian. The gentleman who held me hooded yesterday told me he has eyes and ears everywhere.'

'Held you hooded?' She saw something change in his face. Saw the clenching of his jaw and the danger in his eyes. 'I think you had better start at the beginning, Phoebe, and tell me all.'

And Phoebe did. She told him of the Messenger at the Tolbooth and how at first the threats had been directed only against her papa. She told him of the letters and of her meeting in the carriage with the gentleman. And of the threats to Hunter…of what they were willing to do to have the ring. Of how she was to steal it and the means of communication. Every last little detail there was to tell.

'Now do you understand why I could not tell you?' she asked. 'I could not risk my father's life. I could not risk yours.' She took his face in her hands feeling the rasp of the beard stubble beneath her fingers. 'What is so special about this ring that it would cost two men their lives?'

'It should hold significance for me alone, Phoebe. My father entrusted it to me as he lay dying.'

'I know what the ring means to you, Sebastian, truly I do.' And her heart was aching with his pain. 'But you must let me give it to them.'

'Never.' The word was unyielding. 'With his last breath my father made me swear to guard the ring with my life. I will not break that oath, Phoebe.'

'Please! Your father would have understood.'

'I will not part with it.' There was such vehemence in his voice that she knew he would not be persuaded and all the fear and panic bubbled up to overflow.

'They will kill you, Sebastian! And they will kill my father, too! Do you not understand?'

He slipped the ring back into his pocket and took her hands in his own.

'Phoebe, trust me in this. I will find another way. Have no fear—for I will see that your father is safe. And I will discover who is behind this and deal with them for what they have done to you.'

He did not understand the power and reach of the men who

wanted the ring. She stared up into his eyes, felt a terrible despair roll through her and wept in earnest.

Hunter gently wiped away her tears and pulled her to him. 'Hush, my love, do not be afraid. All will be well.' He held her to him and stroked her hair and whispered words of reassurance. She cried until there were no more tears, cried until she felt empty, then just stood there in his arms, her face hidden against his chest.

Beneath her cheek she could feel the strong steady beat of his heart and, in the arms that surrounded her, the warmth of his love. He was everything to her: her heart, her love, her life. She raised her eyes to look up into his beloved face.

'I love you, Sebastian. I love you so very much.' She cupped his cheek with her hand, caressing the fine stubble.

'I love you, too, Phoebe.' He turned his face to kiss her fingers and then slid his hand against her scalp, holding her to stare down into her eyes, and there was such love and absolute integrity in his gaze that she could not doubt the truth of it.

Sebastian reached her mouth to his and kissed her with such tenderness. His hands trailed down over her arms to take her hands in his, entwining their fingers as surely as their hearts were entwined.

'You were always my love, Phoebe,' he whispered. 'And you always will be.' And he kissed her again, slowly, meaningfully, as if to substantiate the words of his promise. They kissed and in their kiss there was a merging of their hearts, a merging of their souls. They kissed and she did not let herself think of the danger and darkness and hopelessness that surrounded them. She did not look beyond to all that lay ahead. She loved him. She loved him, and she knew there would only ever be this one night.

All of her joy was in that kiss, and all of her sorrow. All of her passion and despair. Everything she had found and everything she would lose. And as the flame that had burned between them always flared and raged she laid her heart open to its blaze.

He kissed her eyelids, her cheeks, the line of her jaw, capturing her hands to the small of her back and holding them there to support her as he arched her to him. Her head lolled back, exposing her neck all the more to his mouth. He trailed kisses all the way down her throat, nuzzling the hollow in its base, lapping against her, tasting her, kissing her until her breasts were straining against the blue muslin, aching for his touch, longing for it. His lips slid lower over her décolletage, his breath hot and moist through the muslin.

She squirmed, willing him to mouth her breasts, but Sebastian followed back the same route, tilting her upright, claiming her mouth again with his own. He freed her hands and slid his fingers up her back, pulling her to him, deepening the kiss to share his very soul. She knew his gift, knew her life would never be the same again and she clung to him, until at last the kiss ended and they stood there staring into each other's eyes in the soft shadowed candlelight.

'Phoebe.' His voice was strained with emotion.

'Yes,' she said and reached her fingers to stroke down his jawline, feeling the rasp of his beard stubble all the way down to his chin, all the way to dip the tip of one finger into the cleft that nestled there. 'Please, Sebastian,' she whispered; looking up into the dark intensity of his eyes, she grasped his chin and touched her tongue to the cleft, probing it gently, kissing it. She felt the tremor that ran through him and slid her fingers lower, down over the abrasive skin of his neck, over the lump of his Adam's apple and the stiff collar of his shirt. The knot of his cravat parted easily enough and the linen strip fluttered to land forgotten on the floor. Her hands were trembling as she unfastened the collar of his shirt and felt it fall away as she leaned in to touch her mouth to the hollow of his throat, just as he had done to her. Beneath her lips she could feel the fast hard thrum of his pulse.

Sebastian's touch was so light against her back she did not realise that he had unbuttoned her bodice until the dress gaped away from her breast and began to slide from her shoulders. He eased it down her arms and she helped him until the muslin slid with a soft rush to pool around her ankles. One tug of a lace and the white froth of her petticoats tumbled to the same fate. His eyes glittered and smouldered in the flicker of the candlelight as their gaze meandered from her legs, over her shift, all the way up to her stays and the tops of her breasts that it exposed.

'You are beautiful, Phoebe,' he murmured.

And her heart leapt to hear the words even as it was tinged with the shadow of sadness. The kiss was deeper now, giving all the more, worshipping her with the slide of his lips, the tease of his tongue, the graze of his teeth. His hands caressed her hips as he pulled her snug to him so that she felt the press of him low against her belly. She wanted him so much, all of his love, all that could be between them. It felt as they were made to be together, that she had been waiting only for him all of those long lonely years. He completed her. He was the other half of herself. And she told him so in her kiss.

Hunter felt the tremble of her fingers as they struggled with the buttons of his waistcoat and he thought that he had never known such love. It filled his heart to overflowing. Nothing in his life had been right until he found Phoebe. Nothing could ever be right without her. She was his destiny, and part of him had known it from the very first moment their eyes met. He worked the buttons open for her and felt the slide of her hands over the lawn of his shirt, skimming the muscle that lay beneath, and his manhood throbbed for her, and his heart ached for her. And all that he had ever longed for in his life was the woman before him.

'Phoebe,' he whispered, and her eyes were dark and filled with such love and passion. 'Phoebe,' he said, and there were no words to express what he felt, the enormity of it, the towering brilliant force of it. He knew only one way to show her how much he needed her, how very much he loved her.

He stripped off his tailcoat, let his waistcoat fall away to the floor.

His shirt slipped easily over his head so that his chest was bared to her and he shivered with the sweet caress of her fingers against his naked skin. And then he took her in his arms once more and pressed kisses to her forehead, her eyelids, her cheeks and ear.

'My love,' he said as he tongued the soft sweet lobe of her ear. 'My sweet love', as his teeth grazed gently against her throat and followed round to taste the skin at the nape of her neck.

One by one he plucked the pins from her hair, placing them in a pile beside her candle. He revelled in the loosening of that heavy auburn coil, unwinding it to hang loose against her shoulders; slid his hands into its soft length, pressed his nose to it, inhaling its scent. He kissed all the way down those lengths, his hands anchoring around her waist as his mouth caressed the pale mounds of her breasts that peeped from her stays. A soft moan escaped her and in it he heard both her pleasure and her need.

She moaned again as his mouth left her; when he looked in her eyes they were dark and dazed with desire. 'Sebastian,' she pleaded as he turned her away from him.

But he reassured her with soft whispers nuzzled against the edge of her shoulder. Still she did not understand, not until his fingers touched to the laces of her stays. He schooled himself to patience, knowing that she was a virgin, knowing how very much he wanted to pleasure her, for this to be the most wonderful experience of her life. His fingers were shaking as he worked his way slowly, methodically down, unlacing the ribbon one stretch at a time, watching the stiff-boned underwear temptingly slacken and teasingly gape until at last it tumbled to land with a thud on the rug.

She turned to face him and he could see the outline of her breasts through the thin worn material of her shift. And she came into his arms and he kissed her, questing gently at first, then deepening the kiss as he felt the measure of her desire. He rejoiced in the feel of her body, stroking her, touching her to stoke her pleasure all the higher. Beneath his hands her breasts were firm, her nipples nosing at his palms. He rolled their pebbled tips between his thumb and fingers, tugging at them gently until she was gasping out loud.

Hunter knelt before the woman he loved, circled her waist with his arms and then he took one breast into his mouth. Her moan was low and deep and guttural. He kissed her slowly and sensually, flicking his tongue against her hardened nub. She gasped and quivered with the force of sensation, threading her fingers through his hair, and clasping his head to her as if she would suckle him. He licked her, sucked her, mouthed her, caressing her hips as he did so. And everywhere his mouth had been the cotton of her shift clung tight and translucent to the bead of her nipple.

'Phoebe,' he groaned, knowing both torture and delight. He was shaking with his own need for her, his manhood so aroused and aching for release that the pain throbbed with an escalating intensity through his body. Yet he wanted her to be ready. He wanted her pleasure at the moment of their coupling to obscure her pain.

He reached for the ribbon of her shift and the soft worn material slid off her shoulders and down her arms, catching on her nipples before slipping all the way down her legs. She stepped out from it, naked save for her stockings and shoes.

'Phoebe,' he whispered as his mouth slid kisses against her stomach, her abdomen, and lower still until his mouth teased over the auburn triangle of hair between her legs.

'Sebastian,' she gasped and dug her fingers into the muscle of his shoulders.

He gazed up from where he knelt, his eyes sweeping over her with all of the fierce possession and adoration that was in his soul.

'You are mine, Phoebe, now and for ever.' And never taking his eyes from where they locked with hers he stroked his hands against her ankles. 'Just as I am yours.'

'Yes,' she whispered, as his fingers began to edge slowly up the inner edge of her stockings. His caress was soft, the lightest trail of his fingers against the silk, against her calf, over her knee and up farther to the pale blue ribbons of her garters tied. She thought he would untie the bow and let the stockings slide down her legs, but he left them intact, kissing each ribbon so that she felt the warmth of his breath against the bare skin of her thigh as he untied the bows and let the stockings slide down her legs.

His hands stroked her hips, cupping her buttocks, his eyes clinging to hers as he moved his mouth to meet what lay between her legs.

'Sebastian!' she gasped, but he did not release her, just worked magic on that most intimate and secret of places, until she was clutching his head to her, pulling his hair, crying out as pleasure exploded throughout her and her body convulsed and throbbed and her legs were so weak that she would have collapsed had he not stood up and swept her up into his arms.

He carried her to the bed and laid her down on the sheets.

She watched while he stripped off the rest of his clothes, stared at his nakedness, at his strength and his beauty, at a body that was so different in every way from her own. Such pale white skin, such hard defined muscle in his arms and shoulders, abdomen and thighs. His manhood was long and thick and rigid and the sight of it sent a pulsing ache through her woman's core.

He covered her with his body and kissed her, his tongue penetrating her mouth in thrusting strokes that had her gasping and pressing her hips to him, and arching to drive her breasts against the granite of his chest. And then his fingers played upon her where his mouth had worked such magic, where she was wet and throbbing for him, her body pleading its invitation. She shuddered her pleasure again, gasping, reeling, floating, so that she barely noticed the pain amidst the shimmering ecstasy as his manhood pierced her. Two bodies became one.

She clung to him as he held her and kissed her mouth and stroked her face. And when he moved, slowly at first, sliding so gently, she knew that this was their journey, their place, the nearing of their final destination. He moved and she met each driving stroke of his body, pulling him into her all the deeper, needing this union, wanting this man. They moved together in what was always meant to be between them. Walking, then running. Running to reach the place that each could only find with the other. Glorying in their union. Striving for the end, yet prolonging the journey in every way that they could. Until he spilled his seed within her and she was truly his and he was truly hers. A sharing of bodies. A communion of souls. A merging of hearts and minds and beings. And nothing would ever be the same again.

He eased down to lie by her side, breathless, reeling from the wonder of her and the love and passion that was between them. His mouth touched hers with all the reverence and joy and love that he felt. She snuggled against him and he wrapped her in his arms, knowing he would protect her from all the world. Phoebe Allardyce, the woman he would make his wife.

Lying there in the darkness of the night and the warmth of his arms, Phoebe wished she could stop time and make this perfect night last for ever. But the hours were passing too quickly and her mind dreaded what the morning would bring. Sebastian turned in his sleep and the moonlight revealed his pale stark handsome features. He looked so peaceful, vulnerable almost, and her heart welled with love for him.

She knew what the men would do to him, for all his strength and resolution; they were many and he was but one man. And it seemed in the quietness of the night she heard again the whisper of his words.

Do you not know I would lay down my life for you?

And she would lay down hers for him. The thought came unbidden, a quiet certainty that it seemed had never not been there. With it came the knowledge that she could not let them harm him. She could not risk his life. And in that moment Phoebe knew that there was more than one way to lay down a life.

Her heart shrivelled at the thought of what she must do and how much it would hurt him. To think of that hurt was almost unbearable, but better that than what the men would do to him. To lose his love and gain his hatred was a price she would pay for a lifetime to save him.

'Phoebe?' he murmured, half-waking as she stole from beneath the sheets.

'It will soon be dawn and I must not be found in your bed,' she whispered. She brushed a kiss against his lips and the pain squeezed all the tighter in her heart. 'Go back to sleep, Sebastian. I love you. Remember that, whatever should happen.'

'I love you, too, Phoebe,' he said and caught her hand in his own as if to keep her with him. She squeezed it gently, one last touch to last a lifetime, before releasing him. Then she moved quietly through the darkness to where their clothing lay upon the floor.

Chapter Eighteen

Hunter woke in a shaft of early autumn sunshine. He felt bathed in warmth and happiness. He could still smell the scent of Phoebe upon his skin, could almost still feel the softness of her body pressed to his. She was his woman in truth, his one true love. The knowledge made his heart glow and his face smile. And as he lay there a plan formed in his head of how to deal with the men who had blackmailed her.

It involved a certain amount of risk and ingenuity, but Hunter knew it would work. It would protect Phoebe and her father, and flush out the bastards who would steal his father's ring. And he wondered again why anyone else would want the ring so very badly. Not that they had a chance in hell of taking it from him.

The note made no noise as it slipped beneath his door. Hunter saw it and thought again of Phoebe. He smiled and rose to fetch it. Once all this was done and Phoebe was safe, then he would speak to his mother.

Only his given name was written on the outside of the folded paper and the ink smeared beneath his fingers so he knew that she had only just written it and passed it to him with her very own hand. He smiled again at the intimacy of it and at the love they shared, and opened the note to read her secret message.

There were only two words. Two words, and the smile wiped from his face and the dread and the disbelief churned in his stomach. *Forgive me.* So black and stark against the pale paper sheet.

His gaze moved to the pile of abandoned clothing, now devoid of all trace of Phoebe, and his blood ran cold with premonition.

The chain coiled alone in the pocket of his waistcoat. He did not need to search anywhere else to know that the ring was gone. Her words of the night whispered again in his head and he understood their meaning and that last breath of a kiss.

Hunter pulled on his breeches and stormed from the room.

Her bedchamber was empty, just as he had known it would be.

He ran down the stairs, yelling her name.

A maid gave a yelp at the sight of him and scurried away, but Trenton appeared in the hallway.

'Miss Allardyce went out five minutes ago, sir.'

Hunter opened the front door and stepped outside to scan the street. There was no sign of her.

He saw the embarrassment in his butler's face and in his urgency to find her he did not care if the whole world knew he had spent the night loving her.

'Where did she go?' he barked the question.

Trenton shook his head. 'She didn't say where, just that she was going out for a walk.'

'Did she receive any messages this morning?'

'Yes, sir. A letter was delivered for her not ten minutes since. The lad said it was urgent. I took it up to her myself.'

Hunter gave a nod. 'Have Ajax saddled and brought round to the front.' And then he took the stairs two at a time back to her room.

The cupboards and drawers were empty and her travelling bag, the same one mauled by the highwaymen on a moor so long ago, sat fully packed by the foot of the bed. Hunter stood and scanned the room.

The smell of burning hung in the air, yet no fire had been lit. He glanced over at the blackened empty fireplace, then moved closer and saw the paper upon the grate. In her haste to leave she had not stayed to watch its burning. The familiar writing was charred, but still readable.

The corner of Red Lion Street with Paternoster Row at Spitalfields Market. Come by hackney carriage immediately and wear the red shawl. Tie the ring inside a white handkerchief and hold it in your hand.

Five minutes later Hunter was dressed and galloping Ajax down the street. She had a fifteen-minute start on him, but he knew the shortcuts that a hackney carriage could not take, and he knew he could reach Spitalfields first. His face was grim with determination and he spurred his horse all the faster.

Phoebe did not look out at the passing buildings, but kept her eyes upon the white-handkerchief pouch clutched so tightly within her hand. The carriage rumbled and lurched over the road, taking her ever closer to Spitalfields. The day was mild and the red woollen shawl was wrapped around her shoulders, but Phoebe was so cold her teeth chattered from it. She felt numb, frozen, sick with the knowledge of what she was doing. And yet not once did she contemplate turning back. It had to be done, to save Sebastian and to save her father.

She dreaded the moment the betrayal would be complete, and she dreaded even more returning to Grosvenor Street to face Sebastian and all that would stand where love had been. Wrath and hurt and contempt. And she would not blame him, not one little bit, not when she had taken everything of him and betrayed him.

She glanced down at the faded blue muslin of her skirt and she remembered the very first time she had met Sebastian, when he had rescued her from the highwaymen on the moor. All of what was between them had been there from the moment she had looked up into his eyes; she just had not known it.

She loved him. She loved him enough to betray him. And the price of her treachery was her own heart.

From his vantage point beneath the portico of Christ Church, Hunter had a clear view of the junction between Red Lion Street and Paternoster Row. Thursday was market day at Spitalfields and despite the early hour the market place was busy and the streets thronged with people. The villains had chosen well, he thought. No one would notice what was happening, and even if they did they would not care.

This was the East End and, although it had once been the affluent quarters of the Huguenot silk weavers, the area had fallen on hard times so that the faces Hunter saw milling around the market were sharp-eyed and lean-cheeked and rough, and he feared all the more for Phoebe. He could hear the cries of the hawkers and stallholders advertising the bargains and quality to be had. Fruit and vegetables, from blackberries and apples to potatoes and lettuce. Carts and gigs and hackney carriages lined the roads, and there were no sweepers here so the horses had left their business free and plenty afoot. He stayed hidden by the church's great stone columns and he watched and waited and a few minutes later saw the woman he loved step out of the hackney carriage.

The scarlet shawl marked her amidst the dark drabness all around. Something of her stance suggested a woman going to her doom, something of her very stillness was all speaking and the pallor of her face was stark against the brightness of the shawl. Hunter slipped from his hiding place and made his way through the crowd.

He threaded his way steadily closer, never once losing sight of the red shawl. He had almost reached her when he saw the figure move behind her, a fair-haired man with his cap pulled down low over his eyes—the same man he had last seen outside the Tolbooth in Glasgow.

He was so close and yet the throng of people between them barred his way, and he knew he would not reach her in time.

'Phoebe!' he shouted, 'Do not do it!' He saw her face turn to him, saw her shock and her anguish.

'Sebastian!' She began to move towards him just as the man struck, snatching the white handkerchief from her hand.

Phoebe stared in disbelief and wondered for a moment if Sebastian were real or just a figment of her imagination.

She had never seen his eyes look so dark or his face so white with fury. He grabbed hold of her, staring down at her and there was such darkness, such danger and intensity about him to raze all else in its path. Phoebe trembled at the promise she saw in his eyes.

'Are you all right?'

She nodded, not trusting herself to speak.

'Take a carriage home and wait for me there. And do not dare run away from me, Phoebe Allardyce.' He pressed his purse into her hands and then sped off in pursuit of the Messenger.

The man knocked people flying as he fled from Hunter, cutting a swathe through the crowd to reach the road where he dodged through the mêlée of carriages and carts. Hunter did not hesitate, running between the carriages, chasing down his quarry. He ran with a cold determination that made his legs pump all the faster. The man glanced back over his shoulder and Hunter knew the villain was tiring. He pressed on harder. Another glance back and this time it cost the man his footing. The bastard slid in a pile of horse dung and almost fell, before catching his balance and running on. A third glance and Hunter caught him as he ducked into the alleyway.

The man bounced against the brick of the building as Hunter's punch landed hard against the villain's jaw.

'You bastard!' Hunter snarled and made to move in.

But the man cowered away and as he did so Hunter felt a flash of recognition as if he knew this man from somewhere, but could not place him. 'Don't hurt me! Please! Just take it...' the coward pleaded and threw the small white parcel.

Hunter felt the hardness of metal as he caught it, but he had to be sure. He ripped through the cotton of Phoebe's handkerchief and there inside, with its emerald eyes looking up at him, was his father's wolf's-head ring.

He glanced up to see the man sloping away. Their eyes met and the man sprang to action and ran for his life.

Hunter tucked the ring safely away and then started after him.

The man sped from the alley, turning left to nip out onto the street just before a procession of carts and a surge in the crowd.

Hunter cursed, then realised that the villain was heading west towards Bishopsgate and for the first time in a year Hunter was glad of his rakish past, of his misspent nights in the low-life gaming dens of Spitalfields and Whitechapel. He knew the lanes round here like the back of his hand. He slipped into Duke Street and then cut along Artillery Lane, taking a short cut to bring him out on Bishopsgate only twenty yards behind the man who was no longer running, but hurrying. Hunter did not close the distance, just stayed amidst the crowd and followed. And as the market crowd thinned and they entered the banking area of London, Hunter knew the man would lead him to whoever was behind this villainy.

The man hurried on until he came to a quiet leafy street lined with a few large houses, a street down which Hunter had never travelled. Hunter hung back, knowing that in the emptiness the man would be sure to see him if he followed too close, then used the ancient sycamores that lined the road as cover to close the distance.

The man hesitated outside the largest of the houses and, with a furtive glance around him, ran up the front steps and disappeared inside the opened door. Upon a black stone plaque on its wall the words *Obsidian House* had been carved and beneath the words were the same symbols that were carved into the lintels above the front doors of both Blackloch and his town house in Grosvenor Street. And Hunter felt the stirring of something dark.

Only once the man was inside the house did he follow. The main doors stood open, caught back and secured with a hook. There was a small porch area followed by a set of glass interior doors that led into the hallway. The glass doors were closed, but Hunter was up the stairs and his back pressed flat against the wall at the edge of the outer doors that he might inch his head round and gain a view.

Inside in the hallway, the man was talking to a gentleman. And now Hunter knew why the fair-haired villain's face had seemed so vaguely familiar. He was a footman. And the gentleman at his side was his master. A gentleman Hunter knew very well. A gentleman Hunter had considered a friend: James Edingham, Viscount Bullford.

There were more men appearing in the hallway now. Men that Hunter or his father had counted friends. Rich men, powerful men. A high court judge, an archbishop, a member of the cabinet, even a member of the royal family. A duke clapped his hand against Bullford's back in a gesture of friendship. And they began filing down a corridor that led straight ahead.

They were smiling. And they were all of them wearing long black ceremonial robes identical to that of the man in the painting in Hunter's bedchamber at Blackloch.

His eyes dropped from the receding black figures to the floor of the porch. Not tiled or wooden, but a mosaic and depicting the same hunting scene from classical antiquity as was carved into the stone fireplace of his study in his town house.

Hunter saw the footmen that came to close the outer doors. He dodged back out of the way and jumped down behind the bushes that grew in the narrow soil strips on either side of the house. Once the doors were closed he made his way back to Grosvenor Street.

Phoebe was not in her room.

He glanced down at the travelling bag that still sat by the bed and the sudden thought struck him that maybe the footman had had an accomplice waiting there to snatch her from Spitalfields. His stomach dipped with the dread of it.

'Did Miss Allardyce return safely from her morning sojourn?'

Trenton cleared his throat 'Indeed, sir, but she has gone out again on an errand for Mrs Hunter some fifteen minutes ago.'

'An errand?' Hunter frowned.

'Mrs Hunter is suffering from a headache. I believe she dispatched Miss Allardyce to purchase a herbal remedy.'

'From where?'

'I do not know, sir.'

And neither did his mother.

'Inform me immediately that she returns,' he instructed Trenton, and aside from that there was little that Hunter could do, despite all his unease.

He went to his study to wait, blaming himself for not guarding her better, chiding himself for not realising that she would steal the ring to save him.

Phoebe made her purchase of feverfew and betony and had just left the apothecary shop when she was assailed by a familiar voice.

'I say, Miss Allardyce, how nice to see you on this glorious morning.'

Phoebe felt her heart sink. She was in no fit state for conversation.

Her stomach was churning with dread at the thought of what the villains might have done to Hunter. Hunter was tall and strong and fast and she did not doubt that he could best any man, but what chance had he against a pistol or a knife? She would not rest until he had returned, despite all that would ensue. She hid her worries and glanced up to see Lord Bullford's coach stopped by the side of the road and the gentleman himself emerging to stand before her on the footpath.

'Good morning, Lord Bullford,' she said politely and forced a smile to her face.

'You are out and about early this morning, Miss Allardyce...' he glanced around the street paying special attention to the apothecary shop from which she had just emerged '...and without Mrs Hunter?' His expression held all the kind friendliness that it ever had.

'Indeed, sir. I am afraid Mrs Hunter is much distressed with a headache. It is the reason for my journey; I have come to fetch a prescription to relieve her pain.'

'Oh dear,' murmured Lord Bullford with his brow creased in concern. 'Poor Mrs H., how she suffers with her head.'

'Indeed,' said Phoebe. 'Which is why, sir, I must beg your leave and return immediately to Grosvenor Street.'

'Of course.' Lord Bullford nodded. 'But I have a better idea. Please, Miss Allardyce, allow me to convey you home in my coach.'

'Your offer is very kind, my lord, but I should not.' She smiled in earnest to soften her refusal.

'By coach the journey will take but a few minutes. On foot, I imagine a great deal longer. And you did say that Mrs H. is quite unwell... I thought only to relieve the lady's discomfort. But if you would rather walk...'

Phoebe felt a pang of guilt at Bullford's gentle reproach. 'Perhaps you are right, sir.'

'I will have you at Grosvenor Street in no time at all to tend the poor lady.' He smiled, and Phoebe was reassured. He held out his hand and helped her climb up into his coach, and the door slammed shut behind them.

Chapter Nineteen

Hunter stood before the fireplace, thinking of Phoebe. If anything had happened to her… And as he worried, his eye caught the carving on the stone beneath the mantel.

A hunter with a great black dog pursuing evil-eyed foxes and boars and ferrets. It was a picture that had fascinated Hunter since he was a child. He remembered coming to this house and tracing his fingers against each of the figures of the scenes. He had always thought that lone huntsman astride his horse had been hunting with his dog, but now that he had seen the defined colourful mosaic in Obsidian House he could see that the dog was not a dog at all, but a wolf. And he could see, too, that there was something missing from this carving, a small detail that had been clear in the background of the tiled mosaic version.

Lurking amidst the trees of the forest, the backdrop against which the hunter rode, were six wolves' faces—Hunter knew there were six because it had been his habit to count them as a child. In the mosaic there had been seven. Hunter looked where the seventh should have been on the stone carving, and there in its place, clear now that he was looking for it, was a headless wolf.

And the strangest thought occurred to Hunter. From his pocket he withdrew the wolf's-head ring, and the wolf seemed to look up at him, its emerald eyes sparkling in the morning sunlight. Hunter pressed the silver wolf's head into the hollow where the wolf's head on the carving should have been, and turned, and one of the long wooden panels in the mahogany wall of his study popped open. Behind the hidden door was a room all in darkness. Hunter lit a candle and stepped into the secret room.

The candlelight showed a long narrow room empty save for four Holland-covered paintings that hung upon the wall and a large chest in the corner. Hunter pulled the holland cover from the closest painting. The cream linen slid silently onto the floor to reveal his father staring out from the canvas at him. In the portrait his father's hair was as dark as Hunter's and his face only a little lined. He was dressed in the same long black ceremonial robe that Bullford and the men had worn and on his finger was the wolf's-head ring. And Hunter suddenly knew that his father was the 'monk' in the picture at Blackloch. His gaze dropped to read the plaque fitted to the bottom of the gilt frame—*Mr Edward Hunter, Master of the Order of the Wolf.*

The other three paintings showed Hunter's grandfather, great-grandfather and great-great-grandfather; all three men were garbed in the same black robes and each wore the same wolf's-head ring upon their fingers.

Hunter's heart was thudding as he turned to the chest, and his hands shook as he found the letter addressed to *My Son, Sebastian Hunter.* The writing was that of his father, the seal that of his father's signet ring. He broke the seal, unfolded the paper and began to read.

7th September, 1809
My dearest son
　If you are reading this letter then I am gone from this world to meet my maker, and you have found yourself on the path to the Order.
　Firstly let me say that I love you and have always loved

you and been proud of you as my son, no matter the disagree-ments that we have had. You are a young man, reckless and wild as young men are wont to be; as I myself once was. It is a father's duty to prepare his son, to guide and nurture and train him for the path that lies ahead. And if I have been harsh and hard with you, Sebastian, then it has only ever been with this in mind. As a Hunter your path is already mapped and it is not an easy one.

I am Master of the Order of the Wolf, a secret society founded by your great-great-grandfather in accordance with the instruction of King George II for the good of all Britain, her people and her king, just as my father was master before me, and his father before him...and just as it is your destiny to be. To the Hunters of our line this is the duty to which we are born and must devote our life's work.

Your great-great-grandfather foiled a plot being hatched amongst the nobles against the king and was rewarded with a fortune to rival that of the wealthiest in the land and the honour of establishing and leading this society. The Order exists to work secretly in the shadows to safeguard this great country and her line of monarchs, to fight against tyranny and foreign invasion, injustice and dishonour. We are the hunters that seek out the traitors within. We are the wolves that slay the guilty. There is meaning in our name, indeed, my son.

Forgive me for having deferred bringing you into the Order for so long, but such is the responsibility that I deemed it crit-ical to wait until you had sown your wild oats and calmed your wild ways. And now that I am gone you must find your own way in. But remember always that no man who is not a member may know of the order's existence and live, and this rule is true for you, too, Sebastian.

By virtue of the fact you are reading this then I have al-ready given into your keeping the wolf's-head ring and with

this letter I name you my heir and successor. Whosoever wears
the ring is Master of the Order, so guard it well.

All that you need know of the Order is written in the book
you will find with this letter.

May you fulfil the destiny that is given you as a Hunter.
God bless you, my son.
Your loving father,
Edward Hunter

Hunter wept as he read the words his father had penned only two months before his death. He wept because written in that letter were the words his father had never spoken to him in life—that he loved him, that he was proud of him. He lifted the ancient brown calf-leather-bound book from the chest, and leafed through its pages.

His father was right, everything he needed to know was there. The history and inception of the society, its rules, its purpose, the methods of its operation, initiation ceremonies and trials for new members and much more. At the back of the book were pages and pages of names of men who had been, and still were, members of the Order. The last name entered on the list, written in his father's own hand, made his heart skip a beat, for it was Hunter's own. He took a deep breath, and scanned the list. Linwood was there, marked as an office bearer, which explained his wolf's-head cane, and the viscount's father was listed, too. Francis Edingham, the Marquis of Willaston, Bullford's father, was described as the deputy master. Bullford's name was not amongst them, but Hunter supposed that no one in the Order had had access to the book to add any new members since his father's death.

Hunter knew now why they wanted the ring and he had an inkling why it was Bullford who had been given the task. He took the neatly folded black robes from the chest and then moved back out of the dark chill of the secret room to the sunlit study.

A knock sounded at the study door. He snuffed the candle and, retrieving the ring, slid it onto his finger. The panel pressed easily back into place, the seam of its outline invisible against the rest of the ornate panelling that surrounded it. Then Hunter opened the study door to find Trenton waiting there, a single letter lying upon the silver salver.

'A letter has just been delivered for you, sir. The boy who brought it said it was for your most urgent attention.'

Hunter felt his jaw tense as he lifted the letter and saw his name upon it, for it was penned in the same disguised hand that had been used in all of Bullford's letters to Phoebe. He ripped it open and read the unsigned contents.

If you wish the safe return of Miss Allardyce, then you will leave your father's wolf's-head ring on the gravestone of Abigail Murton in the churchyard of Christ Church, Spitalfields, this afternoon at two o'clock.

He screwed the paper into a ball and threw it onto the grate in the fireplace. Then he readied his pistols, slipped them into his pockets and rang the bell for Trenton.

Phoebe woke to find herself lying in a dark room. Her wrists had been tied behind her back and her ankles bound together and there was a gag around her mouth. She could hear nothing and see nothing; she remembered the carriage and Lord Bullford removing a small brown bottle from his pocket to drip some of its foul-smelling liquid onto his handkerchief. The warning bells had been sounding in her head, not so much at what he was doing, but at the strange expression upon his face.

She heard his words again: *I am sorry, Miss Allardyce, if only you had done as we asked.* And there had been genuine regret within his eyes.

And she had known, then, who it was that had organised the break-ins in Mrs Hunter's Glasgow town house and at Blackloch, and who had sent his Messenger to threaten her papa.

'You!' she whispered in disbelief and tried to flee, but Bullford was across the carriage and pressing the foul-reeking cloth to her nose and mouth. The vapour of it choked her and burned her throat and lungs, and that terrible suffocating sensation was the last that she remembered.

She shifted, trying to ease her body into a more comfortable position.

'You are back with us again, Miss Allardyce.' The voice was not that of Bullford, but it was one she recognised. This man, whoever he was, was the same one who had held her hooded within his coach.

A flint struck against a tinderbox and she saw the spark catch to the tinder and the flame light a candle. The small flickering light seemed too bright against the darkness and she narrowed her eyes and peered through the blackness to see the identity of the man to whom Bullford had delivered her.

There were two men standing looking down at where she lay, but even if the room had been fully lit she would not have known their identities for both men were dressed in plain long black robes, the hoods of which had been pulled up over the heads to leave their faces hidden in shadow.

The stouter man gestured to the other and his associate bent down and released the gag from her mouth, and as he moved she thought she caught a glimpse of a narrow face and shifty grey eyes and she was sure that he was the Messenger.

'Untie me, sir,' she demanded.

'I am afraid we will be keeping you safely trussed for now, my dear,' said the gentleman from the carriage and she realised with a shiver that his voice was not so dissimilar to Bullford's. There was a small silence as he stepped closer to loom over her in the darkness. 'You told Hunter, did you not, Miss Allardyce? Despite all our warnings.'

'No,' she lied. 'I do not know how he came to be in Spitalfields.'

That, at least, was the truth. 'He knows nothing of any of this, I swear it.' She did not know how Sebastian had found her at the marketplace, but she knew with all her heart that she must protect both him and her papa.

The gentleman, whose face remained hidden by the folds of his cowl, gave a small laugh and clapped his hands together in mock applause. 'Very impressive, my dear, but I seem to recall at our last meeting how very anxious you were to protect Mr Hunter from harm.'

'The gentleman is my employer's son,' she countered. 'His welfare affects Mrs Hunter and therefore also, albeit indirectly, myself. I would not see Mrs Hunter's sensibilities distressed.'

'How solicitous of you, Miss Allardyce. If it is not too indelicate of me to say, the gentleman may be your employer's son, but he has engaged your affection, Miss Allardyce, a feeling which, if I am not mistaken, is reciprocated.'

'You are very much mistaken, sir!' she exclaimed, frightened of where this was leading and what it would mean for Sebastian.

'For your own sake, Miss Allardyce, you had better hope that I am not.' There was a chill in his voice as he uttered the soft words.

Her blood ran cold. 'My papa?'

'Your papa remains unharmed and blissfully oblivious to all.' He reached down and stroked a finger against her cheek. 'But what will Hunter give to save the life of the woman he loves?'

She jerked her face away from his touch and stared up at him with defiance. 'He will give you nothing!' It was the truth. Sebastian would not part with the ring even when he had loved her and she had no doubt what his feelings were for her now. A shiver rippled through her at the memory of his face in the marketplace. Whatever Sebastian did, he would not give them the ring.

'Oh, no, my dear Miss Allardyce. I very much suspect he will give us exactly what we want.' She heard the smile in his voice.

'Had we known Hunter would develop such a *tendre* for you, it would have made matters so much easier for us.'

'And if he does not give you the ring?' Her heart was filled with fear and none of it was for herself.

'Let us just hope, for your sake, my dear, that he does.' And then he gestured to Messenger, who knelt down and fixed the gag in place across her mouth.

Then the two black-robed men were gone, taking the candle with them and leaving Phoebe alone in the darkness.

'Lord Bullford is not at home,' the footman said to Hunter, who was standing upon the steps of Bullford's father's house in Henrietta Street.

'Perhaps you wish to reconsider that reply.' Hunter slipped a pistol from his pocket and held it against the footman's ribs. He had seen the shadowy figure of Bullford outlined against the library window as he called the lad over to hold Ajax.

The footman gave a nod and showed him in to the hall where he pointed silently at the library door before hurrying back down beneath stairs.

Bullford was loitering at the side of the window when Hunter opened the library door and stepped inside.

Bullford took one look at Hunter and the pistol in his hand and the colour drained from his face.

'Hunter, old man,' he tried to bluff, 'what on earth are you doing here and with a pistol at the ready?'

But Hunter had no time for games. 'Where is she, Bullford?'

'I have no idea what you are talking about, old man.'

'Then you had better start thinking and fast.' Hunter aimed the barrel of the pistol at Bullford and began to close the space between them.

Bullford backed away, stumbling in the process, but righted himself to keep edging away.

'You blackmailed her, terrorised her, threatened her father.'

'It was not supposed to be like that.' Bullford shook his head. 'We did not think for a minute that Miss Allardyce would not accept the bribe. There are not many women who would have walked away from two thousand pounds. We had made no provision for it. Charles, m'father's footman, made the threat out of desperation. They were just empty words uttered on the spot. We never would have hurt Sir Henry.'

'But you did hurt him. When Miss Allardyce visited him that day he had been beaten.'

'I swear upon my very life, Hunter, that no harm came to her father by our hands. Charles did not understand Miss Allardyce's sudden change of heart when she emerged from the visit that day, but he was not about to look a gift horse in the mouth and start asking questions.'

'So you continued to torture her with threats to her father's safety?'

'I am sorry, Hunter, truly I am. But I needed the ring.'

'Why was acquiring the ring your responsibility?'

Bullford shook his head. 'I cannot tell you, Hunter. I am sworn to secrecy on pain of death.'

'I know all about the Order of the Wolf, so start talking, Bullford.'

Bullford's eyes widened; he made to step back farther, but there was nowhere left to go. He shrank against the library wall and looked as if he had just seen a ghost.

'Let me guess,' said Hunter. 'Part of your initiation ceremony?'

Bullford nodded and something of the fight went out of him. 'My father brought me into the society close to the end of last year.'

'Just after my father's death, if I am not mistaken.'

Bullford nodded again. 'My initiation is not complete until I have passed the task I have been set. I cannot become a full member until I bring them the ring.'

'And Miss Allardyce?'

'It was not my idea, please believe me, Hunter. They made me do it, but I swear she is unharmed.'

'Where is she being held?'

'Cannot tell you, old man.' The sweat was glistening on Bullford's temple and upper lip and chin.

Hunter experienced the urge to pistol whip Bullford's face and probably would have, had he not learned his father's final harsh lesson.

Instead, he leaned over Bullford and said, 'Ten months ago I learned that in the end there is always a reckoning for one's actions. Your task is the reason for Miss Allardyce's predicament; it was *your* task and thus *your* responsibility. You may not have envisaged the way she would be used, but you went along with it readily enough. And do not delude yourself for a minute that you are but a bystander swept along with events. This is no game, James. Do you honestly think I will let you play with the life of the woman I love and walk away scot-free?

'The Order was established by men of integrity to recruit men of integrity who would be the moral compass when those around were lost. It is a great responsibility and the tasks set were meant to test a man's mettle. So I give you the chance, Bullford, that I never had. Will you put right your mistake? For I tell you now, you *will* take responsibility for your actions this night, one way or another.

'Do you possess the integrity to join the Order in truth? If you do not, I swear by the responsibility given to me by my father, and the responsibility that a man has for the woman he loves, that you will die.'

Hunter touched the muzzle of the pistol to Bullford's forehead. 'Where is Miss Allardyce?'

He saw Bullford's Adam's apple bob nervously. 'You are right, Hunter. I knew it was wicked work and I said nothing. She is in the cellar of Obsidian House. In this I will do right, at least. And if they take my life for so doing, then it is just recompense for all that I did to Miss Allardyce.'

'Your first decision worthy of the Order, Bullford, but do you have what it takes to become a member, I wonder?' said Hunter slowly as he lowered the pistol. 'Let us save Miss Allardyce and see if we cannot both complete the initiation tasks set us by our fathers in the process.'

Bullford's brow creased. 'What do you mean?'

'You will take the ring to Obsidian House.'

'That will allow me to join the Order, but how will it help you or Miss Allardyce?' Bullford's puzzlement increased.

'Because I will be wearing the ring when you present it,' replied Hunter with a cold smile.

Chapter Twenty

'Afternoon, sirs.' The footman nodded as Hunter and Bullford slipped into the hallway of Obsidian House.

'Afternoon,' murmured Bullford in reply, then steered Hunter down a corridor and into the first room that was out of sight. There, the two of them pulled the black robes they had brought with them on over their clothes.

'You are sure this will work?' whispered Bullford.

'As sure as I can be,' said Hunter. 'You know what to do...'

Bullford nodded and wiped away the sweat that was glimmering on his face.

Hunter checked his pocket watch, then gave a nod.

They lifted the hoods to cover their heads and slipped out into the corridor to merge amidst the other robed and hooded men walking towards the ceremonial chamber.

The grandfather clock in the corner of the room chimed three and Phoebe knew the deadline had passed. Two hooded men had brought her up from the cellar and tied her to a St Andrew's cross in the centre of a large shadowed hall. High on the wall facing her hung a larger version of Hunter's ring, a great silver-crafted wolf's head. And as the creature's emerald eyes glinted in the flickering wall-candles a stream of black-cowled men filed into the hall to encircle her.

Phoebe strained against the ropes that bound her wrists and ankles to the wood of the cross, but the knots were tight and secure. A wave of panic swept over her at the ever-growing circle, but she was determined to reveal nothing of her fear.

A man appeared by her side. He pushed the hood back and there was the Marquis of Willaston, Bullford's father. The scent of sweet tobacco and sandalwood hit her and she knew that he was the gentleman from the carriage even before he opened his mouth to speak quiet words that were for her ears only.

'It seems you were right, Miss Allardyce. Hunter does not care whether you live or die. He does not deem your life worthy of one paltry ring.'

She closed her eyes. Sebastian was an honourable man. He would not break the oath he had sworn to his dying father. Now that she had seen these hooded men, so many of them, all garbed in their 'monk' robes, now that she knew that even Bullford, who was supposed to be Sebastian's friend, was one of them, and had seen the great silver wolf's head on the wall, she understood that the ring was in some way a part of all this, too. So much so, they were prepared to kill for it. But to Sebastian, who had guarded it so close to his heart for all of the time since his father's death, that small piece of silver with its tiny emerald chips meant something different.

He felt he had failed and disappointed his father and there were no means to prove himself a better son, no way to win his father's love or forgiveness. Death had robbed him of that chance. And, worse than that, Sebastian had carried the guilt for that death all of these months, as surely as he had carried the ring. To break his oath would be to fail his father in the final test. Keeping this faith was the one thing left he could do for his father. Sebastian would not give them the ring, not even to save her life.

Phoebe closed her eyes all the tighter and would not let the tears fall. She understood, yet the realisation broke apart her shattered heart and ground the fragments to dust. Despair wrapped its dark tendrils around her and grew until there was no more light; it no longer mattered that the men would kill her.

'I'll wager that your affection for him has waned, Miss Allardyce, now that you know the truth of him.'

She opened her eyes and looked up to meet the Marquis's gaze. 'I love him.' The words were quiet and certain.

The Marquis looked at her with a strange expression. 'Do you not know what we mean to do with you?'

'I know,' she said in that same calm voice.

He slid a knife from the scabbard that hung from his belt and showed it to her. 'And are you not afraid?'

She slowly shook her head. 'I have nothing left to fear.' It was the truth, for, inside, Phoebe was already dead.

The last of the black-hooded men entered the hall. As the door thudded shut and the footsteps of the footmen echoed away down the corridor, the Marquis sheathed the knife again. He smiled at Phoebe and turned to face the men gathered in the circle around them.

'Welcome, brothers,' he intoned. 'We are gathered here on the matter of the master's ring and the fact that it lies in the hands of one who is not a member. Our latest novice has failed in his task to retrieve the ring and thus we must take matters into our own hands and act for the good of the Order. Remember that whatever takes place here today is a sacrifice we must make for the greater good.' He glanced meaningfully towards Phoebe. 'And thus—'

One of the black-robed figures stepped into the circle and pulled back his hood to reveal himself as Bullford. 'I have not failed in my task, master. I have brought the ring as you required.'

A sudden murmur of voices passed around the circle.

The Marquis gaped at his son. 'You have the ring?'

There was a silence as all of the black-hooded figures turned to face Bullford.

'I do, master.'

'Then bring it to me, boy!' the Marquis bellowed.

Bullford glanced round to his right-hand side and the black-garbed figure stepped into the circle to stand by Bullford's side. He slipped back his hood and the breath caught in Phoebe's throat, for there stood Sebastian, his face pale, his hair black as night and his eyes green and more deadly than she had ever seen.

A gasp went round the circle, and an even louder one when he lifted the black sleeve to reveal his right hand—there on his third finger, for all to see, was the wolf's-head ring.

'Good lord!' exclaimed the Marquis. 'What treachery is this?'

'What treachery, indeed, Willaston?' demanded Sebastian.

'Seize him!' shouted the Marquis.

'On whose authority do you act, sir?' said Sebastian. 'You are not master here. Perhaps you have not noticed, sir, but the ring is upon *my* finger.'

'You are not even a member of our Order!'

'On the contrary, Willaston, I claim my birthright to be not only member, but master.'

'You cannot just claim membership. You must be proposed by one of the office bearers. And have your name written in the book.'

'My name is in the book, written there by my father's own hand.'

'Your father is dead!'

'And I am his successor, named by him. I am the master here, by blood, and birthright and will. I have my father's decree here for any who wish to read it.' Phoebe watched as he pulled out a letter and held it aloft. 'Do any contest my right?' His voice rang out as his eyes roved around the circle waiting for a challenge, but there was not one sound to break the silence.

The Marquis held his hands out in petition to the circle. 'What is wrong with you? Tell him he is wrong. Will you just stand there and let him trick his way in here and take over?'

'Edward always meant to bring him in,' someone said.

'He was wild!' said the Marquis.

'He was young,' came the reply. 'And not that much worse than your own boy.'

'He is the rightful Hunter,' said another.

'He is a damned usurper!' cried the Marquis.

'You are the usurper,' called one of the figures at the far end. And when the Marquis stared in the direction of the voice no one moved. It was as if they were closing ranks against him.

Even Bullford stepped back to resume his place within the circle.

'James?' The Marquis stared at Bullford with shock and anger and hurt.

Sebastian walked forwards to stand before the Marquis. 'You have forgotten the aims of this society and bent the rules to suit your own selfish desires. You have threatened the innocent, and blackmailed and terrorised a woman whose very honour this society should have fought to protect.' He gestured towards Phoebe, his eyes meeting hers briefly across the floor before he turned back to the Marquis. 'As master, I strip you of your office, sir.'

The Marquis gave a hard laugh. 'That is all you can do. You cannot throw me out. Membership is for life. Once one knows our secrets he is either a member—'

'Or dead,' finished Sebastian.

'Are you threatening me?'

'I would not stoop to your level. I mean to rule this Order as my forebears intended and uphold the very values for which it was founded. All that is rotten will be cut away and the Order's integrity restored.' Sebastian held out his hand to the Marquis, as if he were showing him the ring.

Phoebe watched as the Marquis's face flushed puce. He stood

there for a moment with such a look of murder upon his face that she feared for Sebastian's safety and then, to her amazement, the Marquis got down on his knees and kissed the ring.

Hunter longed for nothing more than to go to Phoebe, to cut her down from that awful cross, but he knew that he must first ensure the loyalty of all the members; without that he doubted that either of them would leave the hall alive. His heart tightened as he met her eyes and he could only hope that she understood. He stood there and the first man pushed back his hood, dropped to his knees and vowed his allegiance with his lips upon the ring. The circle began to slowly rotate as each dark figure in turn followed suit.

The swearing ceremony was only half-completed when he heard Phoebe cry out. The circle gave a collective gasp and stopped. Hunter looked up to see Willaston standing behind Phoebe, one hand gripping her hair, wrenching her head back, while the other held a ceremonial knife pressed against her throat. Everything in that moment seemed to slow. Hunter felt his gaze narrow and sharpen. He could hear the call of outraged voices. He could hear the beat of his own heart and that of the woman he loved.

'She knows our secrets,' shouted Willaston. 'And as a woman she cannot be admitted to our order. Therefore Miss Allardyce must die. Unless you wish to tell everyone here how you mean to bend the rules for your own fancy piece, Hunter.'

Hunter's words were like ice. 'The rule states that no *man* may know of our existence and live. Miss Allardyce, as you have just said, is a woman, and she is no fancy piece but the woman who will be my wife.' Hunter turned so that he was facing the Marquis and Phoebe squarely across the chamber. His eyes gauged the distance that separated him from them. Thirty feet of clear space. He could feel Phoebe's gaze, but he did not allow himself look at her. Instead, he kept his focus on Willaston.

'Release her or I will kill you, sir,' Hunter growled.

Willaston was panting heavily; his face was flushed and sweating.

Hunter saw the tiny flicker in the older man's eyes that preceded the movement of his hand. In the space of one heartbeat Hunter had drawn the pistol from his pocket and fired.

There was the flash of the powder in the pan and an almighty deafening roar and through the blue smoke Hunter watched the knife fall away to clatter on the floor. And Willaston crumpled in its wake, a red stain spreading over the arm that had held the knife.

Hunter was across the distance in seconds, grabbing the ceremonial knife and cutting the ropes that bound Phoebe. Relief surged through him and his love was all the fiercer for it. He pulled her into his arms and clutched her to him.

'Phoebe,' he whispered. 'My love.'

'Sebastian.' She clung to him, pressing her face against his chest.

'I am taking you home.'

'No.'

Hunter's heart gave a lurch. And then she looked up into his eyes and he saw the love that was there.

'Not until you finish what must be done here,' she said.

And Hunter wanted to weep for love of her. There had never been a woman like Phoebe Allardyce and there never would be. She had sacrificed her own heart and all chance of happiness for him. She would have given her life for him. She was his heart, his life, his very existence. And their love for each other would burn bright beyond the aeons of time.

He kissed her and, with Phoebe by his side, completed all that his father had asked of him.

The house in Grosvenor Street had been decked in flowers and greenery. The vases in every room were brimful and overflowing. Great garlands festooned the banisters and mirrors and mantels. Outside the sky was a cloudless powder blue and the sun shone in glorious splendour. The events in Obsidian House seemed far in the past, although only two weeks had elapsed.

Phoebe stood before the full-length looking glass in her bedchamber and stared at the woman who looked back with eyes sparkling with such happiness. She looked radiant dressed in Mrs Hunter's gift. The bodice of the new ivory gown seemed to shimmer in a haze of tiny pearls and iridescent beads. Its neckline was square and cut low enough to hint at the swell of her breasts. Its skirt was of smooth Parisian silk that dropped away to hang perfectly and from beneath which peeped the toes of new ivory silk slippers. Her hair had been caught up in a cascade of curls and threaded with fresh cream roses. And on her arms she wore a new pair of long ivory silk gloves.

'You look quite, quite lovely, my dear girl.' Mrs Hunter dabbed a little tear from the corner of her eye. 'I am so glad to be gaining you as a daughter.'

'And I, you as a mother,' said Phoebe and smiled warmly at the woman who had helped her so much.

'You are almost ready to go down to Sebastian, but for one last thing he bade me give to you.'

Mrs Hunter took out a small cream-leather box and pressed it into Phoebe's hands. Within the box was a gold heart-shaped locket with a wolf's head engraved upon it, and when Phoebe opened the locket, there, inside, were two tiny portraits, one of Sebastian and the other of herself.

Mrs Hunter's fingers moved to touch her own dress where her oval locket lay beneath. 'Such things are precious, Phoebe,' she said as she fastened the locket around Phoebe's neck. And the little golden heart lay above the gentle thud of Phoebe's own.

'Quite perfect.' Mrs Hunter smiled.

Phoebe felt the tears well in her eyes.

'Why, whatever is the matter, my dear?' she asked gently.

Phoebe shook her head. 'I was just thinking of my papa and

how much I would give that he could be here this day to see me married.'

'You must be brave on your wedding day, Phoebe. It is what your father would want. And upon our return to Scotland Sebastian will see that Sir Henry's debts are cleared and that he is released.'

Phoebe nodded. 'You are right.' She dried her tears and let Mrs Hunter lead her down the stairs. And as she reached the bottom of the staircase, Mrs Hunter smiled and stepped aside, and there, waiting across the hallway, was her own dear papa, dressed in his best wedding finery. Phoebe ran to him, tears of joy streaming down her cheeks as she threw her arms around him.

'Papa! Oh, Papa!'

'Child!' Sir Henry laughed and hugged her to him as if she were still his little girl. 'Mr Hunter was insistent that a father ought not to miss his daughter's wedding day. And I do believe that he was right.'

Mrs Hunter pressed a posy of flowers into her hands and her papa led her through to the drawing room where two tall dark-haired, dark tailcoated men stood waiting.

The Duke of Arlesford, who was standing by Sebastian's right-hand side, gave her a smile, then looked at Sebastian. Her papa handed her to Sebastian and left her there.

In both Sebastian's and Arlesford's buttonholes was a fine sprig of purple heather.

'From our own moor, Phoebe,' Sebastian whispered as he smiled at her, and Phoebe's heart was flooded with happiness and she thought there had never been a better man in all the world. She faced to the front, where the old priest stood, and she married the man that she loved.

Phoebe and Sebastian had set off back to Blackloch alone the next day. Both had been of the opinion that there was nowhere else in the world that they would rather be for their honeymoon than the beautiful Blackloch Moor.

As their coach travelled over the narrow winding moor road they could see the great dark house that was Blackloch Hall, silhouetted black against the fiery orange glow of the setting sun. On the horizon was the purple haze of the distant islands. The moor was quiet and the breeze gentled in welcome, and the air was sweet and fresh and scented with heather. And when the coach drew to a halt outside the great studded front door Phoebe and Sebastian climbed out.

Sebastian drew her against his chest so that they stood together and stared out over the blushing moorland.

'We are home, Phoebe,' he whispered as he nuzzled her ear.

'To our moor,' she said and the golden heart-shaped locket nestled between her breasts seemed to glow warm as she turned her mouth to meet his.

And Sebastian scooped her up into his arms and carried her, as his dearly beloved wife, across the threshold into Blackloch.

* * * * *

HISTORICAL

Novels coming in September 2011

THE LADY GAMBLES
Carole Mortimer

Incognito at a fashionable gambling club, Lady Copeland is drawn
to a rakish gentleman, whose burning gaze renders her quite
distracted! She can't risk letting anyone close enough to expose
her secret—though her body craves to give in…

LADY ROSABELLA'S RUSE
Ann Lethbridge

Lady Rosabella must pose as a widow to find the inheritance she and
her sisters so desperately need! Baron Garth Evernden is known for
his generosity and is so *very* handsome…surely becoming
mistress to this rake would bring definite advantages?

THE VISCOUNT'S SCANDALOUS RETURN
Anne Ashley

Wrongly accused of murder, Viscount Blackwood left home
disgraced. Now he has returned, and, along with the astute Miss
Isabel Mortimer, he hunts the real culprit—while battling an
ever-growing attraction to his beautiful companion…

THE VIKING'S TOUCH
Joanna Fulford

Courageous widow Lady Anwyn requires the protection of
Wulfgar Ragnarsson, a legendary mercenary and Viking warrior.
Anwyn learns from Wulfgar that not all men are monsters—
but can they melt each other's frozen hearts?